The Knight Brothers

The Knight Brothers

Dria Andersen

Adrienne Andersen

To my husband, who was my sounding board, my cheerleader, my critique partner, and all the things I needed to finish this project. I appreciate every hour, every word of input, and most of all, your unwavering support.

To my family, who had to deal with mommy being on in another world for hours at a time. Thank you for your patience.

To my sister Tina, who reads everything I write and gives me honest feedback and encouragement, thank you mucho mucho. I appreciate your continued support and cheerleading! To my aunt Cathy who gave me my first love of romance stories, I thank you for allowing me to raid your bookshelf.

Thank you to every fan who continues to stick with me while telling the stories playing in my head. I appreciate each and every one of you. Also, I would like to give a special thanks to Pikko House for the feedback and help I get from your alpha readers.

CONTENTS

CONTENTS

CONTENTS

For Her Safety

CONTENTS

To Her Rescue

Author's Note

I want to first start with content warnings. While there is no explicit, or rather acknowledged abuse in the book, Celine is a victim of verbal abuse from her parents. There is also a lil' bit of violence. But, as usual, the book is very low angst. I'm just in the mood for easy love, and I appreciate those of you who are taking the ride with me!

one

The anger rippling through Celine's chest was making it impossible to breathe. Her hands shook, and tears clogged her throat. The tears were from the rage, but helplessness and grief were battling. Grief for the grandfather she'd lost and anger for the predicament his death had put her in. Celine and her mother were gathered in her father's home office, both in differing states of shock. Black bookshelves covered three of the four walls of the stately room, filled to the brim with lengthy, leather-bound tomes. The carpet was thick, equally dark, and suffocating, as were the gray floor-to-ceiling curtains over the windows.

She needed to get out.

"Virgil, is this true?" Her mother stood next to her, facing her father, shock blanching the color from her mother's face. "Celine in no way should inherit my father's holdings."

Celine's hands shook, and she clenched them together in front of her to stop them. She and her mother were clearly shocked for different reasons. Veronica was upset that the inheritance she had banked on would go to her only child. But then, Celine wasn't at all surprised that Veronica was only thinking of herself. Her mother had never really given much thought to Celine unless it was to parade her in front of her grandfather when she needed to ask him for a favor.

"The will states that Celine has to be married before she can inherit. If the terms are not followed, to the letter, it reverts to you and your sisters." Virgil sent Celine an irritated look.

Her father was a handsome man. His rugged countenance was clean-shaven and all sharp angles. His deep-set eyes had never been anything other than hard when aimed her way. Right now, his thick brows were furrowed with aggravation at having the two women in his life questioning him.

"Then fine, she won't get married," Veronica said and flipped her carefully colored, bone-straight hair over her trim shoulder.

Her mother's cocoa skin was rigorously maintained with weekly appointments for facials and shone clear and supple, defying her fifty years on the Earth. The charcoal slacks and crisp white shirt was her version of dressed down, and as Veronica faced her husband, the gold bangles on her wrist clicked against each other, broadcasting her irritation with their current situation.

Celine looked down at her faux leather leggings and white t-shirt. Unlike her parents, she didn't think a meeting with them warranted dressing up. Of course, Veronica had told her all the many ways she was wrong about that.

"I'm not letting your sisters get their hands on Alan's holdings when I can get it all if Celine marries," he gritted out.

So lovely to be considered.

Celine kept that thought to herself. She'd never dare utter something like that where her father could hear. She pushed down on her panther as it tried to infuse its power into her. She didn't need the added stress. She was biting down on her tongue as it was. Her panther's strength would make her say something she would pay for later.

"Do I have any say in this?" Celine asked though she knew it was futile.

Her father's panther lit his eyes, gold breaking through the normal dark brown. "What could you possibly say, Celine? You're twenty-six and making no move to marry on your own. I want those holdings."

"So, you're not concerned that Celine will be taken care of; you're concerned that your precious company will." Veronica spat out.

"I'm going to pick a man from a good family. He won't mistreat her." Virgil sputtered.

Fake.

Both of her parents. Neither of them was concerned with Celine's thoughts or feelings on the matter.

"You don't know that!" Veronica stepped closer to the desk. "And the money belongs to my sisters and me. Not your company."

Case in point.

Celine bent her knees slightly to relieve the pressure on her legs. She'd been standing in this position for an hour while her parents fought over who was the more selfish person.

"You're fighting this more than Celine. She's okay with it." Virgil pointed at her.

Veronica's gaze whipped to her. "Celine?"

What could she say? Her father sent her a deadly glare, the pupil changing shape as his panther slipped its leash. She knew the consequences of denying her father. Hell, Veronica knew the consequences her daughter would face, but money was on the table, so Celine's feelings were moot.

The weight of the silence pushed down on her shoulders. Instead of answering their questioning gazes, she left the room. She couldn't even say she stormed. She hadn't stomped, slammed a door, or shown any outward sign of her anger. Not while she hurried down the long hallway towards the door. Not in the meticulously decorated foyer while she slid into her sneakers. Not even as she calmly closed the heavy glass front door did her anger slip out. It wasn't as though she didn't wish she could.

Jesus, she wished she could slam a hundred doors, curse, and rail, but somewhere along her advanced twenty-six years, she'd forgotten to develop a backbone.

"Celine!" her mother called from the front door. Veronica looked around in case her neighbors were outside. She rushed over to Celine, her steps sure across the gravel. "You can't let your father do this."

"What choice do I have, mom?" Celine sighed and rubbed her forehead. "If I don't do this, then dad takes everything."

"That farm is nothing. We're talking about millions of dollars," Veronica snapped.

"That farm is everything to me. It's how I make my living. Dad won't let me buy it from him, and he holds it over my head at every opportunity. He has me over a barrel. Would you have me live on the streets?" Celine didn't raise her voice.

She would never, despite her frustration.

Veronica scoffed. "You can easily move back home."

Her panther bucked against her control, fighting to comfort her. Celine suppressed it tightly. She wouldn't let her mother's words throw her out of control. Now was not the time. Later, when she was on her own, in her comfort zone, she would allow the animal some leeway. Though the full moon wasn't for weeks, she would shift to soothe the panther. After the afternoon she'd just spent with her parents, she'd earned it. She would never voluntarily live under the same roof as Virgil and Veronica Harris again. She'd barely survived her childhood sane. She would basically flush down years of therapy if she came back home.

"All I can hope is that he picks someone I'll get along with." She managed to say after she regained control.

Celine was going to give in. Why her mother insisted on fighting, she didn't know. Virgil would get what he wanted. Whether it was by persuasion or manipulation, he'd get it. It was the reason she was still under his thumb at her big age. The last time she'd fought him had been to live on her own, out at the ranch. He'd controlled her whole life. Perhaps she should look forward to marriage. Not that she imagined she would be free of her father then, but...a girl could hope.

two

Mason Knight growled as his phone rang for what seemed like the one-hundredth time since he'd left his office half an hour ago. He knew better than to leave in the middle of the day, but his father had summoned him, which was unusual enough to make him drop everything. Added to the sense of urgency, his father had called him all the way over to the Southside of Eastfield. It wasn't unusual for Dallas to hang out in their old neighborhood, but getting from downtown to Arlington this time of day was aggravating. His father was usually a little more considerate.

He parked his Audi as close to the front door as possible. Not that he was worried about someone stealing his shit. Despite the side of town he was on, he had no worries. Dallas Knight still ran the city, so theft was the least of his problems. He just wanted to be able to leave quickly.

He opened the ancient boxing gym door, his eyes quickly adjusting to the dimness as he looked around for his father. The smell of sweat, weed, and warm fur hit him as he went deeper inside. He spotted Dallas near the ring, at a small table, surrounded by the OGs he used to run with. They were smoking both cigars and blunts, playing cards, and most likely gambling. Mason shook his head because if his mother found out what his father was doing, she would get in his ass. She hated that he came back to his old neighborhood, claiming that it kept Dallas wild.

His dad and his friends were legitimate for the most part, but he knew that his father kept his toe in that life, if only to make sure he stayed sharp. Being on the ruling three council was a treacherous job, dangerous in its own right, especially how Dallas Knight ruled. His father didn't quite believe in negotiation, and no amount of polish could make him fit into the high society that he found himself in.

Dallas looked up as he came in the door, his panther right on the surface, as always. His father was an animal, a beast, and made no effort to hide it. Mason's panther reacted, his power raising and meeting his father's. Dallas's smile took on the edge of pride. He knew his father worried that their place in society would soften them.

Mason dapped the elder shifters, Dallas' oldest friends and men Mason considered his Uncles.

"Nephew," they greeted him.

He reached his father and leaned down, rubbing his cheek against the top of his head, allowing his panther to greet Dallas's. "Pop. I take it your mate doesn't know where you are."

"Here you go, coming in here to start shit," Dallas grumbled and stood from the table. "Aye, I'm taking my cards because y'all cheat too damn much."

"Man, what the fuck ever," JuJu said, laughing.

Dallas inclined his head to Mason, and he followed behind his father. They went upstairs to the loft area that held the manager's office. He shut the door behind him.

"You came without security," Dallas fussed.

"They're just a few minutes behind me." He shrugged off his suit jacket and placed it on the back of the chair.

"Behind you ain't keeping you safe."

"I can take care of myself," he reminded his father. "Besides, I wish somebody would try me."

Dallas growled but dropped it, settling in the chair behind the desk. Mason took the chair in front and waited as his father studied him with narrowed eyes. Mason held back a sigh. He knew that look.

Dallas was plotting.

"You remember Celine, Virgil's girl?" Dallas said after a tense moment of silence.

"I know Celine, yeah." Mason frowned.

"Her grandfather died," his father said.

Mason sat back in the chair. "And?" He didn't know the man personally, so he didn't know what it had to do with them.

"Here's the thing, Mason," Dallas started.

He got a sinking feeling.

"Alan was old-fashioned."

Mason snorted at the understatement. All of the men in the Motsi society were Neanderthals; calling them old-fashioned was a compliment.

"So, Virgil's been quietly asking around about getting Celine married off."

"Married off?" Mason sat forward in his chair, alert.

He knew that arranged marriages weren't abnormal in the Motsi, the shifter society they ran in. Especially in the upper echelon, where his family was now enmeshed. They were an insular community, ruled by the Tri-council his father was a part of. It was primarily old money or heavy hitters like his father who had made his way in by brute force. It consisted of a representative of the city's bears, wolves, and cats. Dallas Knight ruled the cats of Eastfield with an iron fist, and as far as he knew, the other two members on the tri-council did the same.

It made finding a mate naturally hard. Most of their society arranged their matings based on what power could be brought into the family. His father had even tried it with his older brother when he'd first ascended to his position. It hadn't worked out, and Mason had a sinking feeling that Dallas was about to try again. He wanted to protest, but...Dallas was talking about Celine.

Sweet, shy Celine.

His panther rose, interested in where this conversation was going.

Dallas sighed again and rubbed his temples. "Well, it's being kept quiet, of course, but I've heard she won't get her inheritance unless she's married."

"Fuck outta here," he murmured.

That was manipulative as hell and, unfortunately, very in line with the way the Motsi operated.

"So you're bringing this to me because...." He had an idea, but he needed to first hear what his father was planning.

Dallas sat back and steepled his fingers, studying Mason. "I like Celine, Mason, and I think it's horrible the way Virgil is going about this."

"What do you want me to do? This can't just be about a marriage contract with the Harrises. You don't even like them."

Dallas smiled, the gold caps he had over his fangs showing. "I'd like you to give some thought to doing it."

"Excuse me?"

"Marriage, Mason, I'd like you to consider marrying Celine."

"I..." he stopped. He didn't like the thought of her being married off, especially since he'd had his own plans for her. But he didn't quite want to show his hand just yet. He knew how Dallas operated and knew it wouldn't be as simple as marrying Celine.

"You tried this with Silas," he reminded his father to stall.

Dallas waved a hand. "This ain't the same thing. Back then, I was trying to merge into this bougie ass society their way. Now, I'm doing shit my way, you feel me?"

"What do you get out of it?"

"We."

Mason sighed. "What do we get out of it?"

Dallas laughed. "Oh, you finna act like you don't be searching out lil' mama when you show up at council events? She's beautiful, thick as hell, and submissive, from what I can tell. What else you need in a mate, son?"

Now see, his father be so out of pocket. Not that it made his words any less accurate. But still... "All that aside, I know you, and you always hustling. Tell me what you get out of this so I can assess before I decide."

"Alan had some shipping holdings that are a part of Celine's inheritance. I want them." Dallas shrugged.

And there it was. Mason watched his father as he decided what he wanted to do. The shipping holdings would add millions to their profit margin, and as the CEO of Knight industries, he was with that. He was also savvy enough to know that controlling the ports would give his father more influence, even if it was just through his son.

Regardless of Dallas's motive, Mason liked Celine, and Dallas was right; he looked for her at every event he attended. He enjoyed spending time with her, but with his busy schedule, he'd made no moves to do anything about it. He'd had plans that didn't allow time for a relationship. It seemed extreme to go straight to marrying. But he always heeded his panther's instincts, and the animal was for it.

"What does Celine think?"

Dallas shrugged. "You know how Virgil Harris operates. I doubt she has a choice."

Mason winced. He didn't like the sound of that. "I'll do it, but only after I talk to Celine." He was surprised the words had come out of his mouth.

Dallas smiled, satisfied that he would get what he wanted. "That's fair. I certainly wouldn't want her to be forced, despite the way her daddy is going about this whole thing."

Mason knew Celine would hate it. The shy woman barely spoke two or three words to other people besides him at the parties where they ended up together. He couldn't imagine what she'd do if forced to marry a stranger. Calm overtook him, and a feeling of rightness.

"Yeah, I'll do it. Start the negotiations with her dad so that he'll stop blasting her all over town."

At least Celine would get a respite from her father's machinations. Dallas nodded, and that was that. Mason left the gym potentially betrothed. He certainly hadn't been expecting that when he woke up this morning.

three

It had been three days since Celine had left her parent's house, and she was getting nervous. The first two days, she'd been avoiding their calls. She knew it wasn't the best solution, but she needed time to think. She was resigned to her fate, but she couldn't help but rail against the universe. Why her? Her grandfather had as good as put a target on her back. Out of all the cousins, why would he leave everything to her? Her mother and aunts were still furious.

She fully expected them to show up on her farm any day now to bully her into doing what they wanted. Too bad for them, her father was a bigger bully. When she'd first heard the stipulations, she had been relieved. No one would marry her, so really, she'd never inherit. No one would marry Virgil Harris' only daughter. Her father's reputation had as good as guaranteed it. Veronica may act like they were beloved members of the Motsi, but she knew they were barely tolerated.

Her father's business deals had alienated them from a lot of people. So, to Celine's thinking, the money and holdings would be passed down to her mother and aunts, and she could live on her farm in peace. That's what had first gone through her mind until she remembered who her father was. Virgil Harris wanted her grandfather's money, and he was selling his daughter to the highest bidder to get it.

Especially since he needed both the capital and the social standing that came with it.

She gently tied her dried herbs together in a bundle, using the chore to calm herself. She'd barely been able to sleep the past few days, waiting on either word from her father or a visit from her cousins or aunts. Maybe she could barricade herself in the barn.

Her panther moved in her body, a warning that someone was near. She raised her head and inhaled, frowning, because she knew that scent. She whipped her head back to the door of the barn.

"Mason?"

He leaned against the door and smiled at her. "Celine. Long time no see."

She gave him a shy smile. What was Mason Knight doing on her farm? Her heart stuttered and thumped in nervousness. Surely he wasn't... She shook her head because, of course not. Her eyes traced his face, reacquainting herself with the face she'd seen many nights in her dreams. His dark skin was smooth and unblemished, a soft, full beard covering the bottom half. It framed his thick lips, and her gaze was immediately drawn there. He smiled, and his straight white teeth contrasted with his skin in a way that sent butterflies through her stomach.

"I can't believe you actually took time off to come see me."

She fell back onto the teasing they did when they were together. It was much easier to deal with than the big feelings making her insides tremble. His unusual visit made her both nervous and hopeful. Could she afford hope?

He chuckled. "How are you, love bug?"

God, she loved when he called her that. It was a joke from a long-ago party.

"What are you doing here?" She asked.

He walked further into the barn and leaned his forearms on the stall door. Celine's panther froze, interested in the powerful and beautiful man invading their space. Mason was always well-groomed, his dark brows neat and trimmed. His hooded gaze met hers, the light of his panther flashing green before settling.

"You can't hide in the barn forever, CeCe." He said instead of answering her question.

She smiled, guilty for thinking that exact thing. "It's worked so far."

He laughed. No one could ever call her funny, but she'd tried to be that, just to see him turn that sexy smile her way. She loved his smile. And loved having it aimed at her. The two of them had bonded at many of the parties her mother had dragged her to over their distaste for high society.

"What are you doing here, Mason?" she asked again.

"My father told me that your father was in the process of shopping you around."

She winced at his words. "That's not a nice way to put it."

"And yet it's the truth."

"Are you in the market for a fertile bride?" She asked bitterly.

"You should know me a little better than that, Celine."

"Sharing hors d'oeuvres with you at society parties doesn't really allow us to know each other all that well."

"That's fair," he conceded.

She returned to her tying, but she could feel his dark eyes watching her intently.

"I don't like to think of you having to do something against your will."

She stopped, dropped the herbs, and turned her full attention to him, surprised...pleased? "I don't have a choice," she said quietly.

"I have my lawyers looking over the will and estate information. I think your father is manipulating the situation to fit his needs and not yours."

She felt hope flare in her chest but then doused it. Her father would never let her get out of the marriage.

"As you said, he's already selling me to the highest bidder."

He wanted her grandfather's money, and if there were a way Virgil could get it without her being married, he would've already scoured the paperwork to do so. She went back to bundling her herbs.

"Come here, love bug."

The command in his voice moved her feet. She stood in front of him at the stall door.

"I told my father that I wouldn't agree to this if you weren't on board."

Her eyes widened, and her heart really started thumping. Mason Knight would marry her?

Mason studied her face. Celine was beautiful in the most natural way, especially with her dark caramel skin glistening from the heat of the barn. She had her curly hair up in a poof, tied back by a colorful scarf. It left her face bare and open. Her eyes were large, tilted at the corners, her cat showing through. High cheekbones, a button nose, and lush, full lips came together beautifully on her rounded face. She was working her bottom lip with her teeth, nervousness interlaced in her scent. Woven in there with it was interest as well. He caught occasional flashes of gold as her cat peered at him through her worried eyes.

"Nothing to say to that, love bug?"

Her eyes got glossy, and she turned from him to hide the tears she was fighting. She'd always been shy. It was one of the reasons he loved teasing her when they ended up at the same parties. Sometimes he sought her out just to listen to her dry wit as both of them worked their way through whatever appetizers were floating around.

"You could have anyone you want, Mason. Why would you..." she cleared her throat and turned back to face him. "Why would you do this?"

He considered his words, deciding to give her a truth that he'd been wrestling with since his father had given him the news.

"The first time I saw you from across the room, you were so beautiful, shy, and delicate. The shit had my panther caught up."

She scoffed.

He cupped her face. "I wanted to take care of you. I wanted to tuck you into me and protect you. It was a first for me."

"Why didn't you do anything before now?"

"I'm trying to build my life in a way that's not simply a reflection of my father. He had his way, and I wanted to make mine. But then I talked to you, and you were so proper, prim... I don't know, Cece;

I didn't want to sully you in a way, I guess. You know that the Motsi barely tolerate my family."

"But now?" she whispered.

He leaned until their lips were almost touching. "I couldn't let some asshole have you. You're mine. To hold, to love on, to devour," he whispered before softly pressing his lips against hers.

He pulled back, smiling at the dazed look on her face.

"Would I be better or worse, you think?"

Her gaze roamed his face, stopping at his eyes only a moment before she looked away. "I don't want your pity."

He leaned over and gripped her chin, bringing her face back to his. "When have I ever offered you pity, love bug?"

"You and that nickname," she murmured, changing the subject.

He smirked, allowing it. "Not my fault you were queen of the insects that night."

She laughed and stepped back. "God, who has an outdoor party in Florida during love bug season?"

"A sadist I believed you called Naomi."

She laughed and covered her face. She sobered a moment later. "He'll take it all if I don't agree, Mason."

His heart hurt for her. His panther wanted her nearer so that he could touch her, could ease the tension tightening her face and shoulders.

"This farm is my life," she whispered.

He nodded, knowing that much from their conversations. They hadn't breached more than the surface when they'd talked at events, but he knew how her face lit up when she spoke of her farm and the plants she lovingly tended. He'd researched her while his father worked on the negotiations with Virgil, and he found that she made a pretty little living off the products she sold from her farm. She sold the herbs she grew to restaurants in the area, not to mention the spices she came up with. He'd been impressed with what he learned and proud.

"Choose me, then, Celine."

Her hands shook, and she stuck them in her pockets to hide them. "And if there's no out clause?"

He shrugged. He wasn't looking for an out. And staring into her beautiful face full of turmoil, he couldn't work up any alarm for the direction of his thoughts.

"You're too powerful. My father would never go for it." She said after a lengthy silence. "He can't run over you, and that's what he wants most of all in a son-in-law."

He crooked his finger, and she came closer, only the bottom half of the wooden door between them. "I ain't worried about your daddy, love bug. My concern is only for you."

She bit her lip, her eyes drifting down his mouth, before popping back up to his eyes. "If it's you, I would be willing," she said softly.

And shit...those words had an immediate effect on his dick. He desperately wanted to close the distance between them and taste her lips again.

"I'll take care of it all, then." He promised her.

Hope flared in her eyes. "You don't have to ruin your—"

He put a finger to her lips. "I got you, love bug. Now relax and know it's handled, hear?"

She nodded. "Thank you, Mason," she said in the sweetest tone.

It hit him right in the center of his chest—another thing he would need to examine. Unable to resist, he dropped a small kiss on her lips.

"Back to your work. I'll call you later, okay?"

She nodded and stepped back. Mason needed to leave before he complicated what was supposed to be a very cut and dried contract.

four

Mason shifted in the leather chair he occupied, fighting to concentrate on the legalese his family's lawyer was droning on about. Dean narrowed his eyes on him and went back to the paperwork. Dallas shook his head and turned back to Dean. His father was here with him because Dallas was a control freak, but Mason would let him rock. He trusted his father's word and always took his advice. Dean continued to read through the contract, and Mason listened with half an ear.

He'd made some life-changing decisions when he'd left Celine's farm. He'd spent so many years with his head down, grinding, pushing everything else to the wayside. Taking a wife, a mate, would mean so many adjustments. He didn't know when his feelings had started changing for her. It had gone from sneaking little moments with her at events to actively searching her out when he went anywhere. He knew she was introverted and hated the events her mother dragged her to. He enjoyed entertaining her. The fact that his father had noticed and commented on it meant that others also had to witness it. That could be good for Celine. It would stop some of the nastier speculations that were sure to be flying around society about their sudden engagement.

His panther had hipped him to game when he went out to her farm. Something he'd never considered in all the time he spent with her. Maybe because work had never really given him much time with her, and he missed the signs, but yesterday, in her space, with her guard down, his panther had showed him why he enjoyed her time.

"Mase," Dean called.

"Yeah, sorry."

"Her grandfather wrote in the will that a divorce can be procured once a child is conceived, so that could be an out clause," Dean told him.

His panther rose. "No."

His dad and Dean both gave him a startled look. Mason ignored it.

"We'll be mated. There's no out."

"You don't have to mate with her, Mason," Dean said. "The will only requires you to marry."

"Next item, Dean," he said, dismissing that.

His panther would have her no other way. Of course, he would give her time to get to know him, to acclimate to their relationship, but she was his, and there would be no out. Mating was permanent.

"You sure, son." His father asked, studying him.

"I'm sure, Pop."

Dallas smiled and nodded. "Well, alright then. Move on, Dean," he ordered.

His friend turned the page, and they started going over assets and how to best take them over. He perked up then.

"Make sure that the money is held in trust for Celine, with her control." He ordered. He told her he would take care of her, and he meant it.

Dean nodded and made a note. "Her grandfather owns extensive real estate in Georgia that can be merged with your assets easily."

"Make sure it's in her name so that she gets the profits once we merge."

Dean paused a beat but kept going. "I'm still working on audits for Alan's holdings and companies. Some of them can be a part of the merger once you marry."

"Virgil is salivating at the chance to get to them. Make sure that it's in the contract and non-negotiable," Dallas said. "I want those holdings under Knight Industries."

Dean nodded. "And the others that don't fit within your son's portfolio."

Dallas waved it off, "I don't care about those. I want his shipping holdings. He owns damn near half the ports on the east coast. I want them for us."

Mason rolled his eyes. "Pop, who's getting married, me or you?"

Dallas gave him a crooked smile. "You're the CEO of Knight industries; you trying to tell me you can't put them ports to use?"

Hell yeah, he could and would use those ports. Logistically it would be a boon to his company. There were many things he could do with some of the other holdings as well. He'd spent the last several days holed up with his executive team going through them, making plans. But, as usual, Dallas was meddling. His father would call it nudging and helping, but he'd worked too damn hard to separate his name from Dallas'. He routinely had to check his father about throwing his weight around on his behalf.

He didn't resent or begrudge it. His father had always told him and his brother that he wanted life to be easier for his sons than it had been for him.

"I'm not the one who needs the reminder of who's CEO." He firmly reminded his father.

Dallas gave him an unrepentant smile. "I'm not trying to step on your toes, baby boy."

He shook his head, steering the conversation back to the contract. "Her father is going to be pissed."

"He may not even sign it," Dean warned.

"He'll sign it," Dallas promised them.

Mason knew then that his father must have something over Harris. Not that he cared. He wanted Celine and would do whatever he had to do to get her. It was a good thing his father was a part of the negotiations because, honestly, he couldn't quite say what he would give up to have her.

*****

Celine squirmed in her chair. She was in her father's downtown office. The large space was intimidating and probably precisely what her father had planned when he decorated the room. She sat in an oversized leather seat next to her father's lawyers as they droned on and on about the contract conditions Mason's lawyer had sent over. She was nervous. Her father had only reluctantly agreed to the marriage to Mason.

She didn't know what Mason had said to him, but Virgil had shown up at her farm furious, accusing her of trying to thwart him. She'd been shaken by the time her father had stormed out, threatening to kick her off the farm if she didn't get Mason to 'act right,' whatever that meant. She didn't know what her father was thinking. How was she supposed to control someone as powerful as Mason?

She frowned as the lawyer's words filtered through her daydreaming. "What?"

"Your grandfather stipulated that you could divorce only after you reproduced, but Mason declined the out clause." The lawyer repeated.

Her heart thumped, and excitement bubbled within her. He didn't want an out? What did that mean for them?

Her father waved that off, "fine, move on."

"He wants the money moved into a trust for Celine with her control over it."

"Absolutely not," Virgil said resolutely. "Next."

His lawyer cleared his throat. "Sir...Dean Powell is an exceptional lawyer. There are no loopholes in this contract."

Virgil slapped his hand down on his desk. "No. That money is mine."

The lawyer sighed, and she could see his frustration. Celine didn't know what was happening, but curiosity got the better of her.

"How much money is it?"

"None of your concern," Virgil snapped.

She shut up. It wasn't worth arguing with him over.

The lawyer turned to her. "We're talking about fifty million dollars, Celine."

Her stomach lurched—God, what she could do with that kind of money.

"Celine will squander it immediately on charity. She cannot have control over that money," her father said.

She didn't consider charities squandering, but that was semantics. She would absolutely disperse that money to people who needed it. Virgil and the lawyer went back and forth, and Celine's mind went back to the lack of out clause. Mason wanted to stay married to her. She was giddy, and nothing would bring her down from that.

"Cancel the whole thing," her father shouted, throwing his coffee mug against the wall.

She flinched, the quick violence snapping her back to attention. Panic bubbled. "What?"

"The shipping holdings belong to Celine. He can't just absorb them into his company," Virgil said.

"According to the will, as her husband, he can," the lawyer corrected.

"Absolutely not. I'll forfeit the entire contract before I hand that over."

Celine spoke up for the first time in her life. "If you do that, I'll refuse to marry."

"You will do what I say," her father told her.

"I'll live on the street before I marry anyone other than Mason," she said softly, fear a lump in her throat. "Or, I'll get another lawyer to draw up the marriage contract, and you won't get a penny."

Where had she gotten the backbone to stand up to her father? Oh, that's right, Mason freaking Knight wanted to marry her. She wouldn't let her father ruin it. He stared her down.

"Then I want control of the rest of the assets." Virgil narrowed his eyes on her, the glow of his cat eerie.

"Celine has—"

"—deal," she cut the lawyer off.

She didn't need money. He could have it all if she could have Mason.

"Celine, that's not in your best interest." The lawyer tried again.

"I want the farm signed over to me, and I want access to enough money to live off. They can fight over the rest," she said in a stronger voice.

The lawyer sighed. "I can probably get away with sign-off permissions from you both on the trust. Will that satisfy you, Mr. Harris?"

Her father stared her down, and she kept eye contact, needing to win this.

Virgil finally growled and cursed. "Fine."

She released a breath, and her eyes fell to her lap. He snatched the paper from the lawyer and scrawled his name.

He slid it across the desk. "Sign it and leave my office," he ordered.

She hastily did as he said and nearly tripped on her way out the door. It wasn't until she got into the elevator has she let her knees give out. She slid to the floor. Holy crap, she was marrying Mason Knight. Giddy, she left her father's building.

five

Celine's hands shook as she peeled potatoes at her kitchen sink. Her phone had been ringing incessantly, and she'd reached the end of her rope. It would be nice if she could say that even half of the calls were well wishes, but there was no such luck. The majority of the calls were from her family, and they were...venomous was probably the nicest word she could come up with. She'd blocked half of them first thing this morning. She froze when her phone rang again but breathed a sigh of relief when she realized who it was.

"Hey, Lace."

"Mason freaking Knight, Celine! You're getting married, and I had to find out from The Ruling Three's social media page. What the hell, girl?"

Celine laughed, her shoulders relaxing. "It just happened, Lacey. And you know how my father is. I couldn't be sure he wouldn't pull out of the deal at the very last minute."

"Oh, so it's a marriage merger? When in the hell did this happen?"

Celine put the phone on speaker and set it on the counter. "It's been crazy. We haven't had a chance to talk since the funeral. Well. Long story short, Grandfather left everything to me, but the will stipulates that I have to be married."

She hurriedly thumbed her way to the internet on her phone and went to the main page of the Ruling Three's website. Her breath caught. There on the front page was a picture of her and Mason someone had taken at a party with a mating announcement. She greedily took in the image, amazed that someone had caught the shot. She hadn't been aware anyone had been paying attention to the two of them. To a casual viewer, it looked like they were together and had been for some time. Giddy excitement filled her.

"Ah, okay. And the Knights, of course, agreed. Your grandfather was extremely wealthy." Lacey said.

The words themselves weren't malicious, but her tone rubbed Celine the wrong way. "I'm sure Mason Knight doesn't need my money."

She put her focus back on dinner, cutting up potatoes.

"Oh, of course, I'm sorry for how that sounded," Lacey hurried and said. "I just meant—"

"I know what you meant," Celine muttered, irritated.

For a moment, she'd gotten caught up in the excitement all over again, but reality intruded. Her grandfather had so many holdings and companies that would benefit Knight Industries. It would be foolish of her to think he wanted her for anything other than that.

"I'm sorry, Celine. I spoke without thinking. I'm really excited for you. If it helps, all the gossip has been about that picture. It makes it seem like the two of you have been secretly dating." Lacey said.

Celine paused. "Really?"

"Really," Lacey confirmed. "But...have you two been secretly dating?"

"Lacey," she chided.

She didn't answer the question, though. She'd much prefer that rumor to people thinking she could only get a man because her grand-father was wealthy. That probably made her petty, but a girl had her pride.

"Are you excited?" Lacey prodded.

She smiled. "Despite everything, yes."

Lacey laughed. "I'm happy for you. I can't believe it!"

Her phone beeped, and Celine peeked down at it. Her heart fluttered. "I gotta go, Lace. That's Mason on the other line."

Lacey squealed. "Yesss, call me later."

Celine promised she would and clicked over to the other call. "Hi."

"Love bug," he greeted. "What you doing?"

"Cooking." She shoveled all the potatoes into a pot and started the water.

"I want to come over," he said.

Celine froze and stared at her phone. "Umm, yeah, that would be fine."

He laughed, and the doorbell rang. Her eyes widened, and she gasped, looking towards the front door.

"You're here now?"

She looked down at the thin t-shirt dress she wore. It was her favorite to lounge around in, and it showed. The thing was damn near see through and clung to her thick body. She grabbed her boobs and let out a sigh of relief. At least she was wearing a bra.

"Come open the door, love bug." He commanded.

Her heart started racing as she fast-walked through the living room. She took a quick look around, very happy that she'd cleaned earlier in the week. It wasn't like she was a junky person, to begin with, so there was that. She took a deep breath when she reached the heavy oak door, standing on her toes to peek out the peephole.

She opened the door and took a step back. Lord have mercy, Mason Knight was fine as hell and standing at her doorstep. He wore a pair of black jeans and a black, short-sleeve button-down that was unbuttoned to the top of his chest. She took a deep breath and closed her eyes as the scent of his cologne filled her senses. Her panther perked up at the wild smell underneath that signaled his animal.

Her gaze finally made it back up to his face, and the dark lust in his eyes as he stared at her caught her breath. Worry about what she was wearing went out the window. The way he stared at her said he liked it, which made her feel incredible...sexy. That was new. She gave him a nervous smile.

"It smells amazing in here," he said, pulling her into his chest.

"I'm cooking," she said into his chest as he pressed them close together. She inhaled again, letting his scent wash over her.

He walked them into the house and shut the door behind him. She stepped out of his arms as he locked the door.

"I'm making herb-crusted pork chop." She waved for him to follow her into the kitchen. "Luckily for you, I make enough for leftovers."

"You want some help?" He looked around, a slight smile on his face.

She scoffed. "I don't think so."

He smiled wider. "Hey, I can cook."

"Um, I remember conversations where you admitted to me that you subsisted on takeout."

He gave her a sheepish smile. She'd never seen that look on his face before. She liked it.

"Plus, I don't like people in the kitchen at the same time as me, getting in my way." She pointed to the cushioned stool at her kitchen island.

"Duly noted," he said as he sat.

She checked the timer on her pork chops and started washing and cutting the green beans she'd picked out of her garden. She was nervous as he watched her work, but at least the task kept her from obsessing.

"The news is out. How are you feeling?" He broke the silence.

"Nervous," she admitted. "I talked to my friend, and the gossip has already started. You want something to drink?"

"I'll take whatever you're drinking." He nodded toward her wine glass.

Her cheeks heated, and she wanted to stick her head in the pot of potatoes she was about to mash.

"What?" He asked, smiling.

She cleared her throat. "It's kool-aid."

He threw his head back and laughed. She couldn't help the wide smile that covered her face at his amusement.

"Celine, I swear you are so damn funny," he said, standing up. "Where you keep the glasses."

She turned from the pot. "I can—"

"I got it, love bug, just keep working." He said, pulling out the pitcher of kool-aid she'd mixed earlier.

"Glasses are in the cabinet right next to the fridge." She told him.

He pulled one down and filled his glass with a chuckle. He sat down and tasted it, laughing again. "Okay, now, tell me how you feel, Celine."

"I'm happy. I like you, and this could've ended so much worse." She bit her lip as soon as the words escaped. She could've worded that a lot better.

He smirked, not in the least insulted. It was one of the reasons they got along so well. He never took offense at the things she'd blurt out. She hadn't quite mastered the public persona.

"I gave my mother your number. She wants to plan the engagement party with you."

She froze, nervous. She didn't do well with parties.

"I told her," he said softly, seeming to read her mind. "But, you know my father's position."

She nodded. Of course, it would have to be a tri-council event. Her hands shook as she prepared the food. Her phone rang, and she sighed at the unknown number. She didn't answer, wouldn't dare in front of Mason. She didn't know which family member it was and had no plans to be embarrassed in front of him. She sent the call to voicemail.

"Do you want a big wedding?" She asked to distract him when the phone started buzzing again.

"I honestly don't care, either way, love bug. I'll leave that up to you." He eyed her phone when it stopped ringing and started again.

She growled and put it on vibrate so the ringer would stop interrupting them. "If it were up to me, we'd get married outside with like maybe six people."

He nodded. "I'll let mom know."

Her eyes widened, and she looked up from what she was doing. "You would..."

"Celine, I want you to be comfortable. If that's what you want, then that's what we'll have."

She nodded, relieved, happy.

"Let's talk about living arrangements."

She took a shaky breath and turned to him. "You work downtown. It's a bit of a commute way out here."

He nodded. "I can swing it for the most part, but there will be some days when I need to stay in the city. Will you be okay with that?"

"Oh," she said.

Of course. If he stayed in the city, then he could have access to the women he'd have to give up because of her. It would be discreet, but her panther swiped at her, not liking the thought of that.

"I'll make sure you get plenty of notice so you can make arrangements here. Maybe we can work out a schedule for your busy season. I'm sure you won't want to be from here long during a busy season."

Her eyes widened. "Oh, you mean...."

He frowned. "What did you think I meant, Celine?"

"I just thought...."

He shook his head, "already trying to get rid of me."

"No," she said hastily.

"I'm joking, love bug."

"Oh," she laughed with him.

Mason studied his soon-to-be wife. She was nervous, but that was expected. They'd have to change their lives within a matter of months. Celine didn't seem like the type that liked change, and this was a major one. They talked while she finished making dinner, and he enjoyed watching her in the kitchen. He mostly enjoyed watching her as Celine reached for stuff. The hem of that shirt dress she wore would lift, and he'd get a look at all that glorious skin. Her thick thighs were beckoning his touch. He wanted to feel her skin.

"Do you want to eat in here, or I can set the dining room table," she asked him. She caught him watching her.

He licked his lips and begged his animal to behave so they could make it out of here without attacking Celine. "Here is fine." He stood to help, but she waved him back into his seat.

His mouth watered at the plate she set in front of him. It smelled and looked amazing. He liked the thought of her cooking for him. Her phone buzzed for what seemed like the fiftieth time. He finally frowned and looked at her.

"Celine, who is calling you like that?"

She looked embarrassed and shrugged. "It could be any one of my family members. They don't want the marriage to go through."

"They want your inheritance."

She nodded. "My mother and her sisters are angry. My Uncles are..." she shuddered. "The money has caused a problem."

"Why did your grandfather leave it to you and not them?"

She shrugged. "According to his lawyer, Grandfather regretted the way he acted in life and thought, I guess, this would make up for how he'd spoiled his children. He said they'd gotten their inheritance during the years he'd been alive. I guess they borrowed a lot of money from Grandfather. Honestly, if you had seen how they circled him when he found out he was dying. They were like vultures. I don't blame him for not giving them anything. My family is not nice."

He grunted because it was true. They were all social climbers, and the things they did to get as far as they had made for scary reading. His father had had the whole family investigated while they were going through contract negotiations, and there was a moment there where Dallas had been tempted to call it off. All it had meant for Mason was that he wanted to get her out of the situation she found herself in. He didn't think her father would be picky about who he chose for Celine.

He said nothing as she prayed over the food.

The phone rang again, and Mason lifted it from the counter before she could grab it. He swiped to accept the call but said nothing. He stared at her as the vitriol from the other end poured in.

"Don't let me find you," he told the person. "Don't take this as a threat because it's a promise. As soon as I match this voice with a face, I'm fucking you up. Make sure the rest of the family gets the message."

The line was quiet before they hung up. The message was received, and that was all that mattered.

Celine's eyes were big, her fork hovering over her plate as she stared at him in disbelief. He waited to see if she would say anything, but she just took a shuddering breath before going back to eating. He smiled because he didn't scent any fear or apprehension from her, simply shock. He could deal with shock. He pulled his phone out and texted his security team. Now that the news of their engagement was out, he worried about what her family would do. He didn't like the tone of those threats, and desperate people did wild things when it came to money.

"Have the threats escalated?"

"Not so far," she told him.

His security manager texted him that they'd have someone on Celine before he left. Satisfied that was taken care of, he went back to his food. They ate and got to know each other, and Mason was reminded of how much he liked her. They would be a good match, and he looked forward to marrying her. He was glad that he'd left the office early to come over. His assistant had stared at him in surprise when he passed them at five. Typically, they beat him out the door.

After dinner, they went into the living room, and she put on a movie. He sat next to Celine as she tried to sit on the other side of the sofa away from him.

That wouldn't do.

"Aht-aht." He pulled her back next to him, sliding her legs onto his lap.

She squirmed for a moment before she settled. Mason slid his hand beneath the shirt dress, feeling her soft thighs and closing his eyes as he fought his panther. He would be between them soon enough. He slid his hands higher, resting them on her soft stomach. He raked his eyes over her curvy body, already imagining the ways he'd take her, which was definitely not a good idea. He was getting worked up.

"Quit touching my pooch," she fussed. "You're making me self-conscious."

He hummed and leaned into her neck, nuzzling her skin. "Your skin is so soft. I can't wait to rest my head here."

She narrowed her eyes at him.

He laughed. She didn't believe him yet... that was fine. He could show her better than he could tell her.

"Not now, it's too close to your pussy, and I'm holding on by a thread as is."

She gasped, and her panther's power filled the space between them as the scent of her arousal rose. Fuck, he needed to go before shit really got out of hand. He moved his hand from under her shirt reluctantly and stood.

"I need to go. I got work in the morning. I'll call you tomorrow, love bug."

She stood with him and walked him to the door. "That's right, busy building that empire."

He smiled at her teasing. "I got security outside for tonight. Tomorrow, we'll work on making the farm a lot safer, okay."

"I don't need—"

He cut her off with a kiss on her full lips. "You're mine now, Celine, and I protect what's mine. That means security, like the rest of us."

She nodded, dazed. "Text me when you get home," she whispered.

"Will do," he leaned down and gave her another kiss, this one a little longer.

Her chin lifted, and she sighed into the kiss. She was so damn sweet.

"Lock the door, so I can leave." He waited as she closed the door, and he heard the deadbolt before he left.

He scanned outside of her house until he spotted his enforcers. Satisfied that she would be okay tonight, he got into the backseat of the blacked-out Escalade, his security getting in after him. Tonight was a good start for his relationship with Celine. Despite the hard-on he was leaving with, he was satisfied.

six

Celine's knee bounced as the chauffeured truck she was riding in cruised through Friday night traffic. She was being driven by her new security guard named Lance. So far, they were getting along. He'd taken over her pool house and sort of... hovered, but he wasn't intrusive, and with the number of calls she was getting from her family, she was very happy to have him there.

They'd had their first hiccup when he'd insisted on driving her to Mason's family's house. He hadn't taken no for an answer, and he'd tried to put her in the back seat. She'd simply rolled her eyes and sat in the front. She hadn't ridden in the backseat of a car since she'd moved out of her parent's house.

Nerves started attacking her stomach the moment they pulled up to an ornate gate. Hard-faced shifters staffed it as security. She objectively knew that being in the tri-council was dangerous, but this level of protection brought it home for her. The guards checked the truck as they sat there, and once they looked into the interior, they waved them through. She nearly gasped as she came to the house.

It was beautiful, stately. They circled the fountain in the front, and Lance pulled her up to the front door. Mason was waiting for her on the front porch. Her heart was racing as he came down the steps to open her door. He held her hand as she stepped down, pulling her into his chest. He leaned down and kissed her, and even after the two weeks they'd been engaged, she was still getting used to his easy affection. Learning and discovering this side of him was amazing.

"Hey, love bug. You look beautiful," he told her.

Her cheeks heated. She'd worn a wrap dress, the maroon color her favorite. She was worried there was a bit too much cleavage, but from the hungry look in Mason's eyes, he wasn't concerned about it. She stood on her toes and kissed him. She didn't know what made her so bold, but he deepened the kiss, and she was glad she had.

He stepped back. "How was your week?"

She nodded. "Fine. You?"

"Busy, or I would've made time to see you again."

"It's fine," she told him. She understood how important his work was to him.

"I'll have to make it up to you." He nuzzled into the side of her neck, his panther brushing across her skin. "Come on. My mother is anxious to see you."

"I'm nervous," she admitted, gripping his hand tightly.

"Don't be. It'll be fine."

He walked her through the door, and she looked around. The place was beautiful. It was opulent but still warm. Pictures of Mason and his brother were displayed prominently in between artwork that she knew cost a pretty penny. His parents stood when they came into the sitting room.

"Celine," his mother greeted, rubbing her cheek against her hair.

Celine's panther raised to return the greeting, and Celine was shocked. Her family didn't live so easily with their animal.

Adina Knight was beautiful, dressed elegantly, her jewelry and clothes tasteful. None of it disguised the panther lurking beneath her skin. Celine had seen her around at council events, but she was still shocked by how closely the older woman wore her animal. She didn't hide what she was. There was no blending into human society for her. The same could be said for his father. He and Mason looked alike, except Dallas was darker skinned and had a white beard. He was handsome, dangerous. He was part of the ruling three, and his power was evident. It was in the way he walked, his dark penetrating stare. Everything about him screamed predator.

She took a deep breath, calming her panther. The curious creature had sat forward, easily giving room and submission to his cat. Dallas Knight was an imposing figure, he looked dangerous, but the smile on his face softened the predator. He and Adina made a very striking match. It made her a little self-conscious. Would she compliment Mason that well? She was nowhere near as personable as him, and she certainly didn't move about society the way he did. She worried that his parents would hold that against her, but they were both warm as they greeted her, nuzzling against the top of her head.

"Congratulations, lil mama," Dallas told her, rubbing his cheek against her hair. "And welcome to our family."

She felt relief because she was confident that Mason would not get the same welcome from her family. They especially wouldn't make an effort to greet his panther. Her family worked very hard to fit into human society. They erased most signs of their animal when out in public.

"Come, dinner is ready." Adina preceded them into a dining room.

Celine and Mason sat across from his parents. They left the head of the table empty, making the dinner more intimate than formal.

"So, Celine, tell us about yourself," Adina said.

She froze, unsure what to say. "Umm, there's not much to tell. I spend most of my time on my farm working."

"Where did you go to school?" She asked as she waved a server over with the first course.

"Well, I took classes at the community college before going to Florida State. By the time I went, it only took me a year to finish the courses I wanted."

She left out the part where her father forced her to take as many courses as possible so that he could hurry her back underneath his thumb.

"How did you react to your grandfather's will," Dallas asked.

She cleared her throat. "There wasn't much I could do about it. My father is a man that doesn't take no for an answer." She looked at

Mason and smiled. "Mason agreeing to it has been a Godsend, if I'm being honest."

Adina smiled. "Yes, any woman would be lucky to have my baby."

"Oh Lord," Dallas murmured.

"What, I can brag on my son. He could've sat in this big ass house and rested on what you built, but instead, he stepped out from under your shadow and built his own." Adina said proudly.

"It's very admirable," Celine agreed.

"Of course, all that building comes with a downside. I didn't think I'd ever get a daughter-in-law between my two sons. He's always so busy."

"Chill out, Ma," Mason said with a smile.

"I researched your farm while we were doing contract negotiations, Celine. I'm impressed with what you've created." Dallas turned the subject to her.

Her eyes widened.

"Emily told me that you couldn't leave without talking to her," Adina said.

Celine warmed, her cheeks heating.

"You purposely put someone else as the face of the company?" Dallas asked,

She nodded. "My family isn't supportive. It's easier for them to forget it exists with Deena as the face. Plus, she's a lot better in front of the camera than I am."

Adina smiled. "I don't know why your parents wouldn't be proud of that."

"Thank you." She glowed under their praise.

"What about the phone calls you were getting?" Dallas' question surprised her.

She looked at Mason. He'd told his father about the calls? She turned back to his parents. "Mason got me a new phone, so they've stopped."

She didn't add that there were now packages left on her doorstep in lieu of the calls.

"Well, thank God for that," Adina said. "You should probably move out there before the wedding, Mason, just to be on the safe side."

Celine's eyes widened.

"It's a good idea, Mason," Dallas chimed in.

She picked up her wine glass and took a big gulp, anxious to see what Mason would say.

"I've already made arrangements. I'm taking care of it, Pop."

Lord have mercy. Mason was moving in before the wedding? She worked to keep her heart rate down and keep her excitement contained. Her leg started bouncing beneath the table. Mason placed a hand there, leaning over and kissing her shoulder.

"Settle," he whispered in her ear.

She nodded and picked up her fork as the next course was served. She would get through this dinner without embarrassing herself...hopefully.

Mason watched Celine as she got more comfortable with his parents. He relaxed and settled. The dinner was going well, and he could tell from his mother's questions that she liked Celine. Not that he had doubts about it. She was sweet, and once a person could get close enough to her, she was naturally witty. She smelled amazing sitting next to him. The dress she wore was driving him crazy. The color contrasted beautifully against her skin, and that little vee in the front was going to get him into trouble. He peeked down her dress again, his mouth-watering. Now that he'd committed to marrying her, it was like feelings he had been suppressing were coming out. His panther took it as a sign that it was go time, and now every time he was near her, the damned animal was reaching for her. He wanted her to himself.

"Mason says that you want a small wedding." His mother's voice broke him out of his fantasies.

Celine nodded. "If that's okay."

Adina waved her hand. "It's perfectly fine. We can have a big engagement party to make up for it. That way, we can just say you wanted something more intimate for the wedding."

His soon-to-be wife relaxed next to him, visibly relieved.

"Should I call your mother to help arrange the engagement party?" Adina asked.

Celine choked on the wine she was drinking. He rubbed her back and grimaced. He had to wonder about the relationship she had with her parents because she made an effort to avoid talking about them.

"Umm..."

Adina gave her a sympathetic smile. "I'll handle the details, don't you worry about it. Your mother can't blame you if I take over."

"You'd be surprised," Celine said softly.

Dallas grunted and gave him a look. Mason raised his eyebrows, on the same page with his father. They both knew how far Cece's parents controlled her.

"I got it," Adina assured her.

Mason quickly changed the subject. The rest of dinner went by quickly, and it wasn't long before he was helping Celine out of her chair. He wanted to rush her, his need for her making his hands shake.

Adina gave him a knowing smile. "Wait, Emily wants to talk to Celine. She's trying to grow an herb garden."

Mason barely stopped himself from groaning. Dallas walked him outside.

"She's sweet, Mason."

"I know, Pop."

"You're still thinking of mating her?"

He nodded. "My panther is insisting on it. I guess I've been so focused on work. I wasn't paying attention to what he'd been trying to tell me about her."

Dallas sucked his teeth. "I done told you about not listening to your instinct."

"I understand."

He looked over at Lance and saw him pacing next to the truck on the phone. He went over.

"What's going on?"

Lance looked nervous. He passed his phone over to Mason. "This happened a few minutes ago."

Mason cursed as he watched some hooded person walk up to Celine's house and throw something through the window, smashing them one after the other. His panther rose, furious, the hair on his arms raising before Mason could get control.

"Has anything else been happening?" He growled.

"I saw someone drop a package off two days in a row. I assumed it was stuff for her farm, but with this, I'm curious to its content."

Mason flexed his hands as his claws pushed against his skin. "Go ahead and handle that. I'll keep Celine with me tonight." He told Lance.

Lance nodded, "I'm going to add another body at the ranch for now."

He thought back to his parents' words. "I'll move in after the engagement party. That will give you two more bodies. Does she have the space?"

"The pool house has two bedrooms, we can make that work, and I'll get with Julian to set up a duty roster."

Mason nodded and turned when the front door opened. "I'll let Celine know. Get someone out there first thing in the morning to replace the windows. Is the system I ordered in place?"

"They're nearly done, but I'll get them out there to finish up tomorrow."

"Celine doesn't want cameras inside," he reminded Lance.

Lance nodded and got into the truck.

Mason walked back towards the house, but Celine met him halfway. She frowned. "Where is Lance going?"

He grabbed her hand and brought her into his chest. "You're coming home with me tonight."

"Why?"

He kissed her lips lightly, "dang, you don't want to spend more time with your fiancé?"

"That's..." she narrowed her eyes. "You're hiding something."

Damn, she was perceptive.

"There was some ruckus at your house, and Lance went to take care of it. You'll stay with me tonight and worry about it in the morning."

"What kind of ruckus? What happened?"

"Unless you want my father involved, let's get in the car and discuss it."

She looked back at his parents. "Yeah, I've heard how your father handles things."

He smiled to hide his anger and didn't bother telling her that his father had taught him well. He would be handling the situation precisely the way Dallas would. He just needed time to find out who'd done it.

"Come, love bug." He walked them back to the porch, and they said their goodbyes to his parents.

He'd barely started the car before she turned to him. "What happened?"

"Someone busted a few of the windows at your house."

"Oh my God," she said. "I want to see."

"In the morning, Cece."

She growled, her panther riled. It was the first time he'd seen her animal in any way of wildness. She suppressed it immediately, and he sighed. He'd have to work on that.

seven

She was quiet the whole way to his apartment. The tension in the car raised the moment he pulled into his garage. He waited until his security waved for him to leave the car before he went around and helped Celine out. As they ascended in the elevator, she clutched his hands, her nervousness broadcasting clearly. He used his key to open the elevator and escorted her through the foyer into his condo.

She looked around, her curious gaze taking in everything. "I love this."

"Good, this is where we'll stay when we need to be in the city."

His eyes followed her as she walked around his space, lightly touching things. The way the skirt swished around her legs was slightly mesmerizing. He could almost feel the soft thickness of them wrapped around his body. She turned to him and lifted her eyebrow, having caught him staring. Her expression was a shy pleasure that he liked on her.

"I don't have anything to change into," she said softly.

His mind went straight to the gutter, but he cleared his expression, hoping the hunger didn't show. "I can find you something. You want to shower?"

Her eyes widened a touch before she nodded. He inclined his head towards the hallway, waiting tensely as she passed him. Her soft scent floated to him as she passed. Celine was slowly seducing him, and she'd done nothing save be herself. Her curious gaze turned back to him, a small smile adorning her face as she stepped into his bedroom. The panther inside him was still, watchful, careful of their next move. Celine was not a woman to rush. They both knew this on an instinctual level.

"Just through here?" She pointed towards his bathroom.

Mason had a guest bathroom that she could've used, but he wanted the scent of her lingering in all the spaces where he would be.

"You can shower in here, and I'll have clothes waiting for you when you're done." His voice was gruff.

He was nervous.

That was a first for him on a couple different levels. For one, he didn't bring women back to the place where he would lay his head. His parents had stressed that. However, they'd each had their different reasons for the advice. Dallas had made his life in the streets and said it was all about safety. Adina...well, female shifters didn't play games, and she'd advised him that his potential mate would take exception to a string of women being in and out of space that would be hers.

Either way, he'd taken the advice to heart. It had made clear boundaries for the women he slept with. Celine was the first and only woman besides his mother that had been inside his condo.

He grabbed her a towel from the linen closet and put it on the sink. She was standing next to it, so his arm grazed her waist, and she sucked in a breath. Tension thickened the air in the bathroom. She stared at him, and he couldn't decipher the expression on her face. She was so good at hiding her feelings. He leaned over into her space, and her sharp inhale made him smile.

"Let me know if you need anything else." He trailed a finger down her skin. "I'll be in the living room."

She nodded but said nothing. He licked his lips, and she mimicked the motion, her eyes dropping down to his mouth. Mason nuzzled against her cheek and inhaled her scent. It calmed him just as much as it riled him. It perfectly summed up his feelings for Celine.

*****

Celine pulled down on the tight shirt Mason had given her. The simple A-shirt clung to her breasts and stomach. The shorts were a little better, not as tight, but she was still a little self-conscious. She wished she had something sexier to wear for her first night with Mason. She snorted and smoothed down the shirt. There was nothing saying they'd sleep together. Hell, she didn't even know if he wanted her like that. She took a deep breath, exited the bathroom, and retraced her steps back to his living room.

The room was semi-dark, the only light coming from the muted television. The screen was big enough to light up most of the room. Mason was on the sofa, his fingers flying over the keys of his laptop, his face a mask of concentration. He was so damn handsome. The light reflected off the deep waves in his hair, and the dark shadows put his features in stark relief. His prominent nose and full lips stood out. The well-groomed beard on his chin looked soft in the dim lighting.

She stood at the end of the sofa, unsure of what to do. Awkwardness assailed her, the dreaded feeling one she was familiar with within social settings. She was ordinarily comfortable with Mason, so she didn't understand why she was being such a dork.

She cleared her throat, and he looked up. "If you're working, I can just go to bed."

He set the laptop on the floor next to him. His eyes narrowed as he got a good look at her, his soft growl making her heart race.

He licked his lips, his gaze caressing her body. "No, it's fine. I'd love to chill with you."

Celine sat gingerly. "What are you watching? Never mind, I forgot. You don't have time to watch t.v."

She turned when he didn't respond to her joke. He crooked his finger and her breath caught at the heat in his eyes. She slid over closer to him.

His lips quirked. "Closer, love bug."

Her heart thumped, her clit matching the rhythm as she did what he asked. She moved until their thighs were touching. The fresh scent of soap wafted from him, along with his cat's deeper, muskier scent. A part of her wanted to cuddle closer and wallow in that scent. Her panther urged her closer, but she shut the wanton creature down.

"How has your week been?" He asked, facing her and throwing his arm across the back of the sofa.

"Not bad. Deena and I have been filling orders all week." She turned to face him. "You?"

He slid his hand across her hair. "Same ol'. How have you handled the news spreading?"

She shrugged. Outside of her family, there wasn't anyone overly concerned with her business. She was sure that there had been shock about the news, but she didn't do social events outside of the ones her mother obligated her to do, so she wasn't privy to any actual gossip.

"Did you get any angry calls from women now that you've taken yourself off the market?" She teased.

"Angry, nah. I ain't on that type of level with anyone. If you remember, I showed up to events alone." He reminded her.

She smiled. "That would explain why you had time to entertain me instead of mingling. I don't know if I've ever thanked you for rescuing me at those things. I can't imagine how much more unbearable they would've been."

"You weren't even trying." He chuckled. "I didn't even have to look around for you. I just looked for the nearest window slash corner combination, and there you were."

A laugh burst from her at that bit of truth. "Fair."

His eyes traced her face. "My father called me out the other day. Said I searched for you at every event I attended. I hadn't realized I was so obvious."

Her breath caught at both his words and the intensity of his gaze.

"Nothing to say to that?"

"There's no way I'm your type." She said finally.

"You're gorgeous."

It was said so matter of fact. The seriousness in his tone suggested that he wasn't just saying it to be flattering. Which made it all the more so...

"I've never seen you with a ...big girlfriend."

"Have you ever seen me with a girlfriend?" he curled her hair around his finger, his gaze intense.

She opened her mouth but then closed it because she had not, not in any of the time she'd known him.

"Exactly," he said, grabbing her chin. "Besides, what type of woman I used to date has no bearing on how gorgeous you are."

Her cheeks burned.

"Say thank you, love bug." He pulled down on her chin, making her lips move as though she were talking.

She laughed because he was so silly. They always had fun together. It was usually just the two of them in the corner eating hors d'oeuvres. She'd lived for those interactions. It pleased her that they kept the same energy even in the predicament they found themselves in.

He smiled and leaned forward, kissing her softly. It took her breath away.

"Mason," she said softly.

"You can't be saying my name like that, love bug."

Butterflies attacked her stomach, and her core clenched in need. He closed his eyes and took a deep breath.

"Now see, I'm trying to behave," he said, leaning over her neck and scraping his teeth down the side. "I can smell the sweet scent of your arousal."

Moisture seeped from her sex, and heat filled her, further filling the air between them. She couldn't hide how much he turned her on. He walked his fingers up her legs to the apex of her thighs. He slipped his fingers into the leg of her shorts and skimmed the lips of her sex. She hissed, waffling between hoping he deepened the touch and a little scared that he would. When he slid a finger across her clit, she moaned.

"On a scale of 'a little bit behaving' to 'full-on wanton,' where does this fall?"

He chuckled, grabbing the back of her neck. "Somewhere in the middle," he whispered before sucking on her neck.

It raised her panther, and the eager animal rubbed against him, her power reaching up to touch against his.

"Oh, she like that," he murmured, bringing her chin around to him.

He kissed her, and gods did he know how to kiss. She's been fantasizing about Mason for a really long time, and even she couldn't have imagined it would be like this. Their tongues tangled, and Mason inserted his finger inside her pussy, and she pulled back, exhaling in pleasure.

"I can't wait to be inside of you, love bug. I got a feeling that your pussy will welcome me and squeeze me tight."

She whimpered, and he kissed her again, his fingers exerting more pressure. He didn't push for more, though. Instead, he took his time kissing her, sucking on her tongue, his pace lazy and decadent. She lost track of time as they made out on the sofa, neither of them in a rush. It gave her hope that their relationship wouldn't just be a business transaction. Soon though, she got impatient, her hips moving forward, needing more.

"I need..." she whispered.

"I got what you need, love bug." Mason thumbed her clit, and she burst, pleasure overtaking her. She closed her eyes, savoring the satisfaction. He kissed her lightly. "I like that look on your face."

He slipped his fingers out and sucked on them. Her channel spasmed in response, wanting him inside. He leaned over and kissed her, and she eagerly met him. She thought he would do more, but he didn't. Simply kissed her. Her body was relaxed and languid, and soon, her eyes were drifting closed. All the nervous tension from her day was finally catching up to her.

"Come, love bug. Bed."

"I want to sleep in your bed," she whispered, scared that he would reject her even after what they'd shared.

He scoffed. "That was a given," he told her, that smile she was coming to love on his face.

eight

Mason drove Celine home the following day. He'd loved waking up to her. He'd snuggled into her warmth, trying to coax her into staying in bed. But she wanted to check on her farm, and he couldn't blame her. She'd made him breakfast, complaining that he didn't keep groceries in the house. He should've felt irritated by the fussing, but he liked it. It made him feel cared for. He promised her that he would stock the fridge on the days she stayed. She'd given him a bemused look but nodded.

They pulled up to the house, and he frowned at the number of workers at her place. All that for broken glass?

Lance met them as they pulled up. "I wish you'd have given me more time, boss." He said as soon as they got out of the car.

Mason's heart rate picked up. "How bad is it?"

Lance glanced at Celine, "they trashed the inside a bit. I called the police once the proximity alarm was breached, so they didn't have long, but it was long enough. I have someone coming to clean up once the window is replaced and the walls fixed."

"Walls?" Celine said and rushed towards the house.

"CeCe," he called after her and raced behind her. He caught her on the porch. "You wait on me," he fussed.

She nodded, her eyes wide with panic. He went into the house first and cursed at the state of it. He was on the phone with his assistant as he entered fully and saw the damage.

"Torrance, start the process of packing up my apartment. I'm going to be moving in with my fiancée earlier than planned."

They promised to get it done, and Mason hung up.

"I need to see my greenhouse," Celine whispered, rushing through the house and to the back door.

The whole thing was still intact, and she let out a relieved breath. He pulled her into his chest.

"I'm having my stuff delivered so I can move in."

She nodded, relief relaxing her face. "Thank you."

"It's nothing, love bug. Go upstairs and check around while I talk with Lance."

Celine rushed upstairs, and Mason waited until she disappeared from his view before he turned towards the back door. Lance met him at the patio doors, inclining his head towards the backyard.

"What did you find out?"

Lance sighed. "Whoever it was was drunk as hell. The whole place was scented with them and whatever they'd drank."

"One of her cousins?" Mason took a look around and noticed that they hadn't gotten to the backyard.

"Most likely. The cameras are up around the whole property, including the woods surrounding the house. We got perimeter alarms set, and I programmed them to go to our phones, including yours." Lance reported.

He nodded, satisfied. "Would you recognize the scent again?"

Lance sucked his teeth in lieu of an answer. Mason had to laugh. He trusted Lance and knew the male was good at his job.

"So I don't have to tell you what to do if they come anywhere near Celine."

Lance gave him a smile that was all teeth. "You giving me permission to bust 'em over the head?"

"Do what you gotta do."

Lance nodded. "I'll get back at it."

*****

Hours later, the house was empty and dark. All the servicemen that had been up and through her space were gone. Celine's animal was still riled, restless. She and Mason had eaten take-out, and both tried to keep their conversation light. But, she'd noticed his own restlessness, his panther's energy erratic and angry. She didn't blame him. She was angry as well.

She'd gone to bed a couple of hours ago. Or rather, she'd tried. But that hadn't worked. She padded into the kitchen, hoping tea would help settle her. She wanted to be in bed with Mason if she were being honest with herself. There had been too much going on earlier, though, so she'd retreated to her room. Maybe she could go to the guest room. She didn't think he'd turn her away.

She frowned as she entered the kitchen. The smell of marijuana was strong. Curious, she walked to the patio door, looking out into the backyard. She spotted Mason sitting around the fire pit. A fire was going, and he had a bottle of whiskey next to him, staring into the flames.

Should she leave him to his brooding? She went through the motions to fix her tea, debating it as she waited on the water to boil. Minutes later, her tea steeped the way she liked, she summoned the courage and walked outside.

"Can I join you?"

He stared at her through the haze of smoke before nodding. He stood up as she got closer, but she waved for him to sit down. She took a deep fortifying breath and sat next to him instead of across the fire.

"Is everything okay?" She asked quietly.

He nodded. "Long week." His voice was husky, and the light of his panther was in his eyes. He was shirtless, in only a pair of sweatpants and bare feet. Tattoos covered his torso. It was hot. She wanted to apologize for adding to his long week, but she swallowed the apology.

"You went running?" She asked.

"I wanted to check out the area."

"Did your security team get settled?" She got nervous and took a sip of tea.

He studied her. "What's wrong?"

She shook her head. "Just restless."

He blew out smoke, and she didn't know how to take him staring at her. Her cat was curious, and she squelched the animal from reaching out to his. He chuckled as though he knew what she was doing.

She gave him a bemused smile. "I usually have a little more control than that."

"It's all good, Celine." He stubbed out his blunt and motioned for her to come to him.

Her eyes widened.

He chuckled. "Am I supposed to act like last night didn't happen? Ain't no going back, CeCe."

She let out a shaky breath. Of course, he was right. She was being skittish for no reason. She put down her teacup, stood, and he pulled on her t-shirt to bring her closer, tugging her into his lap. She was stiff for a few moments, but he made no additional moves, just held her there. He lifted his cup, sipped it, and stared at the fire.

"My parents are mated." His deep voice broke the easy silence. "Before this society shit, they were just two cats from the hood, right."

She turned to face him.

"I don't know anything but that. I grew up with a type of loyalty the people we're around don't know about."

Her heart was thumping because she wasn't sure where he was going with this.

"I guess, what I'm saying, is that I don't share."

Her stomach dipped as he gripped her chin and brought her face to his.

"If we do this, you're mine, ya dig? Beneath the suits I wear to work, I'm the animal my father raised us to be, and I'll fuck anyone up behind you."

She licked her lips, holding her breath. "I'm not...there's no one else." She whispered.

Not in all the years she'd been on her own had she been in a serious relationship. Though her father ignored her, he still had plans for her and ensured that anyone she dated had been thoroughly vetted to the point where it hadn't been worth it to get invested.

"Same for me. I won't disrespect our mating."

"Mating," she whispered. She had hoped after the contract terms had been read, but to hear him say it aloud...

"I told you, that's all I know, love bug. My panther won't accept anything less than full submission."

It felt like a warning. One that sent a thrill down her spine. She nodded. He pecked her on the lips and settled back in his chair, taking another sip. She didn't know what to do with that. She turned her head back to the fire. Did she get up and leave? She was stuck in a sort of indecisive loop. Her anxiety spiraled until she was frustrated with herself. He chuckled again and tugged on her shirt until she laid back on his chest.

"Relax, love bug." He kissed the top of her head, and her panther reached out for his, their power rubbing against each other.

She released a sigh at the heat that filled her. It made her feel safe, and her cat settled. She wrapped her arms around his waist and stared out into the dark night. She could hear his steady heartbeat in her ear, and it lulled her body into a deeper relaxed state. She caught sight of his security as they prowled her land. That would take some getting used to.

Mason leaned down and inhaled the scent of Celine's hair, his panther happy to have her close. The animal was pushing for more, but he would be content to hold her for now. She burrowed deeper into his chest, and he smiled. She may be shy when she was awake, but her panther made promises to his cat while she slept. Her power brushed against his panther, relaying the needs Celine suppressed. He pushed out his own power, reassuring the cat that they would take care of them. She shivered, and he slid his hand underneath her shirt, laying his palm on her back and lending her his heat. He kissed her forehead and rubbed his cheek against her head, marking her with his scent.

"Up, love bug," he told her softly.

She tensed a moment and then looked up, disoriented.

"You can't sleep in my lap all night. At least not in this chair." He told her, smiling.

Her eyes widened as she absorbed his words. "Oh, my God, I'm so sorry, Mason."

"Settle," he gently ordered. "You're getting cold. I didn't want to startle you, that's all."

She nodded and scrambled from his lap. He would've just carried her to bed if the chair wasn't so low. Though, that was dangerous in his state of mind. His panther was feeling on edge, and their skittish mate wasn't quite ready for that.

"You can sleep with me," she said hesitantly. "I should've said so earlier, but I was shaken."

He smiled. "I didn't want to assume."

She nodded. "Of course."

He followed her upstairs and settled into bed with her. He'd told her that it had been a long week, and it had. He was exhausted between getting his company ready for the merger that would go down once they were married and the threats to her. He sidled up behind her, pulling her into his arms. She sighed, and before long, the both of them were sleeping.

nine

Celine could name ten things she would rather be doing than traipsing across Eastfield with her mother, looking for a dress for her engagement party. The whole ride was spent with Veronica trying to bully her into a large wedding. That was buttressed by her aunt Dorothy telling her that she shouldn't get married at all. Because, of course, she couldn't shop for a dress on her own, and Veronica was certainly not letting Mason's mother be the only deciding factor.

It was her fault for telling Veronica that Adina would be joining them. She could only roll her eyes when her aunt and her daughters showed up with her mother. The only good thing about that was her cousin Daniel's wife Kate had tagged along. Kate and Daniel had been the only family members to congratulate Celine on her upcoming wedding. She didn't anticipate much help from her, though, because her aunt kept her kids and their spouses underneath her thumb much the same way Veronica did her.

Adina showing up with her sisters in tow hadn't improved the situation. But, it should be an even scrap if something went down. Celine sighed in relief when they reached the next dress shop. This was shop number three, and she was beyond aggravated.

An employee met them at the door with a glass of champagne, and Celine gladly partook. She didn't usually drink, but she needed something if she was going to get through the rest of the day. No matter what it took, she was finding a dress at this shop. She couldn't do another store with this group. Kate grabbed her arm the moment they were inside. She'd spent the better part of the excursion trying to keep Celine excited about the process.

"Come on, Cece. Hopefully, you find a dress here, and we can avoid an all-out war." Kate dragged her towards the back of the shop and a rack of beautiful dresses.

Celine sighed in relief. "I'm getting a dress out of here. I don't care what it looks like. I can't do this anymore."

Kate snickered. "Mother Dorothy is doing her damnedest to insert herself into this whole process."

Celine rolled her eyes at that bit of understatement. She didn't know how her friend dealt with being married into this family. In her opinion, Daniel wasn't worth the aggravation of dealing with Dorothy as a mother-in-law. She eyed a blush pink, sequined mermaid dress with interest. The ruffle on the bottom was higher in the front and hung low in the back. She didn't normally like her arms out, but the corset top was so beautiful.

"Yesss," Kate said. She waved down the assistant. "Can we see this one?"

"Oh, wait, my mother."

Kate sighed in aggravation. "You know Aunt Veronica will say no. You should've seen your face. This is the one, and I know Mason will swallow his tongue."

She smiled at the thought of that.

"Absolutely not," Veronica snapped, coming up.

"Oh my God, Celine, yes. This is beautiful." Adina said as she joined them. She sent a petty look to Veronica.

Celine swallowed a sigh. She didn't know how much longer she could take the two women arguing.

"They probably don't have it in my size." She said to placate the situation.

Adina scoffed. "Maybe not, but it will be in your size by the time of the party. This shop caters to shifters, unlike the others we visited today." She waved at someone, and the dressmaker came up.

Celine winced at the dig at Veronica.

"Mrs. Knight, did you find one you liked?" The woman asked.

"She wants this one."

"Celine, you are not wearing such a, a...hoochie dress." Veronica interrupted.

Kate snorted. "And here we go," she said as she walked away.

Adina turned and faced her. "I don't want to make you wear this if you're not comfortable."

Celine eyed her mother and swallowed a sigh. "I can see what other dresses she has in my size."

Sensing the turmoil, the dressmaker smiled and jumped in. "I have a few dresses that are similar, but if in the end, you want this one, it can be done," the dressmaker reassured her.

She nodded and put on her public smile. They were led to a private fitting room where there was more champagne, a charcuterie board, and plush sofas surrounding a raised dais. It was quiet as they waited on the dressmaker to wheel in the clothes rack. Celine was amazed at the array of colors and fabrics. For a moment, she had been worried that she'd be limited to a few. Adina stood and marched over to the rack. Veronica was hot on her heels. Celine stayed seated, knowing her mother would take issue with whatever she chose. She rubbed her temples as her mother and Adina went at it. Soon their sisters joined in, rushing to back them.

Kate plopped on the chaise next to Celine. "Next time, we're leaving their asses behind."

She snorted. She absolutely agreed with that.

"You know, I heard some rumors about Mason," Kate said off-handedly.

Celine turned her full attention to her cousin and narrowed her eyes. "What kind of rumors?"

"Well, I didn't want to say anything and start unnecessary drama," Kate whispered, looking around.

Celine was nearing the point of snapping at her to spit it out, but they had way too many ears around. She pulled Kate up and stepped out the door of the shop.

"Ok, spill."

Kate looked chagrined. "I mean, it could very well be a lie."

"What is it, Kate?" she snapped impatiently.

"Keara is telling people that she would take Mason from you. She insinuated that they were sleeping together."

Celine's heart thundered in her chest, and for a moment, the world around her spun. Mason would never...right?

*****

Mason growled when he saw his laptop on the kitchen counter where he'd left it this morning. He was out of sorts and running behind in his daily schedule. It was his fault really. He'd woken up early because he couldn't sleep and worked well into the morning. He and Celine had been living together for two weeks, and although they were getting along great, they hadn't yet had sex. He was horny and frustrated, but he was determined that the next move be hers. Their situation had been taken out of her hands at every step. If he could give her control in at least this one thing, then he would do it.

Unfortunately, his shy mate wasn't catching the hint.

Stuffing the laptop in his bag, he headed out to the front door. Celine came in as he hit the hallway, carrying a dress bag. She walked past him without speaking, stomping up the stairs. His panther riled at her dismissal, and he started to follow her upstairs, but he chilled. She would have to come to him if she had a problem. He checked the time on his watch and debated staying to figure out what was wrong or heading into work.

That irritated him even more.

He needed to be at work, but even without the urging of his panther, he couldn't leave without finding out if she was okay.

She came down before he made his decision and rolled her eyes at him, pouting as she walked into the kitchen. And okay, blame it on the bad day, but that irritated the fuck out of him. He followed her into the kitchen.

"Celine, I don't like games, so if you got something to get off your chest, do that, ma. Pouting don't move me."

She blinked at him and shook her head. She turned to leave, but then she turned around. "I heard about your girlfriend while I was dress shopping."

"I don't have a girlfriend," he said immediately.

"You should tell her that." She tried to stomp past him again, but he grabbed her arm.

"Unh-unh, what did I tell you when I agreed to marry you?"

She looked away and bit her bottom lip. "That you would never disrespect me."

"And have I lied to you about anything?"

She shook her head.

He pulled her into his arms. "Then what you mad for?"

She growled, her cat rising in irritation. "Rumors are going around about you and Keara. She's telling everyone that you're sleeping with her."

"Cece, do I seem like that type of dude?"

She looked away, and he stepped back.

"So you gon' think the worst of me."

"I mean, you and I aren't having sex, and I'm sure you have needs."

"Are you offering, Celine? I've been waiting on your time, so, if you ready, then say that shit."

She whipped her eyes to him, wide. "That's not...I didn't...." She cleared her throat.

He stepped closer to her. "I'm loyal, Celine, don't ever question that. I already told you what was up. I'm ready to give our bond a serious chance whenever you want. Don't ever accuse me of shit off of gossip, hear?"

He lifted her chin and made her look into his eyes. She nodded. He kissed her on the forehead.

"I'm running behind today, so I'll be late coming home."

She sighed, and he could still see the worry in her eyes. He closed his eyes and pushed down on his temper. He had to remember that he was in a relationship now. That meant talking even when it would aggravate him.

"CeCe, what you need to hear from me, love?"

Her eyes lifted to him in surprise.

"Celine," he groaned.

She was so damn stubborn. He couldn't imagine how her father treated her mother if she got surprised every time he tried to take care of her.

"What can I do to reassure you?"

"I'm fine. I believe you."

He stared into her eyes until her cat met his gaze, and he could be sure that she was being truthful. The tension between them gathered, and his animal was ready to push the issue.

"I'm marrying you, Celine, and I'm patient enough to wait. Accusing me of cheating undermines my integrity and the respect I have for us both. I don't want to have a conversation like this again."

She nodded. "I'm sorry," she whispered, and the shit broke his heart a little bit.

She was so fragile, his wife.

He dropped a small kiss on her lips. "Call me if you need something, kay?"

She nodded and lifted on her toes and kissed his lips a little longer this time. He smiled when she pulled away hastily.

"I'll have dinner waiting on you," she promised and left the room.

His gaze followed her, and he debated staying and coaxing his wife into more kisses.

ten

CeCe was cooking to calm herself. That, and she was hoping the elaborate meal would appeal to her soon-to-be husband. She frowned as Kate's words went through her head. Keara was a beautiful woman and a society darling. More like the type of woman she thought would be Mason's type. And yeah, that hurt. But, he'd said the rumor wasn't true, and she refused to be taunted by a what-if.

She sighed as her phone rang. It was Lacey.

"Hi."

"What's wrong?" Lacey asked.

"Nothing's wrong. What's up with you?" She tried to divert the conversation.

"I can hear it in your voice," Lacey said.

"Did you call for a reason?" Celine stood firm.

"I was talking to Kate, and she wanted to go out tonight," Lacey told her.

A night out...that sounded like the perfect something to get her mind off her fight with Mason. But, it did mean that she would be on her guard with Kate there. Anything she did or said had the potential to get back to her parents. She wouldn't be able to talk about Mason with Lacey, which wasn't a bad thing. She didn't want to do or say anything that could feed into the reputation he and his family already had.

Plus, she was still irritated with Kate for bringing that rumor to her.

"You're thinking way too hard over there. Tell me what's wrong." Lacey ordered.

Cece sighed. "I got into a little fight with Mason."

"About what?"

"There is a rumor going around that Keara is sleeping with Mason."

"Ugh, that bitch," Lacey said immediately.

"Right. But Mason said it's not true." Celine grumbled.

"She's so jealous," Lacey snickered. "Keara has always wanted Mason, but her daddy would never merge their family with the Knights."

Celine growled.

"Don't get mad at me. Half of the Motsi is scared of Councilman Knight, and the other half still considers them outsiders."

It was true but no less irritating to her. "Well, she seems to think she can take him from me."

She bit her lip, hating that she had let that bit of insecurity slip.

Lacey snorted. "Please, Keara can say whatever she wants, but I have never heard those types of rumors about Mason."

A part of her felt better, though a part of her wondered if that meant it would just be harder to catch him. She thought back to the anger on his face. He looked offended that she would think he'd disrespect her. That made her feel better. She touched her lips, remembering that she had kissed him. He told her whenever she was ready. How did she show him she was ready? She thought she'd shown her willingness at his house, but maybe she needed to say it. She bit her lip, nervous at the prospect.

"You need to get out of the house," Lacey said.

Celine tuned back into the conversation. "What?"

"Let's go out. We can go to Banjos, line dance a bit, and it will give you space to think."

She gnawed her bottom lip. What would Mason say? It's not like he'd object to her going out...at least, she didn't think he would. She knew that he would probably be upset if she left the house without security, though.

"We have to take Lance."

"Who's Lance?"

"My new security."

"Oh, wow, I forgot you're rolling in the big leagues now." She laughed. "Okay, we'll be ready at eight."

"Okay, great! See you soon!" Lacey said happily.

She hung up with her friend. She debated telling Mason she would go out as she finished dinner. But he could tell her, no, and then she'd be stuck at home, in her head. She shook her head and texted Lance to be ready to leave at 8. He didn't ask questions, just texted back, *'Bet.'*

Okay, then.

She finished dinner and went to get dressed. At seven, her doorbell rang, and she let Lacey in. Lacey carried a bag with her.

"What's that for?"

"I already know you're going to wear jeans and a frumpy top. That's not happening tonight."

"Lacey," she muttered. "I'm about to be married. I can't be going out dressing like y'all."

"Your husband needs to know his wife is thick in all the right places, and you need the ego boost, so stop all that whining."

An hour later, she came downstairs in cut-off shorts, the strings trailing her thighs, and a t-shirt with her favorite country band on it that was Lacey's only compromise. It wasn't tight or revealing, but Lacey cut it so that it hung off her shoulder.

Lance smirked when she came downstairs. "Alright now, Mason gon' get on your ass when he sees you."

Her eyes widened. "Should I change," she bit her lip.

"Hell no," Lacey said. "Put those boots on, and let's go. Kate's going to meet us there."

Celine slid into her favorite black cowboy boots and followed her friend. Lance chuckled as he helped them into the truck.

"With your security driving, that means you can drink," Lacey cheered.

"I am not getting drunk." She warned her friend.

*****

Mason came into the house close to eleven, tired and frustrated. He'd wanted to be home hours ago, but with the merger happening, he had tons of paperwork to get through. He could also admit to being sad that he missed time with Celine. He had gotten a text from Lance hours ago that she was out with her friends. Though he didn't like coming home to an empty house, he was glad she was out having fun.

Which was just foolish. He'd lived alone for all of his adult life. Still, the weeks he'd been here with Celine had him used to her presence.

He saw the note on the kitchen table, peeked in the small fridge CeCe used to thaw out food, and found a plate made for him. He smiled. He liked that she took care of him. He liked being spoiled; he had to admit. He took a shower, and when he came out, his phone was ringing on the bed. He smiled as he saw who it was.

"What's going on, love bug?"

"Not your love bug! Cece wants you to come out to Banjos with us."

Mason frowned because he didn't recognize the voice. "Who is this?"

"Her friend Kate. CeCe's drinking and having a good time! You coming?"

Was his mate drunk? He smiled, not even able to picture that. "Yeah, I'll be there." He hung up and called Celine's security.

Lance answered immediately. "Boss?"

"You got eyes on my mate?" The title slipped right from his lips, natural. It felt right, so he didn't trip.

Lance chuckled. "Her and her goofy ass friends. They straight."

"I'm headed to come get them," he told him.

"Bet. See you in a bit." Lance said.

He texted his security, and they met him at the truck.

He sighed. "I don't need both."

Jules shot him a look and got in the car. They drove to the country bar that was way on the other side of town. Jules pulled his truck up next to Lance's. There was still a line outside the country bar when he drove up. He shook his head and walked to the front, wondering what

Celine's sheltered ass knew about this place. The patrons were primarily shifters and mostly white. Not his scene, but he was no stranger to it. More than likely, the scattering of humans were here to gawk at the shifters. Mason preferred the shifter-only clubs for that reason. Security waved him in, recognizing him. He went inside, and it was crowded.

He spotted his shy wife and her friends right away, as they were the center of attention, with two of them dancing on the bar. He recognized Lacey Hanson because her father was on Dallas' advisory board and a longtime member of the Motsi. The other woman, he was going to assume, was Kate. She also looked familiar. More than likely, she had family that was a part of the Motsi. He knew the Harris's wouldn't have allowed Celine to hang out with anyone outside of that.

His wife was below, smiling and dancing. She damn well knew better than to be wildin out like her friends. He narrowed his eyes when he got a good look at her. She was wearing shorts that showed all her thick thighs. His panther sat up, one part possessive, the other part turned on as hell. She turned and saw him and her face suffused with joy. It clenched his heart.

He made his way to her and helped her friends down from the bar. "You ladies called for a ride?"

Lacey and Kate cheered.

Celine smiled and grabbed his hand. "One dance...please."

Asked shyly, he definitely couldn't tell her no. Her eyes were glassy. She was obviously drunk but still steady on her feet.

"One, then home." He pinched her chin and kissed her.

He was glad they'd cleared the air after their argument. Her friends hooted behind them.

She sighed and smiled. "One."

She dragged him out to the dance floor, and there was a fast two-step playing. Her eyes widened when he fell into the steps.

"You can dance. Of course, you can dance. You're perfect," she said with a dreamy look on her face.

He didn't care for her thinking he was perfect, but he did like that look in her eye. He led her through the dance, spinning her, and despite her being drunk, she kept up. They danced well together. He pulled her close, and they danced as though they'd done so for a hundred years. The song changed, and she stopped in the middle of the floor and stared at him. He had to taste her. He leaned over and kissed her and the room faded.

Someone bumped into them, and he pulled up, growling, flashing his canines. The human apologized, and Mason waved off his security as they headed toward them. Celine's eyes were dazed, missing that entire interaction. Yeah, she was gone.

"I really like kissing you," she whispered. "We should start sleeping together."

"Ok, home with you."

She gave him a mischievous smile. "Yes, home for sex."

His dick certainly agreed, but he tamped down his lust. "Home for sleep, you minx. Let's go. And we gon' talk about this damn outfit the minute you sober, hear?"

He corralled her friends, them dancing the whole way out the door. He held CeCe's hand as she sang and danced next to him. He frowned when he heard the sound of an engine revving. Mason knew that sound. He immediately pulled Celine closer to him, speeding his pace. His guards raced past them and swung the door to the truck open.

"Move, now, love bug," He told her, pushing her ahead of him. He did the same with her friends. "Into the truck!"

He pulled out his burner as a matte black SUV swung into the parking lot. All three ladies screamed at the sound of the gunshots. Mason fired back, Jules, Lance, and Al doing the same. The SUV peeled out, dodging screaming patrons as they scattered to their cars.

"Let's go, Mase," Jules ordered. "Lance."

"On it," Lance said, pulling Kate and Lacey from the SUV and transferring them to the truck they drove up in.

"Wait, where is he taking them?" Celine asked, her eyes wide, her body trembling.

"He's taking them home. You're with me, love bug." He told her, sliding into the back seat beside her.

"Are you okay?" she whispered, her hands tracing his body.

"I'm good, CeCe." He leaned down and kissed the top of her head. "It's handled."

"You're bleeding," she hissed, looking around for something to staunch the blood.

As soon as she said it, he felt the burning where the bullet grazed his arm. "A scratch, love. Settle."

She crawled into his lap, clutching him tightly, her arms wrapping around his neck. He rubbed her back and nuzzled into her neck. He held her as Jules drove them back to the farm. By the time they reached, she was sleeping in his arms. Jules opened the door for him.

"Want me to grab her?"

Mason clutched her tight. "I got her."

He swung his legs around and slipped from the back seat, holding his mate close.

"You good with your arm?" Jules moved to his left side and parted the rip in his shirt. "Never mind, it's already healed."

"Like I told her, it was just a scratch. Let me know when you get word." Mason ordered, headed for the house without waiting on an answer.

He'd been friends with Jules his whole life and trusted him. He would get it done.

He tucked her in bed, changing her into one of his oversized t-shirts. His nerves were all over the place. He should go for a run and let his cat out. That would help dissipate some of the adrenaline; instead, he headed back downstairs to the kitchen. He pulled out the food Celine had left for him, warming it in the microwave. He sighed when his phone rang, already knowing who it was.

"I'm straight, Pop."

Dallas sucked his teeth. "The hell were you doing over on that side of town anyway?"

"Out with my mate," he answered, sitting down at the table with his plate.

"Mate, huh?"

"I'm in it, Pop."

"I'll let your mother know you're fine. She's gonna want to see your face," Dallas warned.

He looked up as he scented Celine. "I'll come by this week." He promised. His eyes followed Cece's path into the kitchen. "I'll holla at you."

He hung up the phone and watched her. "I left you sleeping."

She gave him a shy look. "I was thirsty."

She walked over and tiptoed for a glass. The t-shirt he put her in lifted, her ass peeking out from the bottom of it. He growled, his fingers flexing.

"How you feeling?"

She filled up her glass and walked over to him, setting the glass on the table. "A little shaken, but I'll be fine.

He grabbed her around the waist and swung her into his lap. "Does this happen often?"

Her eyebrow raised. "The shooting or the drinking?"

Mason chuckled. "You got jokes."

"I'm always designated driver, but since Lance was with us, I thought it would be okay to have one drink." She smiled at him, her eyes still glazed.

"Just one, huh?"

"It might have turned into more."

He smiled and nuzzled into her neck. "You're drunk, love bug, admit it."

She giggled and stood up to get her water. She looked at him as she drank it.

"What?" he said.

"What you said earlier."

"Earlier when, ma?"

"When we were arguing. You're leaving the decision on whether we sleep together up to me."

He nodded, wondering where she was going.

"And if I say yes?"

"You already know, love bug. But not tonight. Not while you're drunk," he told her.

She nodded and leaned down, gripping the sides of his face. She slowly descended, and he let her have control. Up until her lips touched his, that is. Then, he took over, ravaging her mouth. She moaned, and he pulled back.

"Back to bed, love bug, and behave." He slapped her ass. "And burn them damn shorts," he yelled as she ascended the stairs.

A giggle was her answer.

eleven

Celine wanted to curse.

Her head was thumping, and her mouth was dry. Reaching over to the cup of water she kept at her bedside; she frowned when she didn't encounter it. Lifting her head and squinting, she realized she hadn't left her cup where she usually did. She sat up with a gasp, moaning when the room spun slightly. She hated drinking. She looked down at the shirt she wore, lifting it to her nose. It was Mason's. She smiled and reluctantly rolled from the bed.

Her morning routine took a lot longer than usual as she trudged through, waiting on the aspirin to kick in. She slowly made her way downstairs, her eyes widening as she saw Mason still at the island, having coffee. He seemed to sense her, smiling at her and turning back to his tablet. He was dressed for work, the striped shirt fitting his chest perfectly. Her heart started thumping just from the sight of him.

She stumbled into the kitchen, smoothing her hair to ensure her bun was in place. Mason smirked at her and got up, packing his briefcase.

"You gonna be okay today?"

She waved him away, heading for the coffee machine. "I'm just going to go upstairs and die if that's okay with you."

He chuckled and pulled her into his arms. "You can't handle your liquor, farm girl."

He kissed her neck, and she shuddered, grabbing his head.

"I'm going to say no."

He lifted her chin and looked into her eyes, giving her a mysterious but playful smile. "Let me know when last night comes back to you." He kissed her softly and backed away. "I'm headed to work."

She waved him off and stared after him.

He turned around when he got to the door leading out to the garage. "Oh, yeah. And don't think I forgot about you going out last night dressed like you ain't got a man at home."

Heat crawled up her face, making her cheeks sting. "It was just shorts."

He growled lowly and made his way back to her. "Just shorts, on this ass," he gripped her butt. "Nah, you can't go out without me in nothing like that no more."

She giggled. "Okay, deal."

"I'm not playing with you, love bug. I'll toss you over my shoulder and drag you out of whatever club you may be in, hear?"

She laughed and kissed him. "I don't even go out like that."

"Mmhmm." He kissed her lips and left her standing there.

Celine touched her lips and smiled. She'd always known that Mason was charming. Even though many in the Motsi turned their noses up at his family, he still moved about society, his charm drawing people to him. It felt good to have it aimed at her. She was about to go back upstairs and sleep, but she sighed when her friend and business partner pulled into the yard.

They didn't move in the same circles and had met purely on accident nearly four years ago. It had been right after she got her farm and was deciding what to plant. She'd bumped into Deena, and the two of them sparked a conversation and hit it off. Three years later, they had a thriving business and friendship. Cece stood on the porch, her cup of coffee in hand, waiting on her friend to get out of the car.

Deena hauled a box from her passenger side, her eyes widening when a panther walked by. "Girl, is that another guard?"

Cece nodded and sucked in a breath as she realized what happened last night and why the extra guards were roaming the property.

"What happened?" Deena asked, setting the box down on the porch.

"A shoot out last night," Cece said.

What?" Deena grabbed her shoulder. "Here?"

She shook her head. "At Banjos."

Deena sucked her teeth and picked up the box, going inside. "That's what you get for hanging out with them damn rednecks."

"It's not just rednecks," she defended.

"You right. It's rednecks and y'all Black asses. I'm assuming Lacey dragged you there." Deena said, rolling her eyes.

"Lacey and Kate." She admitted, peering into the box Deena brought with her.

"Staging stuff," Deena answered her unspoken question about the box's contents. "You hard-headed."

Celine knew what she was talking about and pinched her lips together.

"Nothing to say to that?"

"She's my cousin's wife, Deena. And I've known Lacey since boarding school."

"That's not a point for either of them. I told you, them bitches shady." Deena said, laying out various fall-themed kitchen flatware and tools.

Deciding a subject change was in order. "What's this all for?"

"I want to do a spice loaf, and since the holidays are coming soon. We can stage for Thanksgiving." She put her hands on her hips and studied Celine. "You gon' be able to work? You look a mess."

Celine snorted. "Hungover, but I can work."

*****

Despite the shit that went down last night, Mason was in a good mood when he exited the elevator onto the executive floor. The department store he owned took up the two bottom floors of the building, but the third and fourth were for the corporate staff. He could've easily kept his offices in one of the many other buildings he owned, but many of his employees had been with him from the beginning and lived closest to their flagship store. Eastfield's traffic was its own villain, and if he could lessen their commute, he would. He nodded to his assistant.

"Jules beat you to the office. Said he needed to talk to you. I pushed back your conference call by an hour."

The young shifter was straight out of college and worth every penny he paid them. They were efficient as hell, both with a computer and the nine they kept in the desk drawer. He grunted and entered his office.

Jules stood at his window, looking out over the parking lot.

"What's the word?" Mason settled into the chair behind his desk.

Jules leaned his back against the window as Mason spun to face him. "Got some trouble."

He wiped a hand down his face. "Someone coming for dad?"

Mason knew it was a risk that the family took for his father's position, but he never wanted Celine to be mixed up in it.

Jules shook his head. "There's a hit out on Celine. I'm still chasing down details, but it didn't originate in the streets."

Mason gripped the side of his chair, hissing as his claws tore from his hands. Fury filled him. "Who would dare?"

"A bunch of rogues, most likely. We hit one in the attack last night. I found him in an underground shifter clinic."

"Those still operate?"

"There's some of us who still don't trust humans. Plus, all hospitals report gunshot injuries to the police. That's shifter or human-run alike." Jules answered.

Mason grunted. "Did you take him?"

"You know I did, which is why I know he's from out of town. It's also why I say it didn't come from the streets. You know how we handle shit here."

Mason nodded, unable to speak through his anger. The shifters from their neck of the woods handled shit for themselves. No outsider would come in and say they'd done some shit for the cat shifters in Florida. It wasn't done. They handled their own.

Jules walked over to his desk and put his phone down, displaying a picture of the injured rogue. Mason didn't recognize him.

"Where is he now?"

"Being questioned. So far, all we got is the fact that there is a hit. I'll let you know if we get anything else. In the meantime, I sent a whole team out to Celine's. It helps that she's a homebody." Jules picked his phone back up.

Mason's mind was spinning with possibilities. If it wasn't someone from his father's past or coming for the tri-council position, then who the hell could his mate have angered that much. But then he froze.

Fuck.

"Check her family." He ordered.

Jules studied him before nodding, not questioning the order.

Mason grunted. "Thank you, Jules."

His friend gave him a salute and left the office. Mason cursed and called Silas first. His brother answered immediately.

"What it do?"

"Aye, Silas, I got a problem, and I ain't want you to hear from anyone but me."

"What kind of problem?" His brother asked.

"I think Celine's people put a hit out on her. But, they're using rogues from out of town, so it'll take Jules and them a minute to trace who's behind it."

"Fuck that. I'm on my way." Silas said easily.

"Nah, I know you working. I just want you to hit up some of your contacts and see what you can find." The last thing Mason wanted was his wild ass big brother descending.

"I'll see what I can find out. You good in the meantime?"

"I'm straight," he told him. "I'll keep you posted."

"You better. You know I don't play about my baby brother."

Mason snorted. "I'll holla."

He hung up with his brother and took a deep breath. He debated if he could skip his next call. After last night, it might be better to tell his parents what was going on in person. He was the baby of the family, and his parents were way more protective of him than they were of Silas, so he could only imagine how they would react.

He pulled up his father's number.

"Baby boy," Dallas greeted.

Mason rolled his eyes. "Jules got word that there's a hit out on Celine."

Dallas got really quiet on the other end. Mason could feel his father's fury.

"I'll take care of it."

"I got it, for now, Pop." He told him quickly.

"You already know who's behind it. Lock Celine down if that's what you're doing, Mase." Dallas ordered.

Mason rubbed a hand down his face. "I wanted to give her more time."

"They're more than likely doing this because if they kill her before the two of you are mated, then the money reverts to the family. If she's yours, mark her. I know you wanted to marry first to give her time, but that won't be tight enough. No one can reverse a mating."

"I'll talk to her."

"Now, Mase. Ain't but so long I'ma sit here with a threat hanging over you. You want to handle it, gone and do that, because if I do, I'll paint blood all over this shit."

Mason smiled. "We gotta prove it first, Pop."

Dallas grunted. "You know if I tell your mama, it's over."

Mason laughed. Dallas was a savage, yes, but Adina controlled that savage and, when she wanted, loosed and aimed him at her whim.

"I called Silas to see if he could find out anything. As soon as I can trace it back, I'll spin the block on their ass myself." He promised his father.

"Keep yourself safe, son."

"Love you too, Pop."

Mason knew he wouldn't get any work done today. "Torrance, what's on the schedule that can be moved?"

He wanted to get home.

twelve

The sun was beating down on the back of her neck, her panther was fed up, and Celine was dragging as she kneeled next to the lavender bush she was clipping. Deena stood over her, going over the orders they needed for the upcoming week. Celine was listening with half an ear.

Deena sucked her teeth. "You need more caffeine."

Celine had to smile and lower her head. "Remind me never to go out drinking on a school night."

Deena snickered. "I don't know what you were thinking. You never drink."

"Peer pressure, Dee," she admitted.

"Well, now you're paying the price."

"It won't happen again," Celine promised.

Deena scoffed and went back to the tablet. "The herbs we need for this week's order are already in the dry shed. You can put this off until this evening when you're feeling more yourself, or we can do it tomorrow."

"Why am I down here instead of up there with the tablet?"

Deena snorted. "Because my rows are done, you're the one dragging."

"Oh, yeah." She sighed. "Forget it. I'm done." She grabbed the basket that she'd already half-filled and stood. "Let's go hang these and then take the rest of the afternoon off."

Deena closed the case over the tablet. "Perfect, then we can have some coffee, and you tell me about this hot shifter you're marrying."

Celine smiled, thinking about Mason flirting with her this morning. She'd loved it. He'd been polite and careful around her with their engagement. It was great to see him return to the charming man he'd been when they met. She followed Deena to their dry shed, and the two of them got to work tying twine around bunches of lavender and the other herbs they'd picked today.

"It's Mason." She said, breaking the silence.

Deena swung around to her, a huge smile on her face. "The guy you're always talking about from the events?"

She nodded. Deena wasn't a high society shifter, so she wasn't privy to all the things that happened at Motsi events.

"So, tell me about him."

"Mason is…" she shook her head. "He's amazing. Like, I'm so excited about getting married to him. I didn't…when Grandfather's will was read, I was sure my life was over. I couldn't imagine in a million years that Mason would rescue me."

Deena made a humming sound for her to keep going.

"You've seen him before, right?" Celine asked.

"What's his last name?" Deena asked absently.

"Knight."

Deena spun around and gripped her shoulders. "Holy shit, you're marrying one of the Knight brothers? Lead with that, Celine. Them boys fine as hell!"

Celine laughed at her friend's expression. "It's a marriage merger."

"Who gives a fuck? You're marrying Mason Knight, which means you get to sleep with him, and I will need every detail of that."

Celine laughed outright, relieved that her friend wasn't judging the way it felt like Lacey had. It could be because Deena never wanted to be a part of the Motsi. She was way more down to Earth than her society friends.

"You don't think I should feel some type of way that we're only getting married to merge assets?" she asked quietly.

Deena snickered. "Yesss, merge them assets, girl. The more merging, the better."

Celine busted out laughing, bending over at the lascivious look on Deena's face. She was so happy she'd told her friend.

"And here I was worried you'd be laid up with a hangover." Mason's deep voice said from the doorway.

She swung around and gasped. Had he heard what they'd said? His eyes were glittering with amusement.

She cleared her throat. "Ummm, Hey Mason."

"Biiiitch," Deena whispered under her breath.

Celine tucked her lips to keep from laughing again. "What are you doing home so early?"

He walked over to her and leaned down to kiss her. "I came to check on you."

"I'm feeling better."

"She been dragging all day," Deena supplied.

Celine shook her head and laughed. "Okay, yes, I've been slow. Mason, this is my friend and partner, Deena Michaels. Dee, my fiancé, Mason Knight."

Mason held out his hand. "Nice to meet you."

"Nice to finally meet you. CeCe talks about you often," Deena said, waggling her eyebrows.

Celine's cheeks heated. She rushed to change the subject. "I just need to finish this, and then we're taking the afternoon off."

He turned and observed the herbs drying all over the shed. Though, shed was underselling it. It was a huge barn. She'd renovated the horse stalls into separate drying areas. There was now a stall designated for the different conditions each herb needed for drying and preserving.

"It smells amazing in here," he commented. "You two do all this yourself?"

"For the most part," Deena answered. "We only pick what we need for orders, so it's not a giant harvesting situation."

"I'm impressed, love bug," he said, walking around.

"Love bug?" Deena mouthed, eyes wide.

She snickered and swatted at her friend. Mason walked back over to her and pulled her into his arms.

"I'll be at the house when you're done then." He lifted her chin and kissed her.

It wasn't a small kiss either. It melted all over her, and she dropped the bundle she held in her hand. He pulled back and smiled, a cocky smile that heated her further. He walked away, and she stood there stunned.

"Chile, marriage merger, my ass," Deena said.

It shook Celine out of her stupor. "Oh my God," she whispered.

Deena gave her a sly smile. "That man is fine as hell, and from the look in his eyes, he ain't worried about no damn assets."

Celine was starting to think her friend was right.

*****

Mason dropped his leather messenger bag next to the kitchen counter and loosened his tie. He raked his eyes over the house to ensure everything was in place. He'd spotted the extra security when he was outside with Celine, some in their animal form, which satisfied him. Jules had come through for his mate. He pulled out his phone and sent Lance a text message. He looked up as he came through the back door.

"Everything good?"

"Good, boss, I got everyone set up where they need to be," Lance answered.

"Okay, I'll be home for the rest of the afternoon."

Lance smirked and gave him a look that Mason didn't understand.

"What?"

"First, you chase after her way 'cross town, and now you're off work early...."

Well, shit... "And?"

Lance snickered. "Just noting, boss. I'm around if you need me."

Mason grabbed a cup and filled it with Celine's kool-aid, smiling. He hadn't had kool-aid since he was a child, and his grown ass mate kept it in her refrigerator at all times. Lance's words circled his head, and he had to admit that he'd been moving different since he agreed to the marriage merger with Celine. Not that he was complaining. He loved spending time with her.

Celine came through the front door as though he'd conjured her with his thoughts. She looked happy, if not a little tired. He hated the news he had to drop on her.

She spotted him in the kitchen and turned from the stairs to him. She walked to him, wrapping her arms around his waist, resting her head on his chest.

"I'm sleepy," she said.

He kissed the top of her head and tightened his arm around her waist, reveling in the feel of her curves against him. He set his glass down so he could hold her with both arms.

"Mmhmm, that's what you get for going out gallivanting in them lil ass shorts you had on."

She laughed and tiptoed to slide her cheek against his. "Let it go, Mason Knight."

He grabbed her ass. "All this mine. Ain't gon' be no more showing it off to other people."

She chuckled, and he lifted her chin, loving the smile on her face. He dropped a small kiss on her lips.

"We can spend the rest of the afternoon in bed."

Her cat rubbed against his, and her smile became wistful, heat filling her eyes. "I would love that," she said softly.

He kissed her again, this time deeper, their tongues dancing. He pulled back after a long moment.

"I need to talk to you first."

She pouted, and he promptly kissed her again.

"What I told you about pouting?" He teased.

"'That pouting shit don't move me,'" she said in a deep voice, mocking him.

He laughed. Gods, he loved this silly woman. His heart started racing as he realized where his thoughts went. Shit, when had that happened? He stared at her, thunderstruck by that realization.

She smiled, and he nuzzled against her cheek.

"What's wrong, my love?" she asked.

He kissed her neck and shuddered as his cat filled him, need for her taking over. "You've never called me by a pet name."

"You use enough pet names for the both of us." She teased, but her eyebrows were bunched in confusion. "You want a pet name?"

"No, that's not what's wrong. We have to talk."

She groaned. "That sounds serious. Can I take a shower first?"

His panther slammed against his cage. "Not yet," he managed to get out.

She tried to back away, but he held tight. Worry filled her eyes. "Ok."

"We have a problem."

"With?"

"Your family," he told her.

She sighed and nodded. "What happened? Is my father trying to renege? We can always get me another lawyer to negotiate. I'm not marrying anyone else."

It warmed his heart, and unfortunately, his cat went crazier, demanding. He pinned down the magic, forcing his animal to step back.

"My security team got word that there was a hit put out on you."

Her eyes widened. "I don't understand. Someone was hired to go after me. Why?"

"I think they're after your inheritance," he said solemnly.

"Then they can have it." She stepped back from his arms. "I won't risk you getting hurt."

That her first concern was for him warmed him, and it made his panther all the more determined for their next step.

He pulled her back into his arms. "That's one answer, though, I don't want to reward that behavior."

"What can we do?"

He heard the fear in her voice, and it shredded him.

"We can mate."

Her eyes widened, and her heartbeat thundered loud enough for his hearing to pick it up.

"I thought you wanted to wait."

"On you, love," he reminded her.

"You..." she licked her lips and looked away. "You would really mate with me? Even though this was just supposed to be a marriage merger?"

"My panther picked you way before I understood what was going on, Celine." He told her, and as he said it, he realized how true it was. From the moment his father told him that she was getting married off, his panther had been in a state. "Had I not had my head up my ass and buried in work, I more than likely would've noticed months ago."

She gasped, her eyes shooting back to his. "You're serious."

He nodded, studying her face for a clue to how she felt. Celine kept her feelings tight, her panther more so, so it was hard to judge what she was thinking.

"What if I wanted to give my inheritance back? Would you still mate with me?" she whispered.

He cupped her cheeks so that he was staring into her eyes. "I would have you in whatever way I could."

Her eyes started watering. "Okay," she whispered.

"That easy?"

"I want you," she admitted softly. "Have always wanted you. You were my secret fantasy. I never thought—"

His kiss cut her off. Hearing that, knowing that they could've mated sooner had he not buried himself in work, before all the danger to her... He was angry with himself, yes, but mostly, need for Celine, for his mate, heated his body. She went up to her toes to deepen their kiss. Power filled his body, and the insatiable need he'd been holding back for her overwhelmed him. He needed her, and he needed her now.

thirteen

Urgent need bubbled to the surface, drowning Mason in a fiery wave. He deepened their kiss, dominating her. Celine moaned and raised to her toes, her tongue tangling with his. His panther pushed forward insistently, his fingertips aching from the press of his claws trying to come forward. Instead of fighting it, he gave in to the animal, using those claws to rid Celine of the shirt she wore.

She gasped, her eyes widening, but no fear entered her scent. Freed from her mouth, Mason kissed his way down her neck, sucking on her shoulder.

"I'm sweaty," she complained, her fingers digging into his shoulder.

He hummed, raking his teeth across the front of her neck. Celine threw her head back, giving him the submission he demanded, which set him off even more. He could smell the herbs from her drying shed, along with a scent that was a mix of her and her panther.

He wanted to consume her.

He slid his hands into her yoga pants and found her wet. There was a moment when reason tried to rear its head, but his cat pushed it down, and Mason couldn't find it in him to slow down. He nipped her chin before sucking her bottom lip into his mouth. Celine met his aggressive kiss head-on, giving him back the same energy. He hooked his fingers into her sex and closed his eyes at the hot clasp of her sheath.

She gasped and went up on her toes. "Mason," she whispered.

"When you say my name like that, love bug..." he used his thumb to press down on her clit, and she went up in flames.

Her pussy squeezed down on his fingers, and the mewl she released with her orgasm had him going full-on caveman. He used his claws on his other hand and ripped her pants off. She laughed, the sound dark and husky. Yeah, she liked that shit. He pulled his dick out impatiently, driving her back towards the sofa.

"Ass up, love bug." His voice was barely human. His panther was damn near in control.

Like the good girl she was, she bent over and arched her back, showing off her dripping wet pussy. She looked back at him, and a hungry growl rattled his chest. He gripped her hips and drove forward.

Fuck.

The feel of her as her walls clamped down on him. He would chase this woman to the ends of the Earth. He wanted their first time to be a soft, affirming experience but it was too far gone for that. With every hard stroke he delivered to Celine, she met his thrust, her greedy sex gripping him. She reached back and grabbed his thighs, her claws scraping against his skin. Her panther reached up between them and rubbed against his own. The heat from their animals ratcheted up the need another thousand degrees.

Her back arched deeper, and she screamed his name, her nails digging into his thighs, marking him as hers. He reached around and grabbed the front of her neck, driving deep. His canines lowered, his panther pushing him to claim her. He licked across her shoulder, slowing his strokes to savor the moment. He fit his teeth right at the crook of her neck, his heart hammering in anticipation.

The moment he bit down and her taste filled his mouth, he was done. Their bond slammed into place, blinding him, frantic carnal heat filling him until his knees went weak. Wild, chaotic power flared and made a mockery of all the feelings he thought he had before. He loved her, yes, but this...

It was obsession.

Celine screamed and climaxed, her scorching pussy pulsing, clamping down on his dick until he yelled out, the pleasured sound ripped from him. He fucked her, stroking deep, hard, wishing he could get even closer to her. Celine took his strokes, throwing her ass back at him, urging him deeper. He'd suspected that his quiet and shy mate had a different side to her, but he hadn't expected the hellion that bucked beneath him taking every inch.

Energy!

He couldn't help but be in love with her.

"Oh God, I'm coming again," she hissed.

Her panther rose, and now that their bond was in place, he could feel her pleasure along with his own. It was too much! His back arched, and the orgasm Celine pulled from him blurred his vision. He cursed as his strokes became erratic, chasing the high and just wanting to stay inside her. Mason held her hips down as he came, her name a desperate whisper on his lips.

Fuck he loved this woman.

He collapsed on her back, their breath sawing in and out of them. He didn't pull out, didn't release his hold on her hips. He couldn't. It wasn't even his panther this time. The animal inside of him was content, smug at their connection with Celine. It was the man. He wanted to wallow in his mate. He slid his cheek against her bare back, rubbing his scent on her soft skin. He scraped his teeth down her spine, wanting to mark every square inch of her body. Never had he felt so possessive.

Celine sighed beneath him, reaching her arm back to stroke the top of his head.

"Heavy, my love," she said, her voice soft and content.

"Fine," he grumbled, lifting from her body.

He slipped out of her, sighing at the loss. He should've done this in her bed, not that he had any regrets.

She turned and cupped his cheek. "Not you pouting."

He smiled and shook his head. "I clearly ain't fuck you hard enough if you got time for jokes."

Her eyes lit. "I can't tease my mate?"

Her mate.

That shit sounded incredible. He leaned over and kissed her, devouring her mouth. She backed off and put a hand on his chest.

"Unh-unh, I'm getting a shower before round two."

He spun her around and slapped her ass, pushing her lightly towards the stairs. "You get a head start. If you make it to the shower before I catch you, then you can get your shower."

The smile she threw over her shoulder was mischievous. "And if I don't?"

His panther bucked, and Mason snarled. "Then you get fucked, wherever I catch you."

Celine sucked in a hungry breath, her heart racing. The intense feelings flowing down their mate bond had her waffling between tears of joy and outright lust. Mason was a sexy man, that could not be denied, but this aggressive, dominating male that he was in the throes of sex was a whole other animal. Her sex clenched, and need for him had electricity dancing across her skin. She's just had him, and his words had set her aflame, starving for another taste of him.

"Run, love bug." His voice was soft, menacing...

Hungry.

"One."

She turned back and took off for the stairs at his countdown. She didn't know how many seconds he would give her, but she had a feeling the panther beneath his skin would catch her in no time. Giddy happiness bubbled inside her, and she felt drunk off of it. She ought to know since she'd just spent last night drunk. This time she wouldn't have a hangover when she awoke.

Hopefully.

No telling how sore she would be in the morning.

She squealed and laughed when she heard his hard footsteps on the stairs. She sped up, sliding into the bathroom. He growled and caught her just as she reached the shower door. A smile covered her face as he stalked towards her, backing into the cold glass of the door. Her heart raced from the running but also from the intensity she could feel from him. It set off her animal; the shameless cat beckoned him closer.

"Oh my God," she whispered as his power filled the bathroom. Her panther reached for him through their bond, and his answered, wrapping her in the most secure feeling she'd ever felt.

He grabbed her thighs and lifted her. "Legs around me, love bug."

She obeyed him, wrapping her legs around his waist. He turned until she was pressed against the wall. He stared down at her, his face open, his heart more so. The love he sent down their bond melted her. Celine cupped his cheek, sending him the same, baring her every vulnerability. He rubbed their cheeks together, his purring vibrating her chest.

"I got you, Celine. Always." He promised.

Her heart clenched, and her throat was tight with unshed tears. He absolutely undid her. She could only nod and clutch him tight, words stuck behind the lump in her throat. Mason leaned down and lifted her breast, licking across her nipple. She arched her back as he sucked it into the heated cavern of his mouth. Her panther pushed forward, reminding her that they hadn't left their mark on him yet. Her gums tingled, and she released her fangs, salivating for her first taste of him.

She leaned forward and scraped her teeth across his shoulder. His head lifted, and she shuddered at the searing look he gave her. That look promised her so many wicked things. She licked his skin, sucking on his shoulder. Mason fitted his erection right at the opening of her sex, sliding back and forth, rubbing against her clit.

"She's so wet for me," he murmured.

She arched her hips, urging him. He quickly obliged, pushing in to the hilt. Her pussy clamped down greedily, wanting every inch. Mason chuckled and started moving in slow, deep strokes. She scraped her teeth over his shoulder again before biting down.

"Fuck!" Mason hissed.

She sucked on the skin of his shoulder, biting deeper, leaving a mark that satisfied her and her panther. She pulled back and licked over it to close the bite, smug and deeply content. She wrapped her arms around Mason's neck and cupped the back of his head, bringing him closer.

"Mine," she whispered, rolling her hips to take him deeper.

"That's right, claim that shit, love bug."

Celine screamed as an orgasm dragged her under, catching her completely by surprise. Her moans echoed in the bathroom, surrounded them along with the wet sounds of his strokes.

"Mason," she called.

"Yeah, just like that, love bug. Call my name just like that."

She did it again, loving the way he growled. He powered into her, in and out, until she was all feeling and no thoughts. From the tip of her toes to the very top of her head, her nerve endings were raw until even the brush of air over her skin added another dimension to their love-making.

Celine knew then that he owned every part of her.

It seemed inevitable from the moment he agreed to marry her. Maybe even before that. Her crush on him felt childish compared to the love thumping through her heart, consuming her from the inside out. Every kiss he lavished on her, every time his fingers softly brushed her skin, she fell deeper into him. Her stomach tightened, and power swelled inside of her. Mason whispered in her ear, all gibberish since she could only concentrate on the ravenous climax overtaking her senses. Mason licked across the mark he'd made earlier, and she was sent flying, her body breaking apart. She screamed and clutched him tight.

"Mine," she whispered right before she blacked out.

fourteen

There were people everywhere. Every corner of the tri-council ball-room seemed filled. Well, except for the small corner she'd found and was currently hiding in. She was a little overwhelmed by the press of bodies. There was extra security circling the party as well. She was safe enough, but she couldn't help but feel a little stifled and paranoid. There were shifters of every kind in the room, and the energy from their animals filled the space. It was like that at every Motsi event, and one of the main reasons Celine avoided them. It was hard to suppress her panther when the wild magic flowed freely through the room.

Her eyes raked over the crowd while she ruthlessly crushed her aggravation with it all. She and her mother were at odds, Veronica swinging wildly from bullying her into calling off the whole thing to demanding the wedding be a huge society event. This party seemed to be the compromise. She could have her small wedding, but her mother would have the glittering Motsi event that she wanted. The room was full of people Celine didn't know, but Veronica was in her element, taking congratulations as though the party was for her. She watched as her mother made the rounds.

Veronica hid all that festering anger well.

Celine rubbed her arms where she could still feel the phantom pain of her mother's grip. She'd asked Veronica hours ago if she knew about the hit, and the look in her mother's eyes had scared her. She had vehemently denied it, but Celine had seen the small moment of guilt.

Would her mother get down to that level to get access to the money?

Her parents weren't high in the Motsi hierarchy, and without her grandfather's money and influence, they wouldn't have been a part of the Motsi at all. Virgil Harris burned a lot of bridges in his business dealings, and were it not for her mother, they would've surely been shunned by society by now. It was more than likely the reason her father was fighting so hard for Alan's money. Her family needed it to stay relevant and keep hold of their social position.

So, she knew her parents were desperate, but still, at some point, she'd hoped Veronica would consider her daughter's feelings. That seemed unlikely to ever happen. She looked down at her bared arms, wondering if they would bruise. She prayed not because she didn't want to imagine what Mason would do if he knew what her mother had done.

She took a deep breath and settled into the corner, happy to be alone finally. She was thirsty, but that would mean giving up her hiding spot, so instead of seeking out one of the roving waiters, she slid a little further back into the shadows. She was nearly at the end of her social rope. Her smile had fallen, and she'd backed herself almost to the patio doors.

Hiding had been hard all night. Especially since Adina worked to make sure she wasn't alone in the crowd of people she didn't know. His family had been good about making sure someone was with her. She really liked Mason's mother. Her new mother-in-law was doing it to be kind...but Celine had wanted to be alone.

It was easier to disappear into the background when she was.

She adjusted the dress's bodice, the deep cleavage new for her. The low neckline had her breasts near to bursting from the top. She personally wouldn't have picked the dress for herself. There was way too much skin showing. But, she'd gotten a petty pleasure picking it over her mother's objection. She smoothed her hand down the satin skirt nervously. It was such a departure from the demure gowns she'd worn in the past.

She'd found a red hue that set off her dark skin well but still blended in with the sea of reds that the other party-goers wore. Red was the color of the Motsi, representing the blood the shifters shed to take their place in the world among the humans. All members wore the color when they attended society events.

And despite the party being for her and Mason, traditions still had to be followed.

Her panther rose and bristled as she looked up. Celine swallowed a growl as Keara and a friend stalked toward her. From their expressions, they weren't coming to offer congratulations. She lamented the loss of her hiding spot.

"You must be satisfied with yourself. Mason is quite a catch." Keara's friend said.

She gave them a wan smile.

"Of course, I can't imagine a mouse like yourself will be able to keep his attention for long. I know his animal won't even bother bonding with you, so I'm sure he'll be looking for entertainment soon. I feel sorry for him being trapped." Keara said.

That barb would've hurt her days ago, but now that she was bonded with him, she knew how he felt about her. Mason was now hers, and there wasn't anything the other woman could do about it. Celine reached out for their mating bond just because she could, thrilled to feel Mason even though he was nowhere near her.

She smiled at the two smug women, sliding her hair to the side to show off her mating mark. "I take it you're mad at me because you still couldn't trap him despite chasing him like a thirst bucket."

She had Mason's cousins to thank for that particular bit of slang.

Keara and her friend both sucked in a surprised breath. Celine was never one to fight back. They'd expected her to suffer through their taunts as she'd done all the times before.

"My mate is happy, so you can keep your pity," Celine informed them smugly.

"He mated you?" Keara's mouth tightened. "A little nothing like you?"

Mason slid up to her left side and grabbed Celine's arm. She hadn't even realized that she'd tensed it to strike. That was so unlike her, but she was on a hair trigger. She was done being social. She wanted to be in bed with Mason in comfy pajamas, not in the sky-high heels and tight shapewear.

He kissed her shoulder and slid a champagne flute into the other hand. "I found grapefruit juice for you."

She sighed and relaxed her body. The women turned their attention to Mason and gave him a simpering smile that pissed Celine off more. Her panther was already riled. She was seconds away from slinging the contents of her drink in their face.

"Mason," Keara stepped closer to him.

Mason stepped back and brought Celine with him. Mason growled, his cat ready to act up. "Move around before I hurt your feelings, girl."

Celine took pleasure in him defending her, but she didn't want any more attention being thrown their way. "Don't," she whispered, her hand on his chest.

It channeled his anger into lust immediately.

His eyes lit, and he mugged her, showing his teeth, the canines growing as his panther pushed forward. Heat filled her, loosening her muscles. He inhaled, his tongue swiping across his lips as he scented her arousal. It wasn't like she could hide it. Especially not from someone like him, who kept his animal so close to the surface.

Keara scoffed, and Mason turned back to her, his chest rumbling. Catching the hint quickly, the two women stormed off.

Mason leaned down into Celine's face. "The fact that you don't like scenes is the only thing keeping my mouth closed," he said softly against her lips. "I deserve a reward for that."

He pulled her out to the balcony and closed the door. Her eyes widened, and she shivered as cold air brushed over her skin.

"What's my reward?" He slid his hand up the long slit of her full skirt. "Got your thighs all out. You asking for it, love bug," he murmured, rubbing his cheek against hers.

She laughed. "I thought you were going to attack me at the house."

"It was a close call," he smiled. "My reward, CeCe. I ain't forget."

She laughed again, so happy with him. She cupped his cheeks and brought his face to hers. She kissed him, and her knees went weak as he took over. His tongue plunged into her mouth, and a moan escaped as her insides turned to liquid. The way the man kissed should be illegal.

They broke apart when they heard a throat clear. It was his mother. Heat rose to her face.

"You two are supposed to be mingling." Adina grabbed Celine's arm. "Come on, daughter."

Celine sighed, knowing her hiding time was at an end. She laughed as Mason growled and reached for her hand.

"Aht-aht, carry your ass on, Mason Knight," Adina fussed.

Celine's smile was full of satisfaction when she saw the way his eyes followed her as his mother dragged her back into the party.

*****

Mason watched his mate as she talked with his mother. That damn dress she wore was gonna get Celine fucked the minute they left this shindig. All that thigh she had out. Lord have mercy. He damn near didn't let her leave the house. Lucky for her, her best friend was there helping her get dressed because had it been up to him, they would've skipped all this shit.

He stared her down as she mingled with his family. They all seemed to get along, his cousins were entertaining her, and he liked that. Celine laughed, and the sound carried to him.

"Please tell me you got a blunt on you." Silas stopped next to him.

"Y'all don't get piss tests in DC?"

"Fuck you, baby brother. Who finna say something to me?"

Mason chuckled. "Nan person."

"Exactly."

They both laughed, and Mason handed his brother the blunt he had from the inside of his tuxedo jacket.

"Boys!"

Well, there was one person. They both exchanged guilty looks.

Adina narrowed her eyes at them. "What have I told the both of you about talking like that in public? And a blunt?"

"Ma, these people gon' still call us names behind our back even if I speak like I graduated from Harvard," Mason said.

She sucked her teeth, "as much as we paid for you to go to Harvard, you better try to sound like it."

He shook his head. Adina had worked her ass off to make sure her boys integrated into high society, but unfortunately for her, they were the products of their father. Because Dallas had earned his seat on the tri-council using a long-forgotten trial by combat, the Motsi treated their family like usurpers. And had for the ten years their father had had his seat.

She sent him a sly smile. "Let me go get my daughter-in-law. Maybe she can get you to act right in public."

Silas cracked up, and Mason shot his brother a look.

He opened his mouth to cuss out his brother, but one of Celine's cousins walked up to them, reeking of alcohol.

"You're just like your father, forcing your way into Motsi society. Everyone knows you're marrying Celine for money," the male slurred.

Adina growled, and Mason held her back with a hand. It wasn't worth correcting. Mason had his own money, ten times what Celine would bring to the table, but he didn't have shit to prove to these people. His brother spoke before he could.

"If you don't carry your ass on," Silas said with a shake of his head.

Arthur narrowed his eyes and swayed on his feet. "If you think my family will stand for this."

Silas sucked his teeth. "Fuck your family."

Mason shrugged. "All y'all can come see me. If I catch one of y'all on our property again, it's on sight."

"You can't prove anything," Arthur slurred.

Mason studied Arthur's face, seeing the guilt before the man suppressed it with anger. Yeah, her family was responsible for the shit that Celine had been dealing with.

Silas sparked up and chuckled, lifting the blunt to his mouth. "We ain't gotta prove shit. Show up and see what the fuck happens."

"Silas," Adina chided.

Celine's aunt Dorothy stomped towards them, her face livid. She shook her head and grabbed her son's arm. "Ignore them, Arthur. They're ghetto trash. All of them."

"Lady, be glad my mama taught me better," he said and shooed her off with one hand while he carefully used the other to keep his mother from lunging.

Adina brushed his hand off, her fangs dropping. "I ain't never been trash, but I got something for your ass."

"What does that mean?" Dorothy snapped.

"You'll find out when you try to get into any other Motsi event in this town." Adina purred.

The woman blanched, her mouth dropping open in shock.

Celine came over and put her arm around Mason's waist. "What's going on?"

He kissed the top of her head and felt the heat of her panther. She was obviously irritated. That shit was turning him on. He glanced down at the cleavage that was sitting up in her dress.

"You will never get to marry her." Arthur sneered as his mother tried to pull him away.

"Too late." Celine told him, stepping in front of Mason. "We've already mated."

Arthur cursed and balled up his hands, breaking away from Dorothy. "You mated this trashy thug?"

Celine gasped and slapped the shit out of Arthur before Mason could stop her. Her claws had come out with the slap, leaving a line of welts across her cousin's face.

"I know that's right, sis-in-law," Silas said with a laugh, "fuck him up."

"Leave," Celine growled, anger tightening her body.

Her mother rushed forward. "Celine, what has gotten into you? You know better than to act like this."

"Say what you want about me—"

"—the fuck you will," Mason interjected.

"—but I will not let you disrespect my mate and his family." Celine finished.

Veronica and her aunt gasped. "Mate? You stooped so low as to mate with him."

Celine stepped forward, but Mason pulled her back into his chest and dropped his chin on her shoulder.

He gave her family a taunting look. "She's mine and ain't shit y'all can do about it."

Silas snickered.

"I'll speak plainly, so there's no misunderstanding," Adina stepped in front of Celine. "You get one warning. If anything happens to Celine or Mason, I will burn all of your shit to the ground with you in it."

"Get 'em, mama," Silas egged on.

Mason turned his head to keep from laughing at his fool brother. Veronica looked around at the attention they were getting, biting her tongue. She gathered her sister's arm.

"Let's go. We don't have to stoop to their level."

Celine was shaking, and Mason grabbed her arm, cutting through the gathering crowd until they were back outside.

"Breathe, love bug. It's okay." He held her shoulders.

Her eyes were watering.

"Don't cry for them."

"I'm not. I'm angry. It'll pass in a sec." She took deep breaths, the fight with her panther on her face. Her eyes lit, then darkened, back and forth with every shuddering breath.

He pulled her into his chest. "We'll go running when we get home, work that right out of your system."

She wiped her face. "I only shift on the full moon."

He shook his head, "Nah, we not with suppressing our animals this way."

She sighed and put her arms around his waist, her body still trembling.

"You stuck up for me, love bug."

She chuckled. "I wanted to do way worst to him. His words were disgusting."

He laughed. "Ain't nothing my family hasn't heard before."

"And I hate that." She clutched him tighter. "How much longer do we have to stay?"

He sensed her pain along their bond now that he was focused on her. He lifted her chin. "What's wrong?"

"Cramps."

He growled, "Please tell me you didn't wear this dress knowing I would have to go to sleep on brick tonight."

She snickered. "I can still take care of you."

He nipped the skin of her neck. "I'm trying to be deep in your shit tonight, though, love bug."

She shuddered, and her lids lowered as her panther's hungry gaze showed through her eyes. Her battle with the animal officially lost. "Then we should probably leave before it starts."

His panther filled his body, and lust overtook him. "Say less." He kissed the top of her head. "We can go now."

She sighed in relief, and he went to talk to his mother.

fifteen

Celine's body should've been pleasantly relaxed after what Mason put on her after the party, but she woke up with cramps, which irritated her. It meant she'd be out of commission for the next seven days. And she was addicted to her mate, so that was highly unfair. Her thoughts went back to the party and the chaos that had ensued before they left. Her family was bound and determined to make every step of the process torture. At least the calls and the scary packages had stopped, and she knew it was all thanks to Mason, and she was thankful.

She started the kettle, pausing as scents from the backyard wafted to her. She knew that Mason smoked weed, but it was stronger tonight than usual. She walked over to the back door and peered out into the dark backyard. She found Mason sitting next to the fire pit, same as she usually found him after a run. His older brother was sitting next to him, and the two of them were passing a blunt back and forth between them.

She smiled. She loved to see her mate relaxed, especially in a space that was hers. He hadn't demanded she move from the farm she loved, instead adjusting his life to live outside the city. She loved him for it.

He caught her watching and waved her over.

She eased outside, wrapping her thin robe across her body tight. She was happy when she reached the heat of the fire. He pulled her into his lap once she was close.

"What's wrong?"

"Stomach cramping," she answered honestly. "I just came down for some aspirin and tea. I didn't mean to intrude."

He kissed the side of her head. "Which side?"

"Left," she said in surprise.

He pulled her closer, and she fell into his chest, settling her head into the crook of his neck. Her back was to his brother. She tensed as Mason's hand slid beneath the band of her pajama pants. Her breath hitched as he skimmed the top of her sex, but he didn't do anything sexual. Instead, the warmth of his palm cupped the left side of her abdomen below her stomach. Her body relaxed as the heat seeped through her skin. The power from his panther reached out to her own, and the animal settled, heating her body. She cuddled deeper into his chest, and he kissed the top of her head.

"Better?" he murmured.

She nodded and closed her eyes. The rumbling of his deep voice lulled her as she settled against his chest. He and his brother discussed shifter politics, and she blocked it out as her body relaxed.

*****

Silas stared at him in amusement.

"What?"

"I never thought to see you settled." His brother answered.

Mason snorted. "Ain't like I was running from it. It just took a lot of my concentration to build Knight Industries, know what I mean?"

"I feel you. Y'all getting along, then?"

"Our situation is very different from yours," Mason told him.

Silas scoffed. "You ain't gotta tell me that. I can see the difference. Lil mama seem like she don't play about you."

Mason laughed. If his brother only knew how hard Cece had to work to be able to stand up to her family like that.

"Y'all still going through with the wedding?"

Mason sighed. "We're mated, so it's unnecessary, but I want to make sure she still gets her day."

Silas snorted and reached for the blunt. "What about that hit shit?"

Mason growled. "It's been quiet so far, but I don't trust it. You saw how they were at the party. I feel like they're just waiting on me to slip up."

"That ain't gone happen, so don't stress. Between all of us, we'll keep her safe," Silas promised.

Mason appreciated the way his family stood with each other. It was in stark contrast to Celine's life. He hurt for her and couldn't imagine how lonely that felt. That was in the past, though. She had him now and his family by default. He would be damned if anything happened to her.

"They a trip. I don't know how you plan to deal with that shit for the rest of your life." Silas said.

"I'll deal with anything for her."

Silas studied him, his panther glowing in his eyes. "I'm happy for you, baby brother."

"How long you in town?"

Silas shrugged. "I'd planned to be here through your wedding."

Mason grunted. "How much longer you got in DC?"

"I don't know, man. Congress be on some bullshit, but I want that adoption bill to go through."

Mason knew the driving force behind Silas' passion. He both admired and hurt for his big brother.

"Any word on that front?"

Silas sighed and rubbed his hand down his face. "Nothing. I don't understand how my daughter just disappeared off the face of the Earth."

"You find Cameron yet?"

"Nope."

"Her family won't talk to me," Mason said. "I done pulled every string I could pull there."

"I appreciate the help."

"I got you for sure, Si."

"Fuck," Silas said softly and took another pull of his blunt. His phone rang, and he looked down. He smiled.

"Oh God," Mason said. "Don't tell me you been in town five minutes and already got a little situation."

"Ain't no call for me to be lonely while I'm here."

Mason snorted. "Man, gone."

Silas stood and dapped his brother. "See you later."

"Be careful."

"Always, baby brother."

He sat outside a little longer, enjoying the weight of his mate on him and the feel of her curves against him. He loved her, and he was happy that they were together. He just really wanted her family to act right. He could see the frustration and sadness every time she dealt with them. It tore him up, but he would make sure she was good, no matter what.

He adjusted in the chair until he could stand with her in his arms. He carried her upstairs and settled her in bed. He hurriedly made the rounds in the house, making sure the windows and doors were locked. Her panther reached for his as he settled into bed behind her minutes later. He brought her back into his chest, leaned down, and inhaled her scent, kissing the back of her neck and settled to sleep.

sixteen

One thing Mason did have to say about living out so far from the city, it gave him space and opportunity to release his panther. He and his animal had spent many nights exploring their new property after work. Yes, technically, the farm was Celine's, but Mason's panther had marked the property and claimed it. Every scent marker was a warning and a dare to anyone who stepped on it. It satisfied him in a way that even the condo he owned—as much as he loved it— couldn't replicate.

He was stalking through the lines of herbs Celine had planted and froze, the cat loosening its grip on his consciousness for a moment. There were intruders on their land, and the cat wanted the man to identify before he went ham. Mason prodded the cat forward, and they rushed back to the house.

Yes, he recognized the scent. And they needed to get to their mate.

By the time they reached the back patio, his cat quickly relinquished control, and Mason shifted, pulling on the jeans he'd left outside but nothing else. He left the rest of the clothes as he heard the raised voices.

Lance came out of the pool house. "It was her father, so I—"

Mason cut him off. "I got it."

He entered the house, growling as he heard Virgil yelling at his mate.

"Just sign the damned papers. You've mated him before the wedding. The least you could do is sign the money over to me!" Her father demanded.

"I don't owe you control over that money." Celine's voice was shaky.

"You betrayed this family!" Daniel said.

Mason narrowed his eyes on her cousin as he came through the kitchen. He was Kate's husband, and from what Celine had said, she and Daniel had always gotten along.

"Stay out of this, Daniel. It has nothing to do with you." Celine snapped.

"It has to do with all of us, you stupid bitch—"

Mason punched him dead in the mouth, and her cousin staggered back. Virgil's eyes were wide, and Celine gasped. With all the commotion, he guessed they hadn't heard him enter.

"What the fuck?" Daniel hissed, blood dripping down his mouth.

"Call my mate out her name again." He said that shit calmly despite his animal's roiling fury.

His mother was always on him about the way he reacted to things. But the way he saw it, he never did so without provocation, and he for damn sure didn't tolerate disrespect. That shit had to be nipped in the bud asap-tually.

He turned his gaze the Virgil, enraged. Celine's father had moved into her space, using his size to intimidate her.

"Back the fuck up," Mason told him, and Virgil took a hasty step back, putting more space between him and Celine. He turned to Celine and cupped her chin. "Into the other room, love bug," he ordered softly.

Her eyes traced his face, her indecision clear by her expression.

"I can handle it," she said softly.

"What I say, CeCe?"

She sighed and left the room.

He turned back to his father-in-law. "You got one more time to come in our shit like this."

"I can't believe that you convinced her to mate with you." Virgil spat out.

Mason gave him a smile full of fangs. "She's mine now," he reiterated.

"That's not—" Daniel tried interjecting.

Mason's look stopped him cold. "Any business you got with her, you got with me and can go through my lawyers."

"You're refusing to allow me to see my daughter?" Virgil sputtered.

"I said what the fuck I said, Virgil. If you want to see Celine, then you call her and make arrangements, but this shit here... this popping up... It ends today."

Virgil and Daniel shared a look.

"Celine!" Virgil yelled, trying to get past Mason.

Which really pissed him off. He'd told Adina that he would keep his hands off her father, but that was gonna be a little hard at the moment. Virgil tried to step around Mason again, growling when Mason put a hand on his chest.

"You can't keep me from seeing her." Virgil gritted out, his fur rippling across his skin.

"Y'all both need to leave." He warned them, though he almost hoped her father lost control of his panther.

He was always down to fight.

"Celine!" Virgil tried again, reigning in his animal.

Celine stayed in the kitchen, which helped Mason keep his temper tethered. Her defying him would've set his animal all the way off.

"Leave and don't come back until you learn to talk to my wife like you got some sense." Mason grabbed the back of Virgil's shirt and dragged him to the front door.

Daniel tripped over his feet to keep Mason's hands off of him.

"This isn't over," Virgil promised as Mason shoved him out of the house and onto the porch.

Mason slammed the door in their faces when they tried to turn back and say something. He locked it and walked into the kitchen to find Celine starting dinner. Her hands were shaking. He dismissed Lance standing guard over her, and sat at the island.

"Are they gone?" She asked.

"They are. Are you okay?"

She nodded but didn't speak.

"Your panther is mad as shit. At me?"

He could feel the fury from her animal way across the kitchen. She was quiet, so he thought she wouldn't answer, but she turned and stared at him, them gorgeous eyes flashing back and forth between gold and dark brown. Oh, his mate was mad, mad. He shifted in his seat and moved his dick to the side.

"I told you I would handle it. I don't...." She shook her head.

"Get it off your chest, love bug. I can take it."

She sighed. "You give me orders and expect me just to follow them. I don't like it sometimes," she spat out quickly.

He hid his smile. Slowly but surely, he was getting her to come out of her shell. If only he could get her to do it with others.

"I'll be more...aware in the future." He hedged.

She narrowed her eyes. "So you won't even pretend to promise not to do it."

He snorted and stood, going over to her. He leaned down and kissed the spot beneath her ear. She shuddered.

"You said only sometimes you don't like it, love bug. That means the other ninety percent of the time, you do."

She scoffed. "Now, I didn't say anything about ninety percent."

He sucked on her neck, and her hands went to his shoulders, her panther rubbing against him. Yeah, she liked that shit. His prim and proper mate was melting in his arms. He lifted her chin and fit their mouths together, kissing her. She pulled back and laid her head on his shoulder. The fire that was in her moments ago was snuffed out as she gathered her animal back under control. He rubbed her back, already missing the heat.

"I'm never gonna sit around and let a motherfucker disrespect you, Celine, so let's just get that straight right now. But, I'll be careful about the way I talk to you. Is that better?"

She nodded, clutching him tightly. "I just thought it would stop, but he still charged into our house, and I just... I want to be stronger," she ended in a whisper.

He nodded and rubbed his cheek against the top of her head, his panther stroking against hers. She shuddered and then relaxed.

"Start with me. Know that you can always let me know how you really feel. Eventually, you'll get to a place where you'll do it with others."

She nodded. They stood that way for long moments until she pulled back.

"Enough of that," she said softly. "Will lamb work for dinner?"

"Fine by me." He said.

The woman could cook her ass off, so he was down for whatever. He pulled out his phone and walked back over to the stool. He texted the one person that could help his wife outside of him. He was determined to make sure she could take care of herself.

seventeen

Mornings in her greenhouse were usually calming. The perpetual humidity mixed with the earthy scents of the soil and various plants never failed to calm her.

Except for today.

Today she couldn't get the events from yesterday out of her head. She'd known that marriage with Mason wouldn't stop her father from his single-minded focus on her grandfather's money. But, she assumed he would move more carefully.

Foolish her.

She rubbed her arm, remembering his hard grip. He was pissed about the mating, and that was to be expected. As soon as Mason filed the paperwork, her inheritance would officially be in her control. Nothing about it made her relieved. As evidenced by yesterday, her father planned to bully her until she turned over every dime of the money to him. As she told Mason yesterday, she wanted to be stronger.

She tensed as her panther moved through her body in alarm. It sensed danger, and immediately Celine looked around. She spotted Dallas Knight at the door to her greenhouse, leaning against the frame. She should've been relieved because, technically, he didn't represent danger, but her panther was still wary.

She wiped a nervous hand down her pants to clean off the dirt. Since she and Mason had been together, she'd only seen him a handful of times. He'd been no less than polite each time, but she couldn't help but be intimidated by him.

"Councilman Knight."

"Dallas is fine, lil mama." His voice was deep, still carrying the drawl of his country accent.

He never tried to hide where he'd come from, carrying the south side of Eastfield everywhere he went. Despite his years on the council, Dallas had not changed from the man he'd been in the streets, according to the rumors about him. She nodded and took a shaky breath.

"How you doing, Celine?" Dallas asked.

He studied her in a way that made her want to squirm. He was sizing her up, maybe? She felt the same way the last two times she'd met him. Mason had told her that his father was calculated like that, always needing to know each person he dealt with. She was happy she'd never done anything to get on his bad side.

"I'm good. You?"

"Every day above ground is a good day. You busy?"

"Umm," she looked around for something to say she was. Finding nothing, she shook her head.

"Come take a ride with me?" It may have been posed as a question, but there was no doubt that it was an order.

Her eyes widened, and he chuckled.

"Come, Celine, I won't bite. Go change into some workout gear, though."

She nodded and rushed from the greenhouse. It took her ten minutes to throw on some yoga pants and a long T-shirt. He was waiting in front of a heavily tinted Mercedes, his security leaning against the driver's side. She pulled out her phone and sent Mason a text.

Celine: Your dad wants to take me someplace?

Mason: Bet. If it's in the city, come see me.

Okay, so that didn't work. She took a deep breath and shored up her courage. If Mason wasn't worried, then she wouldn't either. She descended the porch steps and thanked Dallas as he opened the door for her. The ride was quiet, her new father-in-law on the phone the whole time. She looked out the window and watched the surrounding scenery, frowning when she realized what side of town they were on.

Her eyes widened when they pulled into the shabby parking lot. The warehouse building loomed large and looked like it had been there longer than she'd been alive. She read the sign, her gaze shooting to Dallas.

A boxing gym?

He smiled. "Sometimes, just knowing how to defend yourself will give you confidence."

"I'm not going to punch my father," she scoffed.

"Tone, lil mama," he warned gently.

She cleared her throat. "The point still stands, though. I don't think I could ever hit anyone, especially my family."

He chuckled and studied her. "That ain't true. I seen the welts on that boy's face."

Her cheeks burned, and he laughed as he opened the car door.

"Besides, it might make you feel better," he smirked, and she couldn't help returning his smile. "It for sure will make that panther you got on a tight leash feel better."

His eyes bore into her, and for some reason, she felt guilty. Her mother and father both were strict about shifting. Only on the full moon and one had to have absolute control over the animal. Even though shifters had been out and mixing among humans for almost forty years, her parents still operated as though they still had to blend in with them.

Dallas didn't wait on her response, stepping out of the car. His driver opened her door, and she thanked him, hastening her steps to catch up with him.

She gaped as she walked in. There were two massive boxing rings, and along the walls of the building, punching bags hung, with various shifters in different states of dress working out. Dallas was greeted as they came in. He marched towards the ring with a single male standing in the middle, geared up.

"My position brings a lot of heat to this family, and you'll need to be able to handle yourself. Your father failed you there, but I won't let it go on for much longer. I raised my kids by a different code. You one of mine now, which means you need to be able to flip shit over when it's called for." He told her as they stood ringside.

She felt touched that he would think of her that way. Her fuzzy feelings were short-lived, though.

Dallas turned to her and nodded towards the ring. "Up you go, lil mama."

Her eyes widened, and she stared at the male, gasping as she recognized a shirtless Silas. He was lean and looked like he had been carved from marble. He smiled, showing off the mouth guard he wore. His eyebrows waggled, his gaze teasing. Her panther raised in curiosity, and for once, she didn't push it down. Especially not under the eye of her intimidating father-in-law. Dallas nodded in encouragement, and she bit her lip, crawling up into the ring.

Silas started her off slow, going through the different types of punches. He was gentle, his teasing helping her relax. Before long, she was punching at the pads he had on his hands with him shouting out punches.

She didn't know how long they'd been at it, but her arms and hands were sore. She was exhilarated, though, and all the tension she'd had stored up from her father's visit dissipated. Dallas was still ringside, giving her encouragement, correcting her form.

Her steps faltered as she felt a familiar energy enter the space. Her mate was here. His presence buzzed through their mating bond.

"Aht-aht, focus," Silas snapped, swinging for her to duck.

She smiled at his gruffness. Hours ago, she would've jumped out of her skin, but she realized they all talked to each other that way. She went back to her drills, still watching in her peripheral as Mason sauntered up ringside and dapped his father.

"Celine," he called.

She stopped and faced him. He crooked his finger, and she smiled. She walked over to him happily, grinning as he pointed to his lips. Gods, she loved this man. She leaned over and dropped a kiss on his mouth.

"You can't come in here distracting my girl, Mase," Dallas grumbled.

"Look at him, Pop. Whipped," Silas teased.

Mason laughed. "Why y'all got my baby in here, Pop?"

She warmed at that. She loved how casually affectionate he was with her. It didn't matter where they were; Mason had no problem telling the world she was his. No matter how many weeks they'd been mated, she still considered herself lucky to have him.

"Teaching her what her father should've," Dallas answered.

Mason grunted, not disagreeing. "I brought a change of clothes for you, love bug," he said, holding up the bag.

She grabbed it and looked at Silas.

He nodded, "we done today, lil mama. Use the shower upstairs. No one goes in there except the manager."

"Thanks," she said, exiting hastily. She didn't want him to change his mind. She was exhausted.

Lance met her at the bottom of the stairs, having come down from inspecting the room. "It's clear. I'll be here at the bottom of the stairs. Holla if you need something."

"Will do." She told him. She felt good, and she had Dallas and Silas to thank.

*****

Mason's eyes followed Celine across the gym and up the stairs until the door closed behind her. His panther was urging him to follow her. It had only been hours since he'd left her home, but he missed her.

"How did she do?" He asked his brother.

"She skittish as hell, but I'll break her out of that," Silas promised him.

"She got her panther in a god-damned chokehold," Dallas fussed.

"Yeah, I'm working on that," Mason murmured.

"That's what happens when you raised by them ol uppity ass shifters," Dallas added.

The Motsi shifters had grown soft as hell compared to the council at its inception. Its members had grown complacent, the shifters under them blending more and more with the humans around them. They'd tried combatting that with their marriage mergers, hoping it would strengthen the shifter unions. But, even that had shifted from being about the strength of families to plain old greed.

It hadn't boded well for his father's predecessor. Dallas had easily slaughtered through the male's advisors and enforcers, taking his head and council seat.

Dallas planned for his family to hold that seat well after he was gone, which meant that his boys were raised a hell of a lot tougher than the Motsi society shifters. It also meant, as his mate, Celine needed to be able to keep up and handle herself. Mason wasn't worried. His love bug was tougher than she appeared. He would make sure she could stand with him. He'd meant what he'd told her last night. She could start with him, enforcing her boundaries and making her voice heard.

"Make sure you take her running, pull that cat out her control," Dallas ordered.

He nodded, already planning to do that.

"She's sweet, and her panther is strong under all that control," Silas told him, removing his gloves and sitting on the edge of the ring.

Mason smiled, pride for her tightening his chest. "I'll get her there."

"No doubt," Silas said. "Your mother call you?"

He chuckled. "Yeah. We'll follow y'all home for dinner." He already knew he would get an earful for not showing his face more.

"You straighten that shit with Virgil?" Dallas asked.

"What shit?" Silas asked.

"He came round the house yelling at Celine yesterday."

"He's trying to get the council to intervene. Says you're taking advantage of his daughter." Dallas shook his head.

"He wants Celine to sign the rest of the money over to him," Mason told them.

Celine had told him over dinner last night.

Dallas perked up. "How much money has he already gotten from her?"

"Ten million," Mason said, shaking his head.

Silas whistled. "I take it his company is not doing as well as he's trying to portray."

"I looked into all that shit. The ten mill she signed over will keep him afloat for a little while, but he's up to his eyeballs in debt and is pissing off shifters all over town." Mason said.

"And you don't think that's motive for the hit?" Dallas asked.

"He's confident he can bully Celine out of all of her money. He wouldn't go that far. At least not yet." Mason shrugged. "I'm watching all of them. They'll have to make a move soon."

"What does Celine say?" Silas wanted to know.

"She not hurting for money. She lives simple, and you know I'll always make sure she's taken care of. At the same time, she doesn't want him to have it. I'm pretty sure it's spite at this point."

Silas snickered. "Good for her."

Dallas nodded. "Any word on the hit?"

Mason growled, reminded of his earlier frustration. The only information Jules had gotten from the hired gun they'd captured was a burner phone number and bag of cash. It was maddening. Especially since he knew it wouldn't be long until they tried again.

"Still working on it." He answered finally. "So far, Jules hasn't been able to track anything down. I planted a few seeds about the lack of funds. I'm hoping that whoever they hire understands there won't be no money in it for them."

Dallas smiled at him. "I already told you what to do about it."

"Can't kill the whole family when we don't even know who did it," Mason reminded his bloodthirsty father.

"Any more attempts?" Silas asked.

"We've been kicking it at the house. It's harder to get to us there, so no."

Dallas grunted but said nothing. His panther sensed when his mate entered the room again. She came downstairs, smelling like the floral lotion he'd packed for her and looking beautiful in a maxi dress that skimmed her curves. His chest rumbled, and he was debating skipping dinner with his parents.

Dallas laughed, probably suspecting what his son was thinking. "You can give your mama a few hours."

Celine walked up to Mason, standing toe to toe with him. She reached his chin in the flat Chucks she wore.

"Mom wants us over for dinner. That good with you?"

She nodded, "of course."

He held out his hand, and she grabbed it. Okay, he couldn't skip dinner, but there wasn't anything saying he couldn't rush through it.

eighteen

Mason dropped his messenger bag on the chair closest to the front door, inhaling the heavenly scents in the air. His stomach was growling, reminding him that he hadn't eaten anything since leaving their house this morning. Celine cooked for him every morning, and he had to admit that it spoiled him.

They'd been mated for two months now, but it felt like they'd been together so much longer. He and Celine had fallen into a comfortable rhythm, each of them working around the other's work schedules. Lately, though, he'd had some long nights, falling back into his pre-mated work patterns. He was getting home later and later, falling into bed with exhaustion. He and his panther hadn't been running in at least two weeks, so he was restless. His panther had been nudging him all day, but he blocked it out as he usually did when he got busy at work.

He'd filed the paperwork with her grandfather's lawyers, legitimizing their mating, and he'd been swamped at work ever since. He walked into the kitchen, the scent of the food Celine cooked still lingering in the air. He smiled, wondering what it was that she'd made. He frowned a few moments later when he realized that there was nothing in the oven or the refrigerator.

No leftovers.

He frowned deeper when he saw Celine on the back patio undressing. She was about to go running without him. Now that he was in her presence, he realized that the mating bond had been dulled all day. He probed at it and frowned as her aggravation broadcasted to him.

But it was dim...almost unnoticeable. Was she closing down the bond between them?

She slipped her shirt over her head, and despite his irritation, his body reacted quickly, need for her changing one hunger into another type.

"What's going on?" he asked, stepping outside.

"With what?"

He cocked his head to the side, sensing her attitude. "It smells like you cooked."

"I did." Was her short answer.

"But you didn't leave me anything...."

"I cooked for the people who could bother to be home at a decent hour." She turned her back to him.

He frowned and looked down at his watch. "It's ten o clock."

That made her angrier. He could feel it as he pushed against their bond in an effort to get her to let him in. Her panther rose, and his did the same, answering her call.

He stopped once he realized she wouldn't let him in. "I'm too tired for this shit, Cece."

She whipped her gaze to him. "You're tired because you've been working insane hours for weeks."

"If that's why you mad, then say that shit. What I told you about the games?" He snapped.

"Just because I'm not catering to you doesn't mean I'm playing games." She changed into her panther and loped off.

He growled, irritated. He could admit that he'd become spoiled, so he couldn't deny that she'd been catering to him. He wiped a hand down his face. He took off his clothes and took off after his mate. His panther was pushing him further into the background, its irritation with him harder to ignore in his animal form. Had this been why his cat had been nudging at him all day?

It took him a minute to catch up with her, and when he did, her animal growled at him, snarling if he got closer. His panther reacted, recognizing the turmoil underneath her outward anger. Celine's panther snapped at him and took off. He chased her down, stalking her through the rows of her plants. Her cat was fast, loping through the bushes. He sped up, cutting her off as she turned, pouncing once he caught her.

He bit the back of her neck to bring her down, and she bucked against him. His panther hissed, careful not to hurt her. He tightened his grip on her, asserting his dominance, willing her to calm down. She fought him a little longer before going limp in exhaustion. Mason released his teeth, licking across her fur in apology. It took considerable effort to coax his animal back so that he could shift into his human form. Mason pulled Celine's panther into his lap before she could take off again. He nuzzled into her neck, rubbing his cheek against her fur.

"Talk to me, love bug," he whispered.

Her turmoil was still there. She nipped his shoulder and took off, this time towards home. He sighed and shifted, giving chase, sending an apology to his cat for ignoring it and its instincts. He caught her on the patio. She shifted, and there was hurt in her eyes when she faced him.

"If you don't want to come home, that's on you."

He stared at her in confusion. "I'm not avoiding home."

"You could've fooled me," she snapped.

He grabbed her arm as she tried to leave. "I say what the hell I mean, Celine. I'm swamped with this merger. That's it. I'm sorry I haven't communicated that better."

Her eyes widened in surprise. Her panther was still mad. He could feel the hot stings of it down their connection. He crowded her space, wrapping his arms around her waist. He couldn't control his body's reaction to her, especially when the scent of her desire rose between them.

He opened his mouth to finish his apology, but she pulled his face down and kissed him. Her kiss blew the top of his head off, her need hot and whipping down their bond. She rose to her toes and moved until his erection was snug against her wet, hot sex. He shuddered, his panther rushing forward to meet her needs. Fur fluttered down his arm and the back of his neck as her nails dug into his skin. The bite of violence fit his mood perfectly.

He gripped her ass, his kiss turning rougher. She moaned, biting at his bottom lip. They went at it, wild and animalistic. For it to only be a kiss, there was a lot of scratching and biting. They barely made it into the house before Mason dropped to his knees, pulling her down onto the kitchen floor. Celine opened her legs, and Mason bit her stomach, scraping his canines across her skin. He growled in pleasure at the welts he'd left behind.

She pushed his head lower, and he chuckled, knowing exactly what the minx wanted. Instead of giving her what she wanted, he took his time, leaving marks up and down her thighs. She growled and slashed at his shoulder, her claws leaving their own marks.

"Quit teasing," she hissed.

Mason nipped the lips of her pussy, and she howled, lifting, begging for more. He slid his tongue across her folds and gave his mate what she'd been begging for. Celine held his head in place, grinding against his mouth. Her hips lifted as she tried to set the rhythm. He pulled back. He wanted her submissive beneath him. She moaned and tried to push him back into place.

"Unh-unh. You come when I say you can come." He grabbed her hands from his shoulder and pinned them down above her head.

She bucked against him which...yeah. His mate was in the mood to fight and would definitely oblige her. He used his other hand to part her thighs wider, slamming into her. She screamed and arched her back, pulsing on his dick.

"Hard," she demanded.

Mason chuckled and did the opposite, fucking into her with deliberate, slow strokes. She turned her head and bit into his forearm, and his panther bucked against him.

"Keep biting me, love bug. I can keep this pace for hours."

She moaned, her lust-filled eyes staring at him in defiance. She lifted her hips, still trying to control the pace. He pulled out, and she protested.

"No, please."

He released her arms and spun her body around before she could grab for him. He pulled her hair with one hand, using the other to pull her hips high. She gasped and pushed her ass into him.

He slapped his hand across her ass, and she moaned, pushing back for more. Her claws released, and she reached for him. He released her hair and pinned her arms behind her back. She growled in frustration.

He leaned over her back and licked across his mark on her shoulder. Her answering whimper swelled his dick, and he was close to giving in to her.

Her panther thrashed inside her, still mad with their mate. Part of her wanted to lift her neck and give him the submission he demanded, and the other wanted him to earn it. That last part had her biting him again, deeper this time until she drew blood. He cursed and slammed his dick into her, which was what they wanted to begin with. She dropped her head as pleasure washed over her in an intense wave.

She needed more.

Mason reached around her and grabbed her breast, pinching her nipple hard enough for her to see stars. Her clit swelled in response, and channel spasmed around him. She bit him again, sucking on his skin. He fucked her harder, his strokes hitting that spot deep inside her that was going to make her body explode.

"Behave," he demanded, scraping his teeth across the back of her neck.

All that did was send her panther into a frenzy. She bucked against him, grunting with the force of his strokes, greedy for more. Her core tightened, and her body trembled in anticipation of the orgasm swelling within her. Mason must have sensed the upcoming bliss and gentled his strokes, pulling her from that edge.

It went on forever. Him spinning up her body at his command, then pulling back right before she teetered over. It felt like torture, but the best kind. She was enjoying every minute. Soon though, she was a puddle of tears and yearning. She lifted her neck, her panther gladly giving their mate their submission.

He growled in satisfaction, releasing her hands and leaning over her back. He brought her chin around, and the kiss he gave her was so full of love and tenderness that tears slipped from her eyes.

"My love bug," he whispered, sliding his hands between the folds of her sex.

The moment the soft pad of his thumb caressed her clit, she splintered. She closed her eyes, too tired to scream. Mason was right behind her, gripping her hips tightly.

Exhausted, Celine could only hum as his body dropped down on top of hers. Mason sighed and rolled over, bringing her on top of him. Her body heated as she realized how many bites and scratches she'd left on him. Her panther had insisted on each and every one. She had her own marks, ones she was not in the least bit regretful for.

He hugged her tight, his tongue lashing across his marks. Her panther preened under the attention.

"You like all these marks, violent ass."

She laughed. "I am not violent."

He chuckled softly and held her. He broke the silence a few minutes later once he caught his breath.

"The bond is stronger." There was relief in his tone. "You've been deliberately holding it back from me?" He asked quietly.

She sighed, and guilt filled her. "I'm sorry. I won't do it again."

"I'm still getting used to being in a relationship. I'll get better at it."

She stared down at him, her panther assessing his words for the truth. "I know how important getting out of Dallas' shadow is, but you gotta give yourself a break."

He turned his gaze, squirming. Celine knew he'd worked his whole adult life to establish his own legacy. His father cast a heavy shadow, both on the streets and throughout Eastfield now that he was on the Tri-council. It couldn't have been easy separating from that.

Celine gripped his chin and turned him back to face her. "Guess what? Ain't a shifter in Eastfield who don't know who you are. Your name carries its own weight. I definitely am not trying to stop your grind, but I...." She paused and lowered her gaze, nervous about what she wanted to say. "I don't want to be an afterthought."

His eyes widened, and his hurt and shame flowed down their bond. She realized that tamping down her side of the bond had effectively cut her off from his feelings as well.

"I never want to make you feel like that. You're my priority, and I'll make sure you know that from now on."

There was no doubt of his sincerity. It was so easy to read across their connection.

"At the same time, you have to talk to me, love bug. I have no way of knowing when you're upset, and lashing at me with your panther is not nice." He told her.

She sighed and dropped her forehead to his chest. "I'm sorry. I was going for a run before you showed up to dissipate some of the anger."

He lifted her chin. "Tell me why you're upset."

"It's done. We don't have to hash it out." They'd already worked it out as far as she and her panther were concerned.

"No, I want words, and I want you used to using them. I don't want whatever cycle you're stuck in with your parents to come into our mating."

She hugged his waist, her eyes watering. It took her a moment, but then she took a shuddering breath. "I don't mind late hours, but I've hardly seen you the past month, and I've had to attend events without you. There have been all these snide comments about you being done with me now that you got what you wanted, and I took it bad."

"Now, see, love bug, how the hell would I have known you had all that going on, especially when you've been withholding on your side of the bond?"

"You need to pay better attention to me before problems get this big." She was only half teasing.

He was right, though; she had done them a disservice. At first, she hadn't realized that she'd done it, but then after a week of him not saying anything, she could admit she'd kept it going in an attempt to punish him.

He stared at her, absorbing that rebuke. "I'll do better."

She sighed again and clutched him tight. "I'll better communicate when I'm feeling a certain type of way."

"When is the next event mama has you attending?"

She sighed. "Tomorrow night."

He grunted. "Okay, I'll be there, if for nothing else, just to show off all these marks you put on me."

Her cheeks heated. "We got a little out of control." She admitted.

"I like that shit," he said, pulling her hips to align with his growing erection. "Be possessive all you want, love bug. I done told you, claim this shit."

He pushed inside her, and she moaned at his fullness. She would never get enough of him.

nineteen

Celine hummed along with the music she and Deena had playing in the background as they worked. They were grinding herbs and working on their herbal blends. Deena was in a full face of makeup because they'd just shot some video content for their socials.

It had been a couple of weeks since she and Mason had argued about his working hours, and it was getting better. They were both getting better at communicating, and Celine couldn't ever remember being as happy as she was now. It seemed like her life was finally in a place she couldn't have imagined in her wildest dreams. At the most, she'd imagined a life without her parents holding her farm over her head. Being mates with Mason went well beyond that.

Deena smiled at her. "Girl, Mason got you around here cheesing."

Celine laughed at her friend. "Everything is going so well. I love Mason, and his family has been amazing."

"His brother still teaching you to fight?" Deena asked.

"Sometimes it's Silas, and sometimes it's some of the other enforcers Dallas has."

Deena hummed. "I've always wondered about Councilman Knight. It's even weird to call him that. He was so heavy in the streets, to see his transition to high society is cool."

"I like him. He's tough, but he's been teaching me all kinds of stuff."

Celine had been spending time with him and Adina, and she really liked them both. The two had all but adopted her.

"What kind of stuff."

Celine laughed, "He's teaching me self-defense, and he even took me shooting."

Deena cackled. "Did you tell him you could shoot a rifle like Calamity Jane since you've been playing farmer?"

"You should've seen his face when he saw my targets afterward." She smiled, remembering his pride fondly.

"You and Mason settling in after your big fight?"

She blushed, still not believing she'd told Deena that. But, her friend had sensed the change in Celine the next day.

"Umm, yeah."

Her heart fluttered at the thought. Mason had been so intentional with her since their fight. He came home at a decent hour and had even made time to take her out on dates. Her cheeks heated as she thought about some of the things they'd done together. It ranged from simple fun like mini-golf to sexier dates where they went dancing and got a hotel afterward. He'd completely seduced her.

Deena snorted. "Where is he now?"

"With his brother. I'm meeting him at his parents' house when we're done here."

It was nearing evening, and the days were getting shorter, so though it was only a little after five, it was getting darker outside. She and Deena both paused when the lights in her house went out. They jumped as Lance came through the back door, his gun drawn.

"What's going on?" Celine asked, her heart racing.

Lance shook his head. "Just stay put until I figure it out."

"What's happening?" Deena asked.

"Someone cut the power. It's being handled."

No sooner than he said that, Celine heard a pop, and Lance dropped to the floor. She gasped and rushed around the island to him.

"Get down!" Deena shouted as the glass to her back sliding doors shattered.

Gunshots sounded, and bullets started to come through the house. Wood splinters from her cabinets rained down around them. Deena crawled on the floor until she reached Celine and Lance. The two of them took an arm and dragged a cursing Lance through the kitchen and into the garage. He hissed as they shuffled to help him stand and into the back seat of the truck she used to haul supplies.

Deena slipped into the front seat, lowering the sun visor until the keys fell into her hands. She cranked up the truck. They could still hear gunshots striking her kitchen.

Celine hit the garage door opener and growled when nothing happened. "The power, we can't lift the garage."

"Fuck that," Deena murmured and put the truck in reverse. "Buckle up."

Celine's seatbelt had barely snapped into place when Deena powered the truck through the door. They both screamed as a man tried to step in front of the truck, gun drawn. Deena hit him and swung the vehicle around to go forward.

Masked men came around the side of her house, aiming their guns at them. But there were also panthers racing through the fields to meet those men. Deena punched it, her face a mask of concentration. Celine looked back at Lance to make sure he was okay.

"Will the others be okay with us leaving? Should we go back and help?" She asked him.

"Keep going. You're our priority." Lance cursed as Deena hit a bump.

He pulled his shirt up, and Celine nearly swayed at the amount of blood. He took off his shirt and wiped his side.

"The bullet went through, but they used silver." His breathing was a little labored as he tried to sit up.

"Stay down," she ordered him, squeaking when something rammed the back of their truck. "Oh my God." Celine hissed, unbuckling her seatbelt and diving into the back seat.

"Oh, fuck you," Deena said and punched the gas more.

Lance pulled out his phone, his thumb flying over its screen as Celine examined him. There wasn't much she could do to help other than staunch the blood flow.

She looked behind them, her heart thundering at the black SUV bearing down on them. "We can lose them on the highway, maybe, but this road is long and empty. I don't know if we can beat them there."

An idea came to her as the SUV swerved into the oncoming lane to try and come up on their side. She reached for Lance's chest holster. Lance grabbed her wrist.

"What are you doing, Celine?"

She grabbed his gun and checked to make sure it was loaded. "Hopefully, buying us time."

Deena cursed as another black SUV barreled down the road, heading towards them from the other direction. "Make it quick whatever you're about to do. We finna have more company in a second."

Celine slid the safety off and took a deep breath. "Ok, Deena, slow a bit so they can come up."

She waited until the front of the SUV was just overtaking the back of the truck. She downed the window and prayed as she aimed. She fired two bullets, each striking the front of their SUV. The driver swerved as she fired again, the SUV plowing into the trees lining the highway.

"Holy shit!" Lance and Deena said together.

Celine pressed the button to lift the window, her panther flooding her body with more adrenaline. Deena didn't let off the gas, flying down the two-lane road.

"I called for back-up," Lance gasped out before passing out.

Celine's hands shook as she touched Lance's torso. It was hot to the touch, and fur rippled onto his skin as his panther pushed forward. He shifted, his clothes tearing, the animal just as unconscious as the man.

"Guys!" Deena called out.

Celine peeked over the seat, her eyes widening as the other SUV swerved in front of them, blocking their way. Deena cursed, slamming on the breaks. Celine tumbled to the floor.

"You got any more bullets in that gun?" Deena asked.

Celine picked herself off the floor and reached for the gun until the doors of the SUV in front of them opened.

Relief hit her so hard that she thought she would throw up. "It's Mason."

Deena laid her head on the steering wheel. "Thank God."

The back door ripped open, and Mason scooped her, his arms wrapping around her tight. Her body was trembling, her heart still racing. He walked them around to the SUV he'd come in, putting her into the back seat. His hands were skimming her body, checking for wounds. He looked more primal than she'd ever seen him. His eyes were emerald green, the pupil a narrow slit, shining bright with his panther. His canines were damn near resting on his bottom lip as his animal fought to take over.

"Are you hurt?"

She shook her head. "Just Lance. They hit him with silver."

Silas came up behind him, his older brother looking just as feral as Mason. He pushed his brother to the side and grabbed her in a hug. "We saw what you did, lil mama. That's what the fuck I'm talking about."

Mason shoved his brother back out the way. "Hands off my mate." He nuzzled into her neck.

The passenger door behind her opened, and Deena slipped into the SUV. Her friend looked shaken, but she shared a smile with her.

"We did that shit."

Celine let out a nervous giggle that had an edge of hysteria. Her mind drifted to the shifters she'd caused to run off the road, and she briefly wondered if they'd escaped the accident alive. But, at the end of the day, she'd done what she had to do to escape with their lives, and that was all that mattered.

twenty

Mason was fuming, and his hands shook with the need to kill something. He'd been in a meeting with Silas when Jules had rushed into his office. At the same time, his phone had blared with the farm's proximity alarm. He'd been frantic as they rode towards the house because he'd been unable to reach neither Celine nor Lance. He couldn't remember ever being that scared in his life. He'd felt some sense of relief when he'd spotted Celine's truck barreling down the road, but the SUV speeding after them had his panther shredding his insides to come out.

Seeing Celine damn near hanging out the window with a gun in her hand had sent a streak of pride through him. So many people underestimated his baby. Speaking of...

He turned his gaze towards the smoking SUV a few yards away. The occupants hadn't left the vehicle, so he wondered how much damage they'd sustained.

"Stay here," he murmured, kissing Celine's forehead. "Jules!"

His security flanked him as he headed toward the truck. His panther moved through him, and Mason unsheathed his claws. The driver was unconscious in the front seat, bloody from the gash on his forehead and what looked like a bullet wound on his shoulder. One of Celine's shots had fired true.

Silas growled next to him. Mason opened the door and cut the seatbelt from around the unconscious male, dragging him onto the ground and leaving him. Julian and Silas had the back door open and were shuffling out two other males. Mason cursed as he got a look at the occupants. He shouldn't have been surprised, but he was. Foolishly, he assumed that her cousins would heed his warning.

He leaned down and grabbed Celine's cousin Arthur around the neck, his claws piercing his skin. "I take it my warning wasn't enough?"

Arthur's eyes were wide with panic, his skin rippling as his panther tried to force a shift. Mason squeezed, taking pleasure in the blood that flowed down his hands.

"We didn't have a choice," Arthur wheezed.

"Who ordered it?" Mason snarled.

Arthur cut his eyes to his brother Daniel, unconscious beneath Silas' foot. "I'll tell you everything. Just...leave my brother out of this."

Mason showed his fangs and growled in Arthur's face. "If your brother wanted to be left out of it, he should've kept his ass at home." He threw him back down to the ground. "Jules put them in the back of the truck and follow me back to the house."

He marched back over to the SUV and hopped into the front seat. Silas jumped into the passenger side, and Mason punched it towards the farm. He looked into the backseat, and Celine met his gaze, giving him a shaky nod.

"Fuuucck," Silas whispered next to him as they drove up.

There were bodies scattered across the yard, and the front of their house was riddled with bullet holes, the windows completely broken. Celine and Deena gasped behind him. His mate's cry of anguish tore him up and sealed her family's fate. He wouldn't let them get away with destroying something so vital to her. Celine reached for the door handle.

"Wait." His tone was firm.

Tears crested her eyes and trailed her cheeks, but she backed away from the door. He and Silas stepped from the truck and inspected the bodies. Two of his guards were still in panther form, their breathing choppy. They'd been shot, probably by silver bullets the same as Lance. He leaned down and ran his hand over their heads.

"Healers are about five minutes out. Just hold on for me," He murmured to them.

"The house is clear," Silas said, coming up to him.

"How many of ours is down?" Mason asked, dreading the answer.

"Just these two. The rest are circling the property to make sure no one else comes up." Silas reported.

"We deading this shit tonight," he promised his brother.

"I'm fucking with you, whatever you want to do," Silas promised.

He nodded and stood when his father's car pulled into the yard. The healer had ridden with Dallas and rushed over to their injured security.

"I got them, Mason," Liam told him.

Mason walked over to the SUV and opened the back door. Celine's tear-streaked face greeted him. She wrapped her arms around him and buried her head in his chest. He rubbed his cheek against the top of her head, his panther soothing her cat, his chest rumbling with his growls.

"Settle, love bug."

She shuddered and looked up at him. "My family is behind this?"

"After tonight, you won't have to worry about it again," he promised her. "Now, I want you to go inside and pack. We'll stay in the city until we get our home cleaned and fixed."

She nodded, and he helped her down. She walked away on wobbling feet. Mason wiped a hand down his face and exhaled; it would be a long night. He instructed one of the guards to take Deena home. He met his father on the porch, and they both surveyed the damage.

"How you want to handle this?" Dallas asked.

"The old way. Disappear they ass." He answered.

Silas stepped up beside them. "Be better to make an example out of them."

Mason growled because, yes, that was the better way to handle it all, but he was infuriated and wanted someone dead. They all turned around as the rumble of multiple cars sounded.

Dallas held up his hand. "My way or Silas' way?"

He wanted them all dead, but he had to think of his mate. They all frowned at the three cars that pulled up.

"The goddamned audacity," Mason grumbled when he realized who it was.

Silas scoffed next to him. "They bold as shit."

Mason grunted and crossed his arms over his chest as Celine's family stepped from their cars and rushed towards them.

"What happened here?" Virgil asked, his eyes raking over all the destruction.

"Why are you here?" Mason asked instead of answering.

"I called them," Celine said quietly, coming out of the house. "I want them to see what their greed has brought into my life."

Mason turned to her and gathered her to his side. He looked past her family and nodded to Jules. Jules dragged both Arthur and Daniel trussed from the back of the truck and tossed them down at her family's feet. Several of them gasped and stepped back. Kate rushed to her husband's side, her hands shaking as she inspected him.

"How dare you!" Dorothy spat.

"I want everyone involved in the hit, or I'm taking out the whole family." Mason declared.

Veronica and Virgil blanched, stepping back. A thick, tense silence blanketed the night.

"No one wants to talk?" He stepped towards Arthur. "You wanted your brother spared earlier in exchange for information. Have you changed your mind now that your life is forfeit?"

"Arthur, no." Dorothy gasped, her hand going to her throat.

Arthur's head lowered. "Kill me, but leave my family."

"Done," Mason hissed, grabbing the male by the throat.

"No!" Dorothy stepped forward. "It was me. I hired the men. We're done if we don't get that money." She rushed forward and reached for her son. "Don't kill him, please."

Mason flashed his fangs and dropped Arthur to the ground. Now they were getting somewhere.

twenty-one

Celine's heart was racing, fear, anger, and betrayal stealing her breath. She didn't know if Mason would really go through with his threat, but in her present state of mind, she wouldn't blame him if he did. Her house, the place where she found refuge, was ruined, and all because her family wanted money that didn't belong to them.

"Who else was involved?" Mason growled, scanning her family.

Dorothy sent a quick look to her mother, and Celine's legs nearly gave out. She swayed, and Dallas was there.

"I'm good," she whispered, but she clung to his hand tightly.

"Somebody better speak up!" Mason barked.

Her mother flinched but said nothing. Dorothy stepped forward, her head high.

"It was all on me. The money belonged to my sisters, and I. Celine had no right to it." Dorothy told them.

"The rest of us have nothing to do with this," Veronica said impatiently.

"You didn't try to stop her when you thought it would work," Kate spoke up, cradling her husband. "All of us need that money, not just Mother Dorothy."

"You did it and now are caught. I can't help you now." Veronica hissed.

Celine growled, and anger filled her to overflow. "You've been smiling in my face, and you knew they were plotting to kill me?"

She jumped at Kate, but Dallas held her back. "Easy, lil mama."

"You set us up at Banjos, didn't you?" Celine fought to get out of his arms, her vision red and hazy.

Kate looked away, guilt written all over her face. Of all the betrayals, Kate's pissed her off the most. She expected her family to treat her like shit, but Kate had pretended to be her friend.

Virgil stepped forward. "My wife and I didn't have anything to do with anything that happened here tonight. It shouldn't affect the contract we have with each other."

Celine stopped fighting as hurt pierced her. She didn't think she could feel worse, but the last vestige of hope went with her father's words. She could've been killed tonight, and all he cared about was getting her money.

"You don't care about me at all, do you?" The ache in her chest increased as both Veronica and Virgil avoided her gaze.

Virgil growled. "What does that have to do with any of this?"

She pointed at her father. "You won't get another dime from me. I want all of you off our property, and the next time any of you try to send someone after us, I won't stop Mason from killing the whole fucking lot of you." She snapped and shook off her father-in-law's arms.

She didn't care what happened to them. She was no longer in the business of putting their needs over her own. She turned her back and went back inside of her trashed house. Celine took in the sofa she'd so lovingly chosen, now ripped with feathers littered around it. The art she'd picked, the furniture that she'd been so proud to buy with her own money. All of it was gone. Her chest heaved as her breathing increased, a panic attack overtaking her. She hurriedly stripped her clothes and raced out the back door. She couldn't be in here anymore.

It wasn't any better outside. The rows and rows of herbs that she'd planted were dug up presumably from the fighting. But, she couldn't be sure what her cousins had done in their petty anger. She ran, her claws digging through the soil she'd toiled. She ran until she reached the end of her property and the pond that separated her from her neighbor. She skidded in the dirt, exhausted and heartbroken.

Her head lifted, and her cat took a deep breath, a familiar scent reaching them. She pushed her ears back as Mason's panther approached them. He stopped a few feet away from her, his head lifted, beckoning her. She watched him through narrowed eyes. He shifted into his human form and held his hands up. He sat down in the grass and watched her. His dark eyes took her in, but he said nothing, giving her and her panther space. She paced, her emotions overwhelming her.

Mason broke the silence. "Come, Celine," he kept his order gentle, but it was an order nevertheless.

It took her panther a moment, but the cat obeyed, stalking over to him with her body low. He ran his hand over to the top of the panther's head and nuzzled across its cheek.

"Out, love bug," He whispered.

She stepped back, and her power buzzed over her body as she shifted back to her human form. She crawled into his lap towards the only safety she'd ever had in her life.

"They tried to kill me, Mason. Over money," she whispered.

He held her as sobs wracked her body. He kissed and loved on her until the hurt within her dissipated, and her tears were reduced to shuddering sighs.

"You got me now, love bug." He swore.

She nuzzled into his neck, exhausted. She couldn't summon the strength to do anything other than lay in his arms.

"Want to go out of town until the repairs on the farm are done?"

"Where?" she whispered, a little spark of happiness blooming in her.

He smiled and lifted her chin. "We got a spot in the Bahamas."

"I've never been." She smiled when he rubbed his nose against hers.

He kissed her deeply, his panther rubbing against hers, their power mingling and sending love up and down their mating bond.

"You good?" He asked her softly.

"I love you," she told him, realizing it was the first time she'd told him that.

His eyes lit, and his smile widened. "I love you too, love bug." He kissed her again.

She sighed and asked the question that would keep her awake. "What will happen to my family?"

He nuzzled her cheek. "I saved who I could."

She shuddered and reared back in surprise.

He chuckled. "Trust me. I'm just as surprised as you. I wanted them all gone, but Silas stepped in. But, you know my father's reputation. Daniel, Dorothy, and Arthur will be dead before the morning. The rest of the family is banished from the city and the Motsi."

She snuggled back into his chest and tried to decide how she felt about that. She was surprised that Dallas had held back on her behalf. He could've taken out the whole family. There were plenty of examples of him doing it to others who came after him. Banishment was a mercy they were lucky to receive.

Her family had worked so hard to get to their current position in the Motsi society, so at the end of the day, the punishment was fitting. Her mother would hate every second of not having access to the lifestyle she'd curated.

"You saved me," she whispered.

"You saved yourself, love bug, and I'm incredibly proud of you for that. Your family tried everything they could to break you, but you still came out of that shit a beautiful and loving soul. That had nothing to do with me and everything to do with your strength. The part I played was small."

She smiled and realized he was right. "You still came to my rescue."

"Always," he promised as he stood and then pulled her up into his arms. "Come, my love. Let's go home."

She wrapped her legs around his waist and settled her head on his shoulder. A sense of safety filled her, and despite what she lost tonight, she knew that he would have her. Always.

epilogue

Celine cinched the towel around her chest tighter and leaned over the sink to peer into the damp mirror. She and Mason had been at the beach for nearly the whole day, and her skin showed it. Despite all the sunscreen she'd slathered across her face, she was noticeably darker. She smiled, liking it. She looked relaxed and well-loved on.

It was a good look for her.

She leaned back and pumped out her moisturizer, rubbing it into her face, going through her nightly routine. She was a little sad that tonight would be their last night. It was time to go back to the real world. Mason had received the call that their house was finished and ready for them to occupy again. She was excited to get back to her plants, but she did enjoy all the time she had Mason to herself.

He still put in some work, but for the most part, he catered to her, taking her around the island and showing her around. She'd had his undivided attention, and she had not wasted it.

Mason stepped out of the shower and wrapped a towel around his waist. Her eyes followed his movements in the mirror. The man was a work of art. He moved with feline grace, his lean body chiseled from what she now knew were workouts with his father and brother. He smiled, catching her looking. He leaned down and nipped her shoulder.

"No tan lines," he commented.

She snorted because it wasn't as though the man had let her keep her swimsuit on. He sucked on her neck, and she sighed in pleasure. She turned around, and he lifted her onto the sink.

"Did you enjoy your vacation?"

"I did," she murmured, dropping small kisses to his mouth.

He slid his hand up her neck, squeezing just a bit. Her panther filled her body and smiled knowingly. "You and your panther ain't had enough?" He rumbled, undoing her towel.

It dropped between them, and he ran his hand down the front of her body, squeezing her stomach before dropping to her sex. She opened her legs wider. He chuckled, sliding his finger across her clit, circling the opening of her pussy. She sucked her teeth as he continued to tease her, sticking out her lip.

"What I tell you about pouting, love bug?" he murmured, nipping her bottom lip.

"Quit teasing me, then." She released her claws and lightly raked his back.

His eyes lit, and he laughed. "I can't believe you hid all that violence behind that shy shit."

She smiled, a hint of fang.

"Claim your shit then, love bug," he said darkly.

*****

Mason held Celine tight against him, his gaze focused out at the ocean just a few yards away. He'd left the curtains opened, and moonlight flooded the otherwise dark bedroom. His hands absently trailed his mate's curves, his mind on everything they'd gone through to get to this point. He'd used the week they'd spent at the beach to make her forget all about the shit with her family. There were a couple of times when he'd catch her a little melancholy, but he knew with the way his family loved on her, they could hopefully do enough to make her okay.

A few times, he'd had to shake away the worry and fear that hit him out of nowhere. He'd nearly lost her more than once, and he vowed to never let it happen again. She'd told him she'd wondered what would've happened had her father successfully married her off to someone else. He quickly dismissed that because ain't no way he was letting anyone else have what belonged to him.

Celine sighed and shuffled, turning onto her back. Her eyes drifted open, her drowsy look stalling his breath. Gods, he loved this woman. He leaned down and kissed her softly. Her arms wrapped around his neck and brought him closer.

"We have a flight in a few hours. Why are you awake?" her voice was soft and husky with sleep.

It stirred his libido, though it was fair to say that everything about her usually stirred his libido. He slid his leg between hers, parting them. She arched in his arms, ready for him.

"I love you, Celine Knight," he whispered against her lips as he pushed inside of his favorite place in the world.

Her answering smile was everything to him.

"I love you, Mason."

He kissed her, sliding his tongue between her lips, a desperate need overtaking him. He would never get enough of her. Their hips moved together, the backdrop of the ocean blending into the sounds of their quiet sighs. He stared down into her eyes, and her loving gaze met his. It deepened their connection and forged their bond tighter. There was no rush, no urgency; just simple pleasure shared between the two of them.

Lifting her leg over his shoulder, he pushed in, his strokes deep. Celine canted her hips, meeting his every stroke, her eyes closing as she clamped down onto him. He knew what it meant but kept his pace slow. On cue, her bottom lip poked out in a pout at what she would consider his teasing her.

"There you go, pouting," he murmured, biting her bottom lip and gripping her hips tighter.

She swiveled her hips, smiling at his words. "Your fault."

He chuckled and sped his hips, giving his mate what she wanted. She hissed in pleasure. Mason watched the play of emotions across her face, as always, fascinated at the way she threw herself wholeheartedly into the pleasure. She pulled her bottom lip into her mouth, her breath catching.

"Almost there," she whispered, raking her nails down the back of his neck.

Mason's gaze caressed her, seeing the moment she hit her peak. The most beautiful expression overtook her face, and the hot clasp of her pussy gripped his dick in hard pulses that caught him off guard. He closed his eyes, his back bowing as he erupted, his shout loud and triumphant. He collapsed on top of her, chuckling at the way the minx always got her way.

"I was trying to take my time," he murmured, burying his head in the crook of her shoulder and breathing her in.

She chuckled, tightening her legs around his waist. "Next time."

He rolled them over, refusing to pull out, even as he was softening. He wanted every second he could get. She burrowed into his chest, rubbing her cheek against his skin.

"Mating with you is the best thing that ever happened to me," she mumbled, easing back into sleep now that she had a comfortable position.

"Same, love bug."

He would deny it until his last breath, but for once, he had to give it to his Pop and his machinations. Without that push from Dallas, he may have let the best thing in his life slip away. He'd worked his ass off to build his company and step from his father's legacy, but it would've been worth nothing if it had cost him Celine. He looked forward to their life together.

epilogue II

Silas Knight figured he would spend the rest of his life as a bachelor. It wasn't something he was overly concerned about, and despite his parents' happiness, he didn't really believe that type of love existed. Still, it didn't mean he couldn't be happy for his brother finding his mate. Mason and Celine radiated love and contentment, and no part of Silas envied him that.

He wasn't a hater.

He just had better and more important things to do than look for a mate. He swung his arm, smiling when his sister-in-law ducked and came back up with a heavy cross. She was getting better. Quicker too, he realized as he brought up his arms to block her next two shots.

"Get him, love bug," his brother taunted from the side of the ring.

Celine laughed and set her feet back into position, ready to go again. They had been at it for half an hour, and she would probably call it quits any minute now. He enjoyed sparring with his new sister. She fit right into their family, her shy sweetness balancing out his brother's rougher qualities.

"Silas," Dallas called, coming up ringside.

He put his arms down and turned his attention to his father. His stomach fluttered at the look on his face. Dallas didn't say anything, just held up his phone.

Silas unsnapped his gloves and took it. "Yeah."

"Your bill passed both the House and the Senate," his assistant Keisha told him excitedly.

Elation filled him, and he clenched his fists. "Is it retroactive?"

"Ex post facto ten years," she told him.

"Thank you, Keisha."

"Congratulations! I'll see you on Monday."

Silas ended the call and shared a look with his family. Mason's eyebrows winged high.

"Well?" Celine asked.

"It passed."

Celine rushed to hug him. "That's great, Silas!"

"Aye now," Mason called at his wife.

Celine stuck out her tongue and squealed as Mason rolled under the rope and came after her.

Silas ignored their horse playing, his heart racing with all the implications of that law passing. He was excited. He wanted that Shifter Adoption law passed, but most importantly, he wanted it retroactive. Doing that would give him access to any shifter adoptions that had happened in the past ten years.

He only needed records from the past six.

Silas still needed to play his cards right. He couldn't imagine a scenario where any court would grant blanket access to the records, retroactive law or not. But, he had lawyers working on it, and between them and his family, he would shake something loose.

"Pop," Silas turned his attention to his father, removing the rest of his safety gear.

"I'm on it, Si. We'll find her." Dallas promised.

Mason carried Celine over his shoulder and came over, dapping Silas. "We'll find her and my niece. Just a little more patience."

Silas snorted. He was a lot of things. Patient wasn't one of them. But, to find his kid...he would be that and more.

Dallas

author's Note

The following short story takes place between Mason and Silas's story and gives a little more context to their story. It's just a short snippet that was added for my newsletter, but I wanted to add as a bonus in the print version.

one

Saturdays were probably Dallas' favorite day of the week. He slept in, at least by his standards. Let his mate tell it, eight in the morning was still early for a weekend day. It was one of the reasons she swatted his hand the moment he slid it across her exposed skin. The gown she wore to sleep in was up around her waist. He skimmed the silky fabric, pushing it up further to rest his hand on her soft stomach.

"Cut it out, D," Adina grumbled in a low voice.

Dallas feathered kisses across her shoulder and neck, pulling her body close to his. He rubbed his head against hers, the silk of her scarf sliding across his skin. She'd straightened her hair a couple of days ago, so she had the long strands tucked away. His hands made the trek past her thighs to her heated center. Her pussy flexed against his fingers the moment he touched her. He chuckled.

"She telling on you," he murmured against her skin.

Adina sighed but burrowed deeper into her pillow. "She don't control me. I'm sleeping."

"Don't even worry about it. I'll put her back to sleep for you," Dallas teased.

She laughed. "You so sickening."

He slid a finger between the folds of her sex, finding her wet and ready for him. Nearly thirty years of being married, and she still responded to him. Her pussy pulsed against his hand, and he went from soft kisses to licking and sucking across his mate's skin. She moaned and pushed her ass into his dick. He pushed her leg forward and up, exposing her wet center. He fit his dick at the opening of her sex and plunged in. Wet and clenching, his mate's body welcomed him inside.

"Look how you take me in, ma."

He was slow with his strokes. He wanted soft and blissful so his baby could go back to sleep once he'd satisfied his craving for her.

She sighed and reached back, and cupped his head. He nuzzled into her neck, rolling her nipple between his fingers. She whispered his name and adjusted her hips so that she could control his strokes. She squeezed down on him, and he cursed, closing his eyes as the tight grip of her pussy sent his animal wild. He would never get enough of this woman.

"That's not fair, DiDi," he whispered as she squeezed again.

She was going to make him come before he was ready. He moved his hand to cup the top of her pussy. He pushed his palm down onto her clit, and she hissed, arching her back. He lost himself in her body, her sleepy strokes soothing and riling at the same time. He tipped her chin back so he could kiss her. She obliged him, the sweet hunger of her kiss clenching his heart. Her eyes were semi-closed, and he chuckled.

"Take your nut, lil baby, so you can go back to sleep."

She moaned and arched her back, her hips rocking against him. Dallas closed his eyes as she did as he instructed. The hot, wet clasp of her pussy dragged across his dick, and there was nothing he could do to stop the climax poised to rip through him. He held her tightly against him, his fingers plucking her clit until she tightened down on him, moaning as she came. He was right with her, holding her tight. He kissed the back of her neck and reluctantly slipped from her warm body.

He kissed her shoulder and left the bed. He returned with a warm cloth, cleaning her as she adjusted, searching for the sleep he'd stolen. He kissed her thigh and then her lips.

"Sleep, mama."

"I love you, Dallas," she whispered, her eyes closing.

"I worship you, Adina."

Her sweet smile satisfied him deeply. He chuckled and kissed her again before heading to the shower. He showered and headed downstairs, already scenting his sons. He would talk shit the moment he saw them, but it pleased him that they still came in and out of his house as though they still lived there. He missed them now that they had their own adult lives.

He entered the kitchen and smiled at Iris puttering around the kitchen. She'd been with them from the moment he'd found out Adina was pregnant. She was Adina's cousin and a vital part of their family. Iris had lost her mate at a young age and had refused to marry again afterward.

Iris set down a cup of coffee and a bowl of grits and eggs with fruit on the side.

"Iris," he sighed.

"No bacon until your blood pressure goes down, Dallas."

He growled because that was the drawback of her being so close to the family. She'd long ago stopped being scared of him. He pulled out his tablet and went through his emails, even though he knew his mate would be mad at him for working on a Saturday. He was halfway through with his food when his sons came in.

"Don't y'all have your own houses?" He asked.

Adina snagged his attention as she breezed into the kitchen, smelling amazing and fully dressed.

"You did all that fussing, and you had to get up anyway," he said, shaking his head.

"Yeah, but I could've gotten another twenty minutes in if you hadn't bothered me," she teased, kissing the top of his head. She sucked in a breath when Mason held out a bunch of fish they'd caught. "Now, didn't I have a whole shed built so y'all wouldn't be dragging shit like this through my house?"

Iris laughed and walked up to the boys, cupping Mason's cheek. "Leave my babies alone. You want me to make that for dinner tonight? I have a great recipe from your mate."

"Yes, ma'am," Mason said, nuzzling the top of Iris' head and shooting his mother a smug look.

Adina scoffed. "Now, you see that. Don't be fussing at me about spoiling the boys when you see who the real culprit is."

"Where you going in that?" Silas asked, rubbing his cheek against his mother's.

Lord, he raised some mama's boys.

"Pop, you finna let her go out in that little ass dress?" Mason narrowed his eyes.

"Watch your mouth, Mason Knight," Adina fussed.

Dallas raked his eyes over his wife's fine ass in the emerald green jacket dress she wore. It came down mid-thigh and was cinched at her waist by a gold Gucci belt. She wore a black turtleneck underneath it with sheer black pantyhose that still showed off her legs, the knee-high boots making his mouth water. The whole outfit was elegant and sexy as hell. His hair was entirely white, but Adina wore hers in streaks of white that looked exotic against her caramel skin. It was straightened and parted down the middle, flowing around her shoulders. She seemed to defy age, her skin supple and smooth though gently lined. Her makeup was applied lightly and expertly. It highlighted her almond-shaped eyes that she'd gifted to their sons.

He'd just had her, and he wanted to kick his boys out to take her again. He licked his lips and reached for her, her full glossy lips beckoning him. She smiled and leaned down and kissed him. He got a little lost in it, coming back because his hating ass boys started fussing about their display of affection.

"Where you going?" he whispered against Adina's lips.

She pulled back and wiped her gloss from his lips. "Brunch meeting for Aunt Winnie's fundraiser."

He nodded.

"I'm going with Celine. Mason got Lance on her, so I'll leave my security behind."

He sucked his teeth because DiDi stayed trying it. He slapped her ass. "Quit playing in my face, woman. Isaac better be in that car when you leave these gates, or you already know what's going to happen."

Lust filled her eyes, and she licked her lips, their gazes clashing. For a moment, he thought he would have to kick their kids out. But then she sighed and rolled her eyes. "Fine. I'll be back in a few hours."

She left the kitchen, and Dallas' eyes followed his mate all the way out.

"I don't like the way you be looking at my mama," Silas told him.

Mason snickered.

"Carry y'all asses on out my house, then," He fussed, and they busted out laughing.

two

Adina slid into the back seat of her Bentley, her fingers flying over her keyboard as she texted the ladies she was meeting today. Though her Aunt Winnie had passed on, the orphanage she'd started in her name was still thriving. Adina took pride in that. The current fundraiser she was planning was for year twenty-five, and she wanted to do it big.

"Are we going to get Celine?" Isaac asked as he slid into the driver's seat.

His partner Kenny slid into the passenger seat, and Adina shook her head. Why her husband insisted she needed two enforcers, she'd never know.

"Celine's going to meet us at the restaurant."

Isaac nodded and started the car. She settled back into her seat and resumed texting. There was a lot to do for the event, and most of it began before the planning committee even got together. She and her sister Katrina had been going back and forth about most of the details for a month. She sighed and dropped her phone back into her purse.

She watched the city go by as Isaac drove towards their meeting place. Even though her body was perfectly relaxed after this morning, her mind was a bit restless. Her mate had woken her up in the best possible way, though. After so many years with him, he still knew how to love on her body. She got to the restaurant and waited until Isaac came around and opened her door. He gave the keys to Kenny, growling as the valet stepped too close. Adina shook her head and looked around. She spotted her daughter inside the doors. The gold satin, wide-legged pants and matching top Celine wore complimented her curvy body. A white trench coat with gold buttons covered the whole outfit setting off her glowing brown skin. She was gorgeous, and Adina couldn't wait to see the beautiful babies they would make together. Lance was hovering near Celine.

The men in their lives were so protective of them.

Celine greeted her by rubbing their cheeks together, their panthers greeting. Adina smiled in satisfaction because months ago, her daughter-in-law would've never let her cat off the leash enough to greet her. Mason was helping her get comfortable with her animal, and the results of it showed. Celine was more confident, standing taller, her face glowing. Though, it could've easily been the flush of love that had Celine's aura glowing.

"Mom," Celine greeted.

"Hi baby, I'm a little late. I left your mate at my house with his brother."

"They went fishing," Celine said as she shook her head. "According to them, my lake is not as good as the one at your house." Celine looped her arm through Adina's. "Does that mean dinner's at your house?"

Adina's heart clenched in happiness. She couldn't have picked a better person for her son. Celine had calmed Mason, fitting into their family as though she were born to it.

"Any ideas for what the fundraiser should be this year?" Celine asked.

"I'm thinking Casino night."

Celine groaned. "That sounds like fun."

Adina laughed aloud. "You'll survive."

Her daughter-in-law hated big gatherings. Adina limited the amount of Motsi events she had to attend, knowing how much Celine hated them. But, with Dallas' position, she had to participate in more than she had prior to mating with Mason. Her mate had worked hard to get to where they were today, and Adina made sure she was behind him maneuvering to keep him there.

The hostess guided them to the private room where they would be dining, informing her that most of her party had already arrived. That was perfect. That meant they could get down to business immediately.

***

The brunch passed with no problem. They were able to choose a venue once everyone agreed on the theme. Adina was excited, but then, she was always enthusiastic about her aunt's fundraiser. That orphanage was special to her, and she would do everything in her power to ensure the young shifters who resided there had the best care they could provide. She'd worked hard to pull herself from her humble upbringing; she made sure to drag others up behind her.

Adina didn't mind the way her life had turned out. She was all about the betterment of shifters and would happily throw her weight behind any cause that benefited them. Besides her aunt's charity, she headed several charitable boards. She was under no illusion that she'd tamed Dallas, but she prayed the good she did balanced out all the things her mate did to take care of their family.

Once the meeting adjourned, she stood and gathered her purse.

"I'm headed home, but I'll see you later," Celine told her.

Adina waved her away. She exited the room with Isaac hot on her heels. Her eyes narrowed as she looked across the restaurant. Her heart stumbled a moment before fury tried to take over. Her panther reacted almost violently, bucking against the control Adina had spent years perfecting. She soothed the animal, stopping in her tracks as she observed the woman across the room. It was Samantha Robinson, the mother of Cameron Robinson.

Silas' baby's mother.

Adina talked her panther down from reacting, fixing her face before the woman saw her reaction. There was so much she wanted to say to the woman and almost none of it with words. Adina wanted to drag the bitch across the restaurant floor. Instead, she put on a small smile, knowing that someone was observing her at all times. Unlike her sons, who didn't care what society thought of them, Adina was raised to care.

Her mother had had a whole list of do's, and dont's for her daughters' behavior when they left the safety of their house. Some things were ingrained, no matter how far removed she was from that country girl. Adina made her boys go to the suitable schools and attend the proper functions, all in the hope that they didn't receive half the scorn she and her mate had when they'd first taken their positions.

Not that it had helped.

Adina marched towards the woman, her feet moving of their own volition. She reminded herself that she was too old to be fighting in these people's restaurant. But, she loosened the dainty gold watch she wore on her wrist, a long-ago present from Dallas. Samantha finally looked up, surprise and alarm crossing her face before she hid it. The woman had looked distraught, but that could've been any number of things. After all, Adina's mate had killed hers. Samantha was rightfully wary around her.

"Adina, hi." Samantha greeted dryly. "How many years has it been?"

"Eight," Adina said succinctly. "That would be about how old my granddaughter is now, right?"

Samantha flinched. "Granddaughter?" She played stupid.

The scent of deception wafted from the woman, a stringent, off-putting perfume in the air between them.

Adina's gums tingled as her cat fought with her. "How is Cameron, by the way? It's been so hard keeping track of her."

Samantha stepped back, and Adina knew she hadn't hidden the rage on her face well enough.

"Oh, you wouldn't have heard. We kept it within the family. We lost my daughter years ago." Samantha said low enough to keep it between them.

Shock and uneasiness turned Adina's stomach. "I'm so sorry to hear that. I can't imagine the pain of losing a child." Adina grabbed her arm, and the other woman flinched and nodded.

"It's been very hard for our family."

Adina made a hum of sympathy, genuinely empathetic about it.

Samantha looked down at her watch. "I really must get going. It was great running into you." She lied and rushed off.

Adina turned to watch her leave. "Isaac," she said softly.

"Yes, ma'am."

"I dropped my watch in her purse."

"I'll get Julian on it," he said, needing no further prodding.

She nodded. "Let's go then."

Dallas had numerous trackers on her that he'd hidden in the many gifts he liked to give her. As long as Samantha didn't find the watch before Julian could put a team on her, they would be fine.

Her mind was going through so many possibilities. She knew that Silas had checked death records in his search for Cameron. Could Samantha be lying, or had they hidden the death that well? She took out her phone when she got in the car and sent messages to the PI she had hired years ago to help Silas with the search. She would look everywhere Samantha had lived and traveled. As far as they knew, Cameron had not been living with her, but no way would a mother allow her child to die while not being there. That meant Samantha had to travel to Cameron. If she could narrow down where Cameron had died, then perhaps she'd get lucky and find records of the child.

Her next debate was whether or not to tell her mate.

three

Dallas tapped a pencil against the top of his desk as he waited on confirmation of his order. He'd only been in his office for an hour, and he hadn't had a moment to breathe since. Mondays were already busy, especially the last Monday of the month. Those were court days. The tri-council would hear grievances from the shifters they ruled over. It was a tedious process, made even more so by the rigmarole the other councilman put their subjects through.

The cats underneath Dallas knew to come to him directly. He was automatically suspicious of any cat shifter that came to Motsi court. He had an open-door policy, and it was known that he took care of shit. So if they came to court, they were likely on bullshit.

Two enforcers stood at his open door, waiting on him to finish his phone call. His assistant walked through the door.

"Councilman Knight, they're ready for you," she told him.

"Just one sec," he held up a finger. "Are we done?" he asked the woman on the phone.

"Yes, sir. It'll go out for delivery in the next couple of hours," she assured him.

Dallas hung up and stood, grabbing his jacket off the back of his chair. The Motsi headquarters was a large building, though most of their offices were underground. When it was first established, they were still warring with the humans, and the underground offices had been a safety precaution. Humans had been determined to eradicate the shifters, not even bothering with trying to live with them. It had been easy at first, all the different packs and prides scattered into their own neighborhoods. The shifters had known the best way to turn the tide was to band together. They'd united all the small packs and prides into three main territories for each shifter group. They had, in effect, taken over the city, cutting the humans down from all sides. Once the other cities and states had heard what the Motsi had done, they followed suit. Now, the shifter network was vast, and the shaky truce they had with the humans was the result.

Dallas passed his son's office and frowned when he found it empty. Had he gone out of town? Silas was a liaison for the shifters and traveled back and forth to Washington for that position. The job had been earned through diplomacy, something he didn't think his wild ass son possessed. But Silas had surprised him, surpassing even his wildest dreams for him. What he couldn't earn with diplomacy, his son earned with the fierceness Dallas had taught both his boys. Silas had fought his way through shifters, large and small, to get to his position. Dallas couldn't be more proud of him.

The court was already filling up when Dallas arrived. The octagonal room was large, the ceilings high, the windows letting light in from outside. They held court above ground. Like human courts, there was a massive table in the front that seated all three council members. There were benches in front where complainants waited for their turns. The reps for the bears and wolves were already in place, their assistants and enforcers standing behind them, when Dallas stepped up onto the dais.

Dallas settled into his chair and got himself mentally ready for the day. Court could last anywhere from three hours to all day. They only had once a month to make their issues known, so sometimes it took a while to settle disputes. Dallas sent Adina a text message to let her know he'd be incommunicado and put his phone on vibrate, handing it off to his assistant.

He lifted the docket and narrowed his eyes when he saw one of Celine's family members first up. He wanted to curse. He should've killed them all. But he hadn't wanted to alienate his new daughter.

Micah, the bear councilman, gave him a look the moment he read the docket. Dallas shrugged and gave the bear an unapologetic look.

"Step forward," Cyrus ordered. The wolf's gruff voice was already aggravated.

Out of the three of them, the wolf had the least amount of patience with the proceedings. From what Dallas had heard and observed, the asshole didn't give a shit about his own wolves, never mind the other shifters of Eastfield. Dallas was waiting on the day one of the hungry shifters under Cyrus cut a swath through the whole wolf council. They were greedy, lazy motherfuckers, so it was just a matter of time.

Fredrick Jackson stepped forward, nervous and wringing his hands. "I'm here on behalf of the Jackson family. We would like to lodge a complaint against Councilman Knight."

Cyrus gave Dallas a smug smile. Ah, so he'd set up this little bit of theater. The wolf's lanky body relaxed. The designer suit he wore was custom-made and showed off Cyrus' wealth, as did the understated but expensive jewelry that covered the wolf's neck and arm. The problem Dallas had with Cyrus, hell, with most of the Motsi, was that they thought that money made them better than the shifters they ruled. In another life, Dallas would've run down on him for all of it.

But he didn't do that anymore.

His mate worked hard to keep him out the streets. But these mother-fuckers be testing his gangsta, and one of these days, he was gon' remind them how he got his position.

"What's the complaint?" Cyrus asked.

"Half of our family was punished unfairly due to the councilman's greed."

"Greed?" Micah asked.

Fredrick cleared his throat. "The councilman set up his son with Celine Harris to get a hold of her inheritance. When the family complained, he killed three of my kin and banished the others."

Micah sighed.

Dallas drummed his fingers on the arm of his chair and said nothing. He didn't plan on explaining his actions to anyone. He'd fuck up the world behind his and didn't give a fuck who complained about it.

"And what would you have this council do about it?" Cyrus asked.

"Our family should be paid damages."

Dallas scoffed. Of course, it came back to the money for these assholes.

Micah pursed his lips. "And money was the only reason Councilman Knight acted out against your family?"

Cyrus stepped in quickly. "It shouldn't matter why he acted. He did so without council approval."

"I don't need council approval to run my territory," Dallas said. He kept his smoldering anger under control.

"For an action like the one you'd taken, you do."

"Oh? And should this council look into the wolf territory for the many actions you've taken without our approval?" Dallas asked.

Cyrus blanched.

"Would we then find a closet full of your adversaries' skeletons?" He further taunted.

Micah coughed to cover his laugh. Cyrus snapped his mouth closed, his jaw working, anger lighting his eyes.

"Answer the question," Dallas snapped at Fredrick.

The cat looked towards Cyrus before answering. Fredrick cleared his throat.

"Go ahead and tell the council that your family tried to kill my daughter when she wouldn't sign over the money to you. Or were you not planning to air out your family's deceit?"

"Well—" Frederick started.

"Fuck out of here. Next complainant." Dallas slapped his gavel against the table. He waved his hand, and the enforcers over the court escorted a belligerent Fredrick from the room.

"Now, wait a damn minute," Cyrus blustered.

Dallas covered his mic and leaned over. "Cyrus, I will drag you across this fucking council room if you don't sit the fuck back and mind your business."

Micah sighed. "I'm not fixing to do this all damn day, you two." The bear warned, shifting his bulky body in the massive chair he sat in. Though Micah also wore a suit that Dallas knew cost a pretty penny, the laid-back bear didn't flaunt his wealth like the wolf did.

"I don't know why you allow this thug to act the way he does," Cyrus complained.

"Cyrus, you know as well as I do that this council does not intervene in anyone's territory unless a complaint is made. What Dallas does on the Southside doesn't have anything to do with us until it does."

"The fuck you think Jackson was?" Cyrus snapped.

"A bullshit complaint more than likely stirred up by you," Dallas argued.

Cyrus growled, and Dallas prayed he jumped because it had been days since he knocked somebody across their head, so he was due.

"That man has the seat! It's been over ten years. Get the fuck over it." Micah hissed before taking a calming breath. He nodded to the enforcer at the podium, "Next complainant."

Dallas flexed his aching fingers and settled back in his chair. Cyrus was on some shit, so he was going to have a long ass day.

four

Adina scribbled into the small notepad as Iris walked around the kitchen, calling off the things she needed from the grocery store. Usually, her cousin went herself, but Adina wanted to get out of the house for a bit. Dallas would be in court all day, and for once, nothing was lined up on her schedule. Normally, when she had a moment to spare, she went shopping, but she wasn't in the mood to wander the mall. Plus, her sisters were all busy, so she would have to go alone, and clothes shopping was always more fun with them.

She grabbed her phone as it vibrated across the kitchen island.

"Mrs. Knight, you have a delivery. I'll bring it up," Kenny informed her.

Eyebrows furrowed, Adina made her way to the front door. She peered through the glass in time to see Kenny drive up in a golf cart with a bouquet of flowers and a big box on the seat next to him. She excitedly opened the door. The beautiful vase of pink peonies was her mate's 'just because' bouquet.

Kenny handed her the bouquet and went back for the box. She set the flowers down on the table and leaned in to smell them with a smile. She remembered the first time he'd sent some to her office when he was trying to run game on her. She grabbed the card as Kenny set the box next to the vase. She thanked him, opening the box. She laughed at the peaches inside. She'd just added them to her list for the grocery store. The man was psychic, and she was spoiled. The scent of the peaches competed with that of the peonies.

"Kenny, let Isaac know I'm ready to leave." She told him as she spotted a smaller box next to the peaches.

She hurriedly opened it, pulling the crystal perfume bottle from the satin-lined box, intrigued. She'd never heard of the brand, so she was anxious to try it. Her mate knew exactly the things she liked.

She opened the card.

You know I never mind tricking off you.

She laughed. God, that man. She couldn't even accuse him of being up to anything. She never had to worry about how Dallas felt about her. He expressed it all the time, and what he couldn't say in words, his panther filled in the blanks. She looked up as the front door announced it was open. Her son came in, his eyes low, his hair long, locking up at the top though the sides looked like they'd been recently cut. The sharp lineup and faded edges framed his handsome face that was nearly the mirror of his father. Silas spotted her and the gifts as he walked through the foyer.

"Oooh, I'm telling my daddy you got a lil boyfriend sending you gifts," he joked.

She laughed. "You get on my nerves."

She popped his hand when he reached into the box of her peaches.

"So stingy. I'm your firstborn, mama."

"My mate bought these for me and only me."

He laughed, though it didn't reach his eyes. She amped up her panther and examined her son, seeing past his facade. Her baby was hurting, and she wanted someone to pay for that. She nuzzled against his cheek, using her panther's power to soothe the animal right under the surface of her son's skin. The cat rushed forward, receiving the comfort, relaying how much hurt Silas was hiding. He shuddered and wrapped his arms around her, soaking up her comfort. She wanted to tell him not to worry, that she would fix it, but it had been seven years.

She stepped back and cupped his cheek. "What brings you by."

"I came by to speak to Pop."

"Dad has court today," she reminded him.

He snapped his fingers, "that's right. I forgot."

"Why aren't you there?" She asked.

Silas was usually with his father on court days. He was next in line for his father's position, and Dallas didn't play about prepping their kids. From the time Dallas took the councilman position when Silas was eighteen, he'd been learning at his father's side.

"I just got back in town. I thought I found Cameron."

She made a sympathetic sound and saw the worry all over his face. "Come on, love. Iris is sending me to the grocery store. You can come with me."

From the way his eyes sat low, Adina could tell her son was high. She was thankful when she saw Rock standing in the doorway. It meant that Silas hadn't driven.

"Rocco," she greeted him, beckoning him forward.

"Mama Di." Rock came up to her and nuzzled the side of her face.

She could sense his bear. The man barely talked, but he was understood. She wore her animal close to the surface, and the older she got, the more she did, so her cat reached out to Rocco's bear, and he settled. She'd known Rock since he was small and lived at her Aunt Winnie's orphanage.

"How are you?"

"Same," he murmured in that deep, scarred voice of his.

She knew that getting attached to the kids at her aunt's orphanage was a bad idea, but there were some that dug into her heart, and Rocco was one of the few of them that had gotten past her walls.

"You can drive us." She told him.

She grabbed her purse and walked past them. Isaac was there with Kenny, ready. She opened her mouth to tell him she'd ride with Silas, but one look from Isaac silenced her. Dallas had assigned Isaac to her years ago, and they were close enough that Adina knew what that look meant. Isaac would never let her go anywhere without him. He was more scared of Dallas than Adina, so she sighed.

But, he did allow Rock to drive Silas' jaguar. He climbed into the front seat once he realized Silas was helping her into the back. She watched her son as he got into the back seat with her.

She cupped his cheek. "Tell me what's wrong, my love."

He nuzzled into her hand and then pulled back, leaning his head against the headrest. "Same shit, different day."

She sighed. "No word?"

"Nothing," he murmured.

She debated her next words. She wanted to handle Cameron's mother alone, but she also knew that if Silas saw her out and about before she gave him a warning, it could really go left. Unlike his brother, Silas took a little longer to anger, but once that fuse was lit, it took a lot to burn it out. He'd been waiting on ten for the Robinson family, and she imagined he wouldn't think twice about approaching Samantha. It had been some years since any of them had seen her.

"I saw Samantha."

He turned to her, and emerald green flashed in his eyes. His body tightened, and Adina stared her son's panther down. Silas's growl bounced off the walls of the car, loud and full of fury.

"You know better than to be growling at me," she chided.

His face cleared, though his panther was still on the surface. "What did she say?"

She sighed because she didn't want to tell him, especially since she wasn't sure if it was true. "Samantha claims to have lost Cameron several years ago."

Shock blanketed Silas' face. "Do you believe her?"

Adina shrugged.

"Then the adoption records are the way to go, as I thought," he murmured, rubbing his chin in thought.

"It was always a good idea." She reassured him.

He nodded and turned his head towards the window. "Something had to bring her back to town." He said after a beat of silence.

"Exactly my thoughts. I have someone following her."

Silas whipped around his boyish smile in place. "Always riding for us." He kissed her cheek, "thank you, mama."

"I know I keep telling you not to worry, but we gon' find my grandbaby. I have no doubt about that."

Rock helped her out of the car once they parked at the grocery store. Silas grabbed a cart and followed behind her. She waved at some of the people who greeted her with a smile. Even before her husband had taken his position on the tri-council, they'd been known in the city. Though they could've easily moved closer to the Motsi headquarters, she'd always felt safer and rooted on the Southside. They both wanted to stay close to the pulse of their people, but their reasons were different. She fussed at her husband when he was in the streets because she knew his wild ass did it for entirely other reasons than her.

They entered the store, and Adina took a deep calming breath. She missed the simple act of shopping without the wall of security at her back, but she would take what she could get.

"How have you been, mama?" Silas asked as he trailed dutifully beside her.

"Planning the annual ball for Winnie's House, so that has me busy at the moment. I'm trying to talk your father into a vacation, but he wants this stuff with Mason and Celine settled before we go."

"They're giving him pushback?"

She shrugged. "You'll have to ask him specifics. I get grunts when I ask."

"They lucky he ain't kill off the whole line," Silas muttered.

"Y'all should've told me what was going on. That mess would've been nipped in the bud." She said casually as she checked items off her list.

"Mama, you too old to be slapping people around."

She hit him in the arm with the box of pasta she was holding. "Now, did you say that to your daddy?" He gave her a charming smile that she loved. "Mmhmm, that's what I thought. I don't know why Dallas still gets to have fun."

"You would've let your panther handle it," Silas told her.

"Exactly, and wouldn't be shit they could say about it. Dallas made the mistake of doing it in their human form. Motsi's rules for shifter fights that end in death are a lot more lenient, but what do I know."

Silas wrapped his arm around her shoulder. "Sorry, mama. If I have any issues, I'll come to you and let your panther eat 'em up."

"As is my right," she said haughty and walked in front of him.

She gasped when she got to the end of the aisle, a little girl and her mother passed by them, and her heart clenched.

Silas rushed up to her. "What's wrong?"

She shook her head. She was starting to let Silas' search get to her. She saw her grandchild in every kid she saw that was around the correct age. Logically she understood that the child couldn't be in the same city and they not know it.

"I'm good," she said aloud, waving to settle their tenseness.

She needed to get it together.

five

Dallas wouldn't say he stomped into the house, but he walked hard as hell. The sun had set hours ago, and the darkness pressing in on him had suited his mood. He didn't bother turning on the lights as he stalked to his bedroom. He was still pissed from court. He was 'bout tired of going around in circles with Cyrus and was nearly at the point where he was finna take him out. The wolf had been too long in his spot and complacent.

Dallas knew he could take him out, but he didn't want a war between the wolves and cats bloodying up the streets. Adina would have something to say about that. He sighed and jerked his suit jacket off when he got to his bedroom. He needed to go running, but he wasn't sure what his cat would do if he let it off its leash. Their house sat on ten acres, and he didn't think running the whole of it would take the edge off his anger.

The day had been irritating, yes, most court days were. But...it was the last complainant they had that set him off. When had Samantha Robinson arrived back in town? Not that the woman had shown her face at Motsi headquarters. She'd been banned when Silas defeated her husband years ago. Instead, she'd sent her nephew to petition on their family's behalf. The stupid jit claimed that Dallas' family had been harassing hers. He demanded his family's banishment be lifted. It was part of the terms of Dallas winning the trial by combat. The immediate family had been banished from the Motsi society.

The young shifter had been stuck on mute when Dallas asked him where his grandchild was.

All of a sudden, the council didn't want to intervene.

They had a lot to say about the Harris and Jackson family, but when it came to finding his granddaughter, they were mum. He'd spent the whole car ride on the phone with Julian and another private security firm he used when he wanted to keep his sons' hands clean. He wanted Samantha found and brought to him. His harassing had been nice. He was done being nice.

He growled when the door to their bedroom opened. Adina walked in a short romper that reminded him so much of when they'd first met. Her body, softened by age and their children, still turned him on. He wasn't in the mood, though.

Adina raised her brow. "Who are you growling at?"

"Not right now, DiDi," he rumbled.

"This room is our place of peace, don't come up in here disrupting it." She walked to him, moved his hands out of the way, and removed his tie, tossing it onto the bed. She unbuttoned his shirt next, her fingers brushing his skin. "You had a bad day, fine, but don't be taking it out on me."

He stared her down as she pushed his shirt off his shoulders, her hands going to his pants. His panther was riled, his claws sliding through his fingers as he fought the animal for control. All the fiery anger swirling through his body was instantly channeled into molten lust. Her phone rang, and she stepped back, pulling it out of her back pocket.

"I need to take this."

He grabbed the phone from her hand and tossed it back onto the bed. "Nah, you done started some shit now."

Her eyes flashed with her panther, and his bucked in response.

"On your knees, lil baby." He ordered.

He couldn't help the growl in his voice, especially when his mate obeyed him, dropping to the floor in front of him. He inclined his chin towards his pants, and her hands quickly removed his belt. He bit his lip as she unbuttoned his slacks, parting the fabric. Her eyes lifted to his, the smoldering lust in them making his knees shake. She would make him pay for the way he talked to her, and gods, he couldn't wait.

She slid his pants down his legs, and he sat down on the bench in front of their bed. She licked his dick from root to tip, teasing him. He growled in warning, his hands gripping her hair. He loved when she wore her hair natural, the curly gray strands surrounding her stunning face. Her claws slid from her fingers, and she used them, scraping across his stomach. She pressed down into his skin, and that bite of danger sent his panther into a frenzy.

Her mouth hovered over the head of his dick. "So impatient," she teased before sucking him into her mouth.

He closed his eyes tight, tensing to keep from fucking his mate's mouth. He wasn't in the mood to be nice. Dallas lost himself in the wet suction. She was methodical and thorough, her tongue swirling over the head like it was her favorite treat.

"Fuck, Di," he hissed, opening his eyes so he could watch. "In this mood, I don't—"

She shushed him by squeezing his dick. "Do your worst, Dallas Knight."

Probably the most dangerous thing she could tell him at the moment.

He grabbed her throat, his claws pressing against her skin. Her eyes glowed, flashing emerald green as her cat responded. The smell of her arousal rose between them, and Dallas smiled. His baby loved that shit. He gripped her just a touch tighter, lifting his hips. He couldn't help the moan that escaped his mouth as she took him down.

"Again, ma. Take me deeper," he husked out.

His hands shook as she did as he ordered. He touched the back of her throat, and Dallas knew he wouldn't last long. He lifted her from his dick and picked her up. He spun until his legs were straddling the bench.

"Ride this shit, DiDi."

Adina slid him into her, chuckling at his moan. "Yeah, I need to fuck that attitude right out of you."

Dallas growled at her taunting, his toes curling as she worked her hips, taking him deep. Her feet were on either side of him, giving her leverage as she rode him. She was merciless, doing precisely what she said she would. She bounced on his dick, giving him the roughness his panther demanded. He gripped the back of her neck and brought her closer, kissing her deeply. She bit his bottom lip before releasing his mouth and dragging her canines down his neck. Fuck, this woman. He held her tighter as he felt electricity surging through his body. Adina licked across her mating mark, and his panther purred.

"My shit," she whispered before biting down.

Dallas damn near blacked out as his mate snatched his soul. His legs locked, his chest tightened, and he growled as his orgasm took him under. Her pussy squeezed down on him tightly as she followed him over the edge. She moaned against his skin, every pulse of her core sending chills down his spine.

He didn't know how long it took them to come down from it, but his body was mush by the time she released her teeth from his shoulder. He laid back on the bench, pulling her down onto his chest.

"Not you came in here and hoed me, ma," he murmured, drunk off her.

She laughed and licked his neck. "I done told you about talking to me rough."

"You like that shit." He smacked her ass.

Her shoulders shook with laughter. God, he loved this woman. Yeah, the sex between them was fantastic, but this was his favorite part. Before Adina, he hadn't realized how fun sex could be. He'd been rough his whole life. She brought a softness that balanced and elevated him.

He hugged her tight, closing his eyes as emotion overwhelmed him. "I'm sorry for bringing that energy into your space, love."

"You just have to tell me what you need," she reminded him gently. She kissed him and sat up. "Shower and then dinner."

He grunted in assent and slid toward the end of the bench. He stood, lifted her, and walked them both to the bathroom. The feel of her skin against his as he walked was riling him once again.

She tightened her legs around his waist, and he turned on the water with her clinging to him. He stepped in before it even warmed, laughing as she yelped.

"Don't get my hair wet," she fussed.

He turned so that he was under the spray and let her down gently. Her nails scraped across his chest, and Dallas shuddered. He watched her as she stepped back, soaped up a wash cloth and started washing his body. Every swipe of her washcloth lessened his tension further.

"Tell me what happened," she demanded softly.

He sighed, his chest rumbling in aggravation. "We can talk at dinner."

She hummed, allowing him time. She separated the smaller shower head and rinsed him off, her hands lingering around his dick, slowly stroking him. Dallas threw his head back. Heat filled him, and his dick rose to the occasion as though he hadn't just had her a moment ago. He stopped her hand and slowly backed her to the wall of the shower stall. He trapped both her hands above her head and leaned into her neck, licking across her shoulder. His mark was still as dark as the moment he'd claimed her. It satisfied his animal deeply. He kissed a trail to her mouth, kissing her lightly.

"You so good to me, baby."

Her sweet smile went straight to his heart. He would go to war to ensure his mate always had a reason to smile at him like that.

six

Adina hummed as she moved around the kitchen. Iris had already finished dinner for her and Dallas. She'd dismissed her cousin for the night, wanting the time alone with her mate. The kitchen was clean, and all she had left was to fix their plates. Instead of eating in the dining room, she set their places on the kitchen island, lighting her favorite candles. The room was dim, intimate, and hopefully the perfect setting for Dallas to relax. She had a lot to tell him and wanted him to stay as relaxed as she had left him after their shower.

She was pouring wine when she felt his presence. Her panther rolled through her body, her skin warming as he entered the kitchen. The heat of his body pressed into her back as he slid his arms around her waist. He tucked his nose into her neck, breathing in deeply. He felt calm, the anger that had filled their bond gone, replaced by contentment.

"Have I told you how much I love your scent?" He murmured against her skin.

She smiled and tilted her head. His love for her flooded their mating bond, and she reciprocated, chuckling as he purred. She turned in his arms, her breath catching as her eyes traced his handsome face. From his chiseled jaw covered by his low-cut beard to his full lips and broad nose, she loved every inch of his face. His dark skin was still smooth, lightly lined with their age. His hair had turned entirely white a couple of years ago, and she loved how it contrasted his skin's chocolate tone.

"Better?" she asked, nuzzling his cheek.

He gripped the back of her neck and gave her a deep kiss that had her hands shaking. "Thank you, love."

She handed him the glass of bourbon that she had poured for him. Her face was warm, her skin surely flushed. Nothing could touch the feeling Dallas gave her. She put space between them because dinner would be long forgotten if she didn't. He read her mind, the devilish smile he gave her melting her: God, this man.

"Sit so we can eat." She ordered, pushing his chest lightly.

He wore a simple t-shirt and basketball shorts, and the way them shorts hung off his waist... Lord have mercy. She was still so in love with her mate even after the many years they'd been together. Adina fixed his plate and sat it in front of him. She sat beside him and said grace, feeling his eyes on her the whole time.

The man was potent, that was for sure.

And the thirty years they'd been together had done nothing to dilute it. They ate in silence, an unspoken but mutual allowance. She was sure he was just as reluctant as her to break up their relaxed mood.

"What happened?" She asked, finally unable to wait.

"Samantha's back in town," he said, irritated. She nodded, and he narrowed his eyes. "You knew?"

"I was going to tell you when you got home this evening. I have someone following her."

Appreciation lit his eyes. "That's why I fucks with you. Find out anything yet?"

"They didn't go back to their family house. They're staying at a hotel." She told him.

Dallas put his fork down and frowned. "So they're not on the Southside at all?"

She shook her head. "The hotel is deep in bear territory."

Dallas hummed. "When Rob was in power, the three areas were heavily divided."

Adina nodded, "she probably doesn't know how close you are to Micah."

He grunted. "I'll get with Julian and find out what he knows so far." He sighed. "Samantha sent Leland to court today to petition for their reinstatement into the Motsi society."

Now that was interesting. "That can't be the only reason she's here." She thought aloud.

He stared at her, and Adina flushed. "What?"

"Nothing. I love you."

She smiled. "What are we going to do about Silas?"

"What about him, my love?"

"He's hurting, Dallas."

He nodded. "We're doing everything we can to help him."

"I want to go over there and tear her face off."

He chuckled and started eating. Dallas probably thought she was joking, but it had taken everything in her not to get dressed and go to the hotel room when Isacc had informed her of where they were staying.

"What's her play?"

Dallas chewed and considered her words. "She must still be pissed about Rob, but she's not strong enough to get his seat back."

"But she could use our granddaughter to do it," she said, sitting straight. "Samantha knows we'll do anything to get Silas' child back. Will they use her as leverage?"

Dallas put down his fork. "So she'll use her to make me turn over my seat? Why now and not earlier when we searched so hard for her?"

Adina's mind was flipping through the many scenarios. "You took out Rob and his three sons. Who's left for her to place in the seat?"

Dallas frowned. "None of the others in her family were strong enough at the time. I would've taken them out before I banished the family. I wouldn't have left the mess to come back and bite us in the ass."

Adina hummed in agreement. Her husband was nothing if not thorough. "Samantha can't take it alone."

"She won't get any help from the bears," Dallas assured her.

"So who?"

"We may be jumping the gun altogether." He cautioned her.

Adina nodded, conceding his point. It was all speculation for the most part, but she felt it. They were on to something.

"Samantha told me that Cameron was dead."

Dallas looked shocked. "When?"

"Years, according to her."

"So the adoption records was the right move."

Adina nodded because Silas had said the same.

Dallas smiled in pride. "That boy's mind."

She couldn't help her smile because her baby would make a fantastic council leader when he took over.

"I want to know why she's in town now," Adina murmured.

"She wants her revenge. And she's willing to go through our children to get it." Dallas mused.

Fury filled Adina. She would burn this city to the ground behind her kids. If Samantha Robinson wanted to rumble, then Adina would give her the fight she wanted. She frowned as Dallas's phone beeped. He usually left it on silent when they were eating. His face lit up, and he smiled, looking up from the phone.

"Want to take a ride with me, lil baby?"

She could feel his satisfaction and excitement. She nodded immediately and moved back from the table. "What's going on?"

"We'll see together." He promised, grabbing her hand.

Adina didn't ask any more questions; she was riding regardless of where they were going. She trusted Dallas implicitly.

seven

Isaac cut the lights to the SUV as they turned onto a residential street. He drove slowly, rolling to a stop and putting the truck in park two houses down from their destination. Dallas looked around the small neighborhood, curious about what the security firm had found. He'd had Julian looking into Samantha's movements, and the text from a little while ago was from him. All it had was an address twenty minutes from their house. He trusted Julian, but Isaac and two of his best enforcers were piled into the SUV, along with him and Adina.

Dallas turned his head as he sensed a shifter walking up to their truck. He tilted his head, taking in the scents from around him. He lifted his hand to stop Kenny from getting out when he recognized Julian. The shifter was Mason's personal enforcer and best friend. Dallas slid the back window down as he approached.

"Mama Di," Julian greeted before nodding his head at Dallas. "Samantha Robinson sent her security team to sit on this house."

"How long have they been here?" Dallas kept his voice low.

"The men I have on them have been watching them for two hours now. I wanted to see what they were doing. It looks like they're settled in to watch the place."

Dallas hummed. Interesting. "Has Samantha been here at all?"

Julian shook his head. "I told my men to stay on it, but I figured you'd want to check out the place yourself."

Dallas nodded in approval.

"Have you seen anything out of the ordinary?" Adina asked, her eyes roaming the dark neighborhood.

It wasn't late enough for the residents to be sleep, but they were all in their houses. It was a new neighborhood, the houses all square, similar, the lawns well-manicured and matching.

"Not so far. But there is something I thought you'd want to see." Julian inclined his head towards the house. "You'll see what I mean shortly. In the meantime, I'm headed to Mason. He and Cici are going out tonight. I wanted to be here when you got here."

"I appreciate your work, Julian," Adina told him, a small smile tilting her lips.

"Any time, Mama Di." He tapped the truck and headed to his car.

Dallas turned his attention back to the house. It was a small one-story, the lights on indicating the residents were in. He inhaled deeply, scenting the various marks the shifter residents had left on their individual territories. He could see a shadow pass the front window now and then on the house they were watching. Adina hummed next to him.

"What?"

"The development is new, but I helped a few of these families into these houses."

Dallas smiled, so proud of his mate. She stood ten toes down for their people, and despite the bullshit they dealt with from the Motsi, couldn't a single person say shit to them about how they took care of the cats in Eastfield. That was largely due to his wife. Yeah, he had respect from the people who didn't fear him, but Adina had their hearts. He'd taken out the Robinsons when he took over the councilman seat, but he hadn't been alone. He'd had the support of the Southside from top to bottom.

She gasped next to him, and he turned his attention to the house they were supposed to be watching.

"Dallas," Adina whispered.

A woman left the house, a bag of trash in her hand. She headed to the trash can she'd put out on the street, talking to a young girl who stood in the doorway of their home. The porch light illuminated the brown oval face of the little girl. His heart sped, and his panther filled him until his claws slid from his hand. He would recognize that face anywhere. The little girl's face was a clone of her father's, from the tone of her brown skin, the shape of her nose, even down to his crooked smile. Everything in him wanted to jump out of the car, but Adina, always in his head, gripped his arm.

"Wait," she whispered, tears in her voice.

For that alone, someone was going to see him.

"A few more minutes, mom," the little girl yelled into the night towards her mother.

"Sariyah, we talked about this." The woman said, dropping the bag into the trash can. She marched back up towards the house, the rest of her words hard to make out.

He frowned as he realized the girl had called her mom.

"That's not Cameron," Adina said, on the same page as him as always.

"So she had been adopted," Dallas said.

"We need to tell Silas."

Dallas's mind raced. They could rush to their son's house and tell him they'd found his daughter, but that would result in Silas rushing here and possibly making an already delicate situation volatile.

"We need information first, Di."

Adina turned to him, her eyes wide with shock. "You have until the morning. I saw him yesterday...the pain he's in Dallas. I can't allow him to sit in that any longer."

He nodded. He knew their son was in pain, and though he didn't feel it as acutely as his mate, he wanted it to end.

"I'll call and have him meet us at Julian's office in the morning. That will give us all night to gather as much information as possible." He conceded.

Adina breathed a sigh of relief. "We found her."

They had, indeed. Now it was up to Silas to bring her back to their family.

For Her Safety

Author's Note

I just want to thank y'all for taking this ride with me. There are a couple of trigger warnings for this story. There is mention of maternal death after the birth of the baby. There is violence, killing, cursing, sex, and a lil bit of emotional baggage. Hopefully, nothing that will make anyone too anxious. If you are signed up for my newsletter, there was a short story sent out about Dallas and Adina, the parents of Silas and Mason. It takes place right between To Her Rescue and For Her Safety. You don't have to read that to follow this story, but it's here if you'd like to read it. I hope you enjoy Silas and Mila's story.

one

So.Many.People

Mila clutched her daughter Sariyah's hand tightly as they maneuvered through the throng of shoppers searching for bargains. Between the Fourth of July and the Christmas in July sale, the department store was packed. What was supposed to be a quick outing to get more stuff for their new home had turned into something totally different. It was strange to see both swimsuits and Santa hats sold at the same time. Her daughter Sariyah had been fascinated with it all, skipping through the decorations covering the home section. She assumed her daughter would get tired after a little while, but no, Sariyah had excitedly taken in every detail.

Knights was one of the largest free-standing department stores in Eastfield. The interior always reminded her of movies from the fifties. Gold accents, shiny mahogany floors, and large, ornate columns had an old-school feel that she and her daughter loved. They had been in Eastfield for six months, and her daughter was always asking to come into the store. She didn't know what about the place drew her, but Sariyah loved everything about it.

Mila smiled absently as her daughter chattered next to her about their finds and all the ways she would decorate their new house. She was on high alert, her gaze bouncing around the store as they made their way around the escalator and toward the exit. Mila couldn't shake the feeling of them being watched. She was probably being paranoid. Not that she didn't have a reason to be. Her late husband's family was after her and her daughter. Ever since Seth's death, they'd been steadily getting more aggressive with her, demanding she give her daughter back to the family.

Finally, she'd followed her friend's advice and moved way across the country. The east coast was different than the Midwest, that was for sure. Florida, in particular. It was a lot wilder out here than she'd anticipated. Her friend Helen was here, and since Mila didn't have family, moving close to her friend had been ideal. Helen had promised that her husband would keep them safe. Mila had never depended on anyone before, and she likely wouldn't start now, but it had felt reassuring.

She'd felt at home from the moment they'd arrived, and Sariyah had said she felt settled here. She and her daughter would be fine. They just needed to keep an eye out for Seth's family. After all, there was no way the Robinsons knew where they were.

At least not yet.

She'd been so careful. It was a risk coming to Eastfield, especially since they were from here. But according to her friend, the Robinsons were banned from the city, so she should be safe. They'd been cooped up in the house for the past few months to be extra cautious. Their only outings had been for supplies. But, once her daughter had discovered Knights, it had been a wrap. They'd been in this same store once a week for the past month. Not even buying things, just walking around. Mila shuddered to think what it would look like when it came time for back-to-school shopping.

Sariyah chattered next to her, excited about decorating.

"I can't wait to put up the inflatable Santa," the seven-year-old gushed.

Mila laughed. "I don't know where we're supposed to put up all these dang-on lights." She was exhausted and couldn't wait to get home. Tonight was a take-out night, for sure. "What do you want for dinner, kiddo?"

"You already know I want nuggets," Sariyah answered.

She rolled her eyes and laughed. Of course, that's what her daughter always asked for. She opened her mouth to tease her when she collided with someone. A big someone. Her breath released in a whoosh as she nearly tumbled. A set of muscular arms reached out and steadied her. So many sensations hit her at once she was overwhelmed. His cologne surrounded her calming her, while the warm skin of his wrists as she gripped him for balance sent heat throughout her body. She looked up...and up. Her mouth dropped, surprise and attraction flustering her. Her heartbeat sped, and her body awakened from its long slumber.

He towered over her five-foot-six frame, his chest blocking anything behind him from her view. His full lips were turned up into a polite smile. A lush pair of eyelashes surrounded his dark eyes, and Mila found herself speechless.

She recognized his face immediately. She'd seen it on T.V., especially lately. His brown skin was smooth, damn near glowing. A dark beard covered the bottom of his face, combining with the mustache to frame a pair of full lips that had her sweating. His dark eyes were hooded, framed by heavy brows, staring down at her with an intensity that had her squirming.

Yes, he was fine. That was clear to see, but the power that radiated from him...

She cleared her throat and straightened her posture. "I'm...I'm sorry," she mumbled.

"You good, mama." His voice was a sexy rumble that traveled down her spine. The southern drawl more pronounced than it was in his T.V. appearances and way more potent.

"Hey, you're Silas Knight!" Sariyah's voice reminded her of where they were. "My mom watches you all the time on TV."

Her face burned. Mila gripped her daughter's hand. "No one needed to know that, Riyah."

He and the security that she was just noticing chuckled. At least for a moment. It took only a second for the smile to leave Silas' face. He dropped to one knee in front of Sariyah, inhaling deeply. Was he scenting her daughter?

"What's your name?" His solemn gaze traced her daughter's face.

"I'm Sariyah. This is my mom, Mila. We think it's cool what you're doing to fight for shifters." Her daughter gave him a big smile.

He turned his eyes back to Mila, his head tilted in thought.

Mila gave a nervous chuckle. "Okay, well, we need to get going. Sorry for bumping into you."

She tugged her daughter's hand and hastily stepped around the kneeling god. There was something about his gaze that made her nervous. It didn't feel dangerous, but all the same. Her heart was racing from their encounter, her skin warm and tingly. She chanced a look back and found him staring at her. The look in his eyes was intense, and Mila shuddered in want, a little warning pinging in her subconscious.

two

Silas watched the woman and her daughter as they walked off, shock still resonating through his system.

"Mila," he said quietly, tasting the name, enjoying the way it sounded.

Her curvy, petite body moved through the crowd of shoppers with a confidence that called to him. Her hair was a mass of natural kinky curls pulled back from her face. A striking face. The lack of makeup highlighted that, and her large dark eyes dominated her face, drawing him in. He wanted to know her. It was the first thought he had when he looked at her. She was clearly human, but his animal didn't seem to care. His hands tingled, and he could swear he still felt the soft skin of her arms.

The little girl... He sucked in a breath.

The little girl.

He would know that face anywhere. Eight years. He'd searched for damn near eight years. His panther was going crazy. He felt off-kilter, untethered, and the further the distance between him and them, the antsier his animal became. His panther was tearing through his body, demanding he go after them. Instead of listening to the instinct, he turned to his best friend and enforcer.

"Follow her, Rock. I need to know who she is," He ordered his security detail.

"Home?"

He nodded. "If you can. Leo, go get the car so you can meet him."

"Boss," Leo protested.

"I'll be straight. My brother has pretty tight security." Silas assured him.

Mason, his brother, was taught the same as Silas. They knew better than to be lax on their security. Dallas Knight didn't play that. His security detail left to do as he ordered. He watched them until they disappeared and then pivoted, skirting the crowd with quick steps as he headed to his brother's office. This Knights location had the home office located on the third floor. He punched in the code for the employee elevator with shaking hands.

He was supposed to go to Julian's office, but he made a detour to his brother.

He nodded at Mason's assistant as he rounded the corner to the executive offices. He walked through the glass doors to his brother's office.

Mason looked up with a frown and ended the call that he was on. "So we not even knocking?" He asked, leaning back in his chair.

"I just ran into a woman, and I need you to find her," Silas said, dropping into the chair in front of his brother's desk.

Mason lifted an eyebrow but didn't move. "Good afternoon, big brother. I'm doing well. Busy, but you know how it goes."

"Mason cut the shit. I'm serious." Silas told him impatiently.

"About me using security footage to find a woman out of the thousands that come through this store?"

Silas swallowed a growl, knowing trying to speed up his brother would just make him dig in his heels. "It just happened a second ago. Find me and trace it back. She had a shorty with her."

Mason frowned at him, "what happened?"

"I think I found her."

The 'her' was understood. Mason's eyes widened, and he leaned forward and started typing. There was only one 'her' he'd been searching for the past seven years, and if his cat were right, he'd finally found her. There were a few moments where the only sound was his brother hastily tapping the return key to cycle through the video before...

"Got it," Mason said quietly.

Silas jumped from his chair and walked around his brother's desk. "There," he pointed.

He took in the beautiful woman first. Her hair was a cloud of textured curls that surrounded her narrow face. His initial impression didn't do her beauty justice. His brother changed camera angles, and Silas' panther reared within him. Her full lips and large dark eyes made an arresting picture.

"This the shorty?" Mason asked, bringing his attention to where it was supposed to be.

Silas swung his gaze to the little girl his panther was telling him was his. His body started trembling, his panther whining, demanding Silas leave.

"Mason," he whispered, unable to keep the longing from his voice.

"I see it," his brother murmured. Mason cursed. "She favors you heavy."

A thrill of excitement shot through him. He'd found her. "I sent Rock after her."

"After her, how?" Mason asked, alarmed.

"Just to follow her home. I can get her info once I have her address." He explained.

Mason grunted as the footage followed her out of the store and through the parking lot. His brother zoomed in on her car and tags. He hit print and then turned his attention to Silas.

"What were you doing here?"

"Meeting with Pop in Julian's office," Silas answered, snatching the paper from the printer behind his brother's desk.

Mason frowned. "What's Pop up to? Last time he called me to the carpet, it was about a marriage merger."

Silas looked up from the license plate and frowned at his brother. "That's not...nah."

"You can never be too sure with Dallas Knight," Mason told him.

Silas cursed because that was true. His father could be up to anything.

three

Silas was trembling by the time he reached Julian's office. His assistant told him they were in a conference room across the hall. That didn't help his nervousness one bit. It didn't make matters better to have both his mother and father waiting for him in the office.

"What's going on?" Mason asked.

"Sit, son." Dallas' gaze never strayed from Silas.

He damn near flopped into the chair. His whole morning was off balance. His panther, where it had been anxious a moment ago, was alert...watchful.

"Let me start with the good news first." Dallas started. "We found your daughter."

Mason cursed and sat down in the chair next to Silas.

"I found her," Silas said in confusion.

Dallas looked at Adina. "What do you mean?"

"Just now. I ran into her shopping downstairs. Wait..." he took a moment and processed what they were saying. "What do you mean you found her?"

"Your mother told you about Samantha."

He nodded.

"Adina had her followed. Samantha sent her security to a house in those new developments over near The Landing. We went to go investigate and saw the girl."

Silas stood, the room spinning. "When?"

"Last night," Adina said, tearful.

"You've known since last night," he whispered.

"I wanted as much information as we could gather before we told you." Dallas hastened to reassure him.

He didn't know how to feel. His claws slipped from under his nails, fur rippling beneath his shirt as his panther fought to come out. Mason stepped next to him and put a hand on his shoulder. His brother's cat lent him soothing energy that kept him from shifting.

"This is why we waited until this morning," Adina told him, her eyes begging him to understand.

And he could...logically, he knew he would've driven straight there, and nothing they could've said would've stopped him. As it was, he was having a hard time with his panther. He was liable to shift and chase them down on foot any moment now. He shook his head and forced the animal into submission.

"The woman," he said hoarsely. He cleared his throat. "Who was the woman with her?" He shouldn't even care, but from his cat's reaction to her, he wanted every bit of information they had on Mila.

"Mila Meyers. We think she's her mother."

"That's not Cameron." That went without saying, but saying it aloud shifted things into perspective for him.

Dallas nodded. He looked to Julian, who slid a folder over to Silas. Silas gripped it and took a breath before looking inside. There was a death record for Cameron, listing child birth as her cause of death. He dropped back into the chair. Guilt and no small amount of regret filled him. He and Cameron hadn't worked out. But he would never wish death on her. She had been running from him, had she not, would she have been able to get the proper care for herself?

His mind went to the letter she'd sent him with a baby picture inside. Had that been the last thing she'd done before her death? The handwriting on the envelope had not matched that of the writing on the letter. It meant to him that someone had sent it for her. He wiped a hand down his face as he sat with that.

"Silas," his mother whispered.

He held up a hand, "I'm good, ma. I just need a second."

He stood and walked out into the hallway. The paper slipped from his hand, and he stared at the wall as memories of Cameron went through his mind. They'd both been young when their parents had proposed the marriage merger. It was supposed to settle the cats after the violent turnover. The two of them had been teenagers, just eighteen, but they were supposed to wait until they were older to marry. Lust being what it was, they'd slipped up before the wedding a couple of years later. Though, he didn't know that at the time.

Cameron's brother had tried to regain their father's position as the head of the Motsi from Dallas and had lost his life. Samantha was livid about that and the banishment of the rest of her family. She and Cameron had left town and called off the marriage. It hadn't mattered in the grand scheme of things as Dallas had the support he needed from the cats of Eastfield.

But...it had cost Silas years with his daughter.

He wiped his face when he scented his brother coming out the door, shocked at the tears that wet his hands. Mason didn't say anything, simply resting his forehead against Silas'. Their panthers reached out, and soothing energy filled Silas.

Mason stepped back. "What you want to do?"

"I want my daughter." Nothing else mattered.

four

Mila was still daydreaming about Silas a whole day later...which was foolish. She'd only interacted with the man for less than a minute. The fact that she could still feel his hands on her told her about the state of her dating life. It was non-existent, so of course, she was losing her mind over the small interaction.

She sighed. She was in her home office working. She should've been concerned with the applicant she was interviewing for her client. Instead, she was fantasizing about a stranger. She'd been lucky to find a career in recruiting. She had her own recruiting firm, and never had she been as happy for it as she was now.

Especially with the turmoil over the last four years. She'd been able to care for her daughter and grieve her husband. She couldn't imagine having to do that in an office. Seth's life insurance had taken them far, covering any gaps that had come from their many moves.

She promised herself that this was the last time.

Sariyah loved this neighborhood, and Mila loved living next door to her best friend. They'd been friends since their days in foster care, and Helen was the only family Mila could claim. She hung up the phone and watched from her desk as her daughter tiptoed down the hallway, happy to have something else to occupy her thoughts.

"I'll assume this means your room is cleaned?"

Sariyah smiled and tossed her braids over her shoulder. "Clean-ish."

Mila got out of her chair, walked to the office door, and leaned a shoulder against the wall. "Back to your room, little girl. You don't go outside until your room is clean."

"I only came out because I saw a car in the yard," Sariyah admitted.

Mila frowned and walked to the living room window. Her daughter just basically told on herself. Sariyah's bedroom was in the back, and neither of her windows faced the front of the house. Likely she'd been in the kitchen sneaking a snack. Her eyebrows bunched as she spotted the black Jaguar with heavily tinted windows parked on the curb in front of their house. How long had it been there? She rubbed her hands against the ratty jeans she wore. She heard the footsteps on the porch a second before the doorbell rang.

Sariyah's eyes widened in excitement, and she ran to the door. "I wonder who it is."

Mila sucked in a shocked breath as she saw who was on the other side. She ran a hand across her hair, the self-conscious act automatic. She was glad she wasn't working in pajamas like she did some days. The worn jeans she wore were the ones she used to work in the garden, and the baggy t-shirt had paint splotches from her and Sariyah's attempt to paint her room. She debated opening the door. It wasn't like she could pretend not to be home. Not only was her car in the driveway, but her daughter was next to her, giggling in excitement. She cursed her lack of makeup and gave up with a heavy sigh.

She opened the door to Silas Knight, and he looked even better than her fantasies remembered.

She pasted a polite smile on her face, hoping to cover the nerves. "Good morning, Mr. Knight. How did you find us?"

Silas cleared his throat, his hands brushing against his slacks in a move that broadcasted his own nervousness. She frowned and found it odd that a man like him would be nervous. The confidence in both his manner and appearance yesterday made her think that not much made this man nervous.

"What can I help you with?"

"Invite him in. You're being rude, mom." Sariyah giggled behind her.

She shook her head. "Of course, my apologies. Come in, please."

He cleared his throat again and walked past her to enter their house. The smell of his cologne sent her pulse skittering. She didn't want to examine why especially in front of her nosy daughter, who took in Mila's every gesture with sharp eyes.

Their guest stood in the middle of her living room—which was thankfully clean— looking at odds. She motioned to the armchair, and he perched on the edge, giving Sariyah a longing look. This time the nerves that danced through her body had nothing to do with attraction.

"Sariyah, back to finish your room, please."

"Aww, man." She complained.

One look from her mother sent her rushing down the hallway with no further protest.

"Would you like coffee or anything to drink?" Though she'd kept her voice controlled, she wanted to yell at him to spit out whatever had him fidgeting in her living room.

He shook his head. "No, thank you."

"Well, let's have it then. There is obviously something weighing on you."

His eyes widened in surprise a moment before he composed his face. Silas pulled a small envelope from his jacket and passed it to her. Mila took it with shaking hands. The envelope had two pictures in it and a folder letter. One photo was of a baby she didn't recognize but who favored her daughter...the other she very much remembered. It was Sariyah, taken at the hospital when she'd been born. Mila looked closer at the picture, and her stomach tumbled as anxiety filled her. She looked up at Silas to find him studying her and her reactions.

"What is..." she whispered. She cleared her throat, "what is this about?"

"One of those is my baby picture. The other is a picture my ex-fiancé sent to me of our baby." Silas said quietly.

Mila dropped the pictures on the table. "What does this mean?" she asked, her voice stronger as fear took root in her heart.

He looked away, a hint of embarrassment on his face before he composed himself. "Eight years ago, I was supposed to get married. There was some politics involved. Long story short, Cameron and her mother left town, and I found out about my daughter from that letter." He pointed to the paper she held in her hand.

Her heart started racing, and her gaze shot back toward the hallway and where her daughter's bedroom would be. Was he saying what she thought he was? She wanted to open the letter, but she'd rather do that in privacy. She'd known about the letter. Seth had had a series of them that Cameron had asked him to distribute after she'd died. She hadn't known what the content was of either of them. Mila had assumed it went to her mother and other family members.

"Our adoption was legal," she said hastily. "Cameron put our names on the birth certificate at the hospital.

He held up a hand. "I'm not accusing you of anything. I'm trying to explain that I didn't know anything about the child until that letter arrived. It took me months to trace it back to where it had come from, and by that time..."

She nodded her head and stood, walking towards the window. She knew what he would say. Mila and Seth had been gone by the time the letters had reached their destinations. It was Cameron's wish to keep the child from being used by Samantha in her schemes. Cameron had extracted their promise to take the child and hide. It had all been a whirlwind. From finding out about the baby, to the complications Cameron had suffered a full day after she'd given birth. There hadn't been any time for planning before they'd been thrust into parenthood.

Mila spotted the security that she assumed he always traveled with leaning against the blacked-out Jaguar. It reminded her that she was dealing with someone powerful.

"Look, I'm sorry for what you went through, Mr. Knight—"

"—Silas."

"Silas," Mila conceded and turned to face him, her arms crossed. "Are you here to take my daughter?"

She was direct, even though her body was trembling with the effort it took her to remain calm. Her mind was racing with the implication of his words. If he could prove that Sariyah was his daughter, then that put her in a precarious position. The legal ramifications of a human adopting a shifter child...she needed to call her best friend immediately.

Seth had only told her he was a shifter after they'd adopted Sariyah. It was one of the reasons she'd run from his family. If the Robinsons had been able to catch them, then shifter law would be on their side, and they would've been able to take Sariyah despite Cameron's dying wishes.

But it seemed that now they were still in the same boat. Except this time, Silas Knight was a force way more powerful than the Robinsons.

Silas blinked in surprise. "I..." he stopped, seeming to compose himself. "I only want the chance to get to know my daughter."

"At what cost?" Mila asked, trying to keep hysteria at bay. "Do I just introduce you to my daughter as her father? Not to mention the dangerous work you do."

Silas ran his hands over his face. "Look, I understand how difficult this is. It's the reason I came by myself instead of involving my lawyers. It would be easier for all involved if we could reach some sort of agreement without having to go to court."

"Court!" Mila breathed deeply and looked away, remembering that Sariyah was probably listening at her door. She lowered her voice. "You have no right to take me to court, our adoption was legal, and I have the paperwork to prove it."

"I should have a right to get to know my daughter, Ms. Meyers. I don't want to wreck the life you made for her, but I've searched for Sariyah since I knew of her existence. That has to count for something," Silas's voice was hard, and Mila could almost feel the fury pouring off of the man.

His hands were clenching and unclenching, and she took another deep breath. There had to be a way to resolve the situation.

"And so you'll just come take her?"

"She is my daughter, so she's a shifter. It will get messy if we have to involve the law. We specifically have laws about humans adopting shifter cubs. I could've come in and 'just taken her' as is my right. I want to work this out in a way that will be easiest for you both."

Her stomach dropped in shock. He was right, and that solidified the fear building in her chest. Plus, she knew next to nothing about shifters and for damn sure didn't know about raising one. Would that hold weight in court? She needed to get the conversation back under control.

"Mr. Knight, Silas, let's calm down. Would you like some coffee?" Mila asked.

"No, thank you." He ran his hands over his face again. "Ms. Meyers—"

"—Mila," she cut in.

"Mila. I can give you a few days to talk with your lawyer and come to terms with what will happen. You can find out your options. You'll see it will be better for us to work it out on our own. I can at least allow you that." He stood to leave.

Mila had the feeling she'd been dismissed. "That's so gracious of you," she said sarcastically.

He raised an eyebrow but said nothing, instead heading for the door. He turned before opening it. "Here is my card. My cellphone number is on the back. Even though I'm backing off to give you space, if you need anything...."

"We'll be fine, Silas. Thank you," she cut him off.

He studied her face, and his eyes flashed green a moment before he got it under control. He sighed.

"I'm leaving security in place for the both of you." He held up his hand to stall her argument. "They'll be unobtrusive."

She nodded. What could she say? She'd just tried to argue that his job was dangerous. She watched as he walked to the car, her eyes roving their street to see if she could spot the security he'd left. Finding nothing, she turned and went back inside. Mila leaned her head against the cold wood and released a sigh. What in the world would she do? She couldn't lose her daughter.

five

Silas paced the plush carpet in his family's lawyer's office four days later, clasping his hands together to keep from throwing something. It had been nearly a week, and Mila still hadn't called. It wasn't that he didn't understand how confusing it all was, but he was anxious to move to the next step. He could've spent the days he was waiting working, but there was no way he could concentrate on the intricacies of his job with everything left incomplete.

"You're telling me I have no rights?" He finally spoke.

Dean sat on the leather sofa in his office, a tumbler of scotch in hand, one leg crossed over the other. He'd grown up with Dean; they had gone to school together. Dean's father had been the family's lawyer before he retired, and now Dean had taken over the family practice.

"I'm a corporate lawyer, Silas, but as far as I can tell, there's nothing you can do to compel Ms. Meyers to give you a DNA test."

"It's fraud. Can't you invalidate the adoption? Not to mention, my daughter is a shifter. I can't just leave her in the care of a human."

"After eight years, Silas, do you think invalidating the adoption is best for the child?" Dean was calm.

He cursed and made another round of the office. He had to think of the child. His daughter. She'd only known the family where she was placed. What kind of monster would he be if he tried to take her from the only mother she knew? And from the reports he was getting from the security he put on her, Mila took great care of the little girl. He'd seen it with his own eyes. Though he'd promised Mila space to think, it hadn't stopped him from stopping by her house to watch her and his daughter.

"Not even visitation?"

Dean sighed. "Your best option would be to try and reason with the mother. Perhaps she will allow you to see the girl."

He wanted to throw something, punch a wall, anything to release the anger currently burning through his chest. "She's mine, Dean!"

"Prove it," Dean told him quietly.

"Fuck!" he roared, fur rising and falling on his arms as his animal reacted to his anger. "I can't prove it without the DNA test."

Which Mila had to consent to.

He saw the unspoken words on his friend's face. He cursed again.

"I understand, Silas. Believe me, I hurt for you, but there is nothing legal we can do right now. You drafted a lot of the shifter laws yourself, so you know firsthand the intricacies of claiming shifter status. Without concrete proof that the child is yours, you can't prove she's a shifter which is the only basis you'd have for invalidating the adoption."

"But she can't know that." Maybe he could scare her with the threat of him going to court. No one wanted to go against his family.

Dean held out his hands, an exasperated sigh lowering his shoulders. "You're not even that type of person."

He sighed. Dean was right, and that made him madder.

"Try and talk to her. The less you bring up lawyers, the better your chances will be. She'll be less defensive, for sure."

"So you're telling me to wait," Silas grumbled.

"Same answer I gave you an hour ago," Dean reminded him.

Silas growled. His phone rang from his coat pocket, distracting him momentarily. He walked over to the coat rack Dean had at the door and fished out his phone. He narrowed his eyes at the unknown number.

"Yeah?"

"Silas?" Mila's voice was soft...tentative.

Both Silas and his panther went still. "Hey, what's up?"

"I was wondering if we could meet somewhere for coffee."

"Yeah, that works for me," he hastily replied. "Are you available now?"

"I am."

"I'll send you the address to a spot I know. Is that okay?" He held his breath.

"Yes, that's perfect. It doesn't take me more than thirty minutes to get to most places here. Will that work?" She asked.

She sounded as anxious as him to meet. Would that be a good sign? "Works for me."

He hung up and sent the text message to a local shifter-run restaurant he knew. It would be safer for him there. He liked to stay as low-key as possible when he could. He slid on his suit jacket.

"I gotta go, Dean."

"Remember what I said, Silas. More flies with honey," Dean warned him.

Silas grunted and left the office. Rock and Leo filed in behind him as he left.

"Where to, Boss?" Leo asked, sliding into the driver's seat.

"Michaels, over off J Turner," he answered.

With traffic, he would make it before thirty minutes. His animal prowled his body in anticipation, but he quelled it. He needed to remain calm if their meeting was to be congenial. He made it to the restaurant in twenty minutes, greeting the hostess by name.

"Your party's already here, Silas. I sat her at your usual table," the young woman said with a smile.

He followed her to the back, rubbing a hand down the front of his shirt in nervousness. She was seated, sipping at a coffee cup when he rounded the corner to the secluded table. The Mila sitting in the chair was very different from the woman he'd met at her house. Instead of ratty jeans and a t-shirt, she wore a tight, cream-colored sleeveless top that hugged her curves in a way that made his mouth water. She stood when she saw him, the dark brown slacks she wore molded to thick, luscious hips before flaring out and reaching the floor.

Lord have mercy.

His heart knocked against his chest, and his breath stilled. Power skittered up and down his skin as his panther asserted itself. He knew what that meant, but now was not the time to act on what his cat was trying to tell him. Still, he mentally juggled around some of the priorities he had to make room for what was an inevitable conclusion.

He wanted Mila.

And it had nothing to do with his daughter. It gave him an idea, but he needed to work out the finer details before acting on it. Mila smiled at him, her glossy lips beckoning him forward. She was beautiful in the casual clothes she'd worn the first two times he'd seen her, but in a full face of makeup and elegant clothes, she was temptation in human form.

He took a deep breath and returned her smile. He needed to remember why they were meeting. He leaned over and kissed her cheek, inhaling her scent and committing it to memory.

"Thank you for meeting me," he said quietly.

Mila sat back down, her hands fidgeting with the water glass. "Thank you. I know it was last minute." She reached into her large purse and pulled out two envelopes, setting them on the table between them.

His eyebrows shot up immediately as he sat. This woman was direct, if nothing else. He was still debating whether or not he liked it.

"Before we get into anything regarding visitation, we need to establish that she is your daughter. If it comes back that she's yours, then we can talk about how we're going to do this."

Well...shit. It didn't get any more direct than that.

six

Mila fought not to squirm in her chair. She'd laid the gauntlet down, and now the test was how he'd react to it. Everything she'd read about him hinted that he wouldn't take it well. He was known in the media as well as in the streets for the iron-clad control he had over his life and his team. Helen's husband had given her the rundown of what he'd heard about Silas, and Mila knew she had to play this carefully.

She didn't imagine he liked having her in control of something this important to him. But, Sariyah was her daughter, and she would be damned if she'd let him come in and take over.

She cleared her throat when he remained silent at her statement. "I don't want to turn our world over, and you're not..." She trailed off. "It's just been me and my daughter for nearly four years."

"That's fair," he finally agreed. He turned over the envelopes.

"I took samples from Sariyah and have sent them to this lab." She pointed to the envelope on the right. "In the second envelope, I have another sample from Sariyah that you can send to whichever lab you prefer."

He looked up and studied her face. "How do I know you're giving me the right sample?"

Mila sighed, "That's a fair question, but if we're already starting this with you not trusting me, then what are we even doing?"

His face was still skeptical, but he slid both envelopes into his brief-case. Mila took a deep breath, relief relaxing her shoulders. She hadn't known what he would say, and while she was prepared to fight for her daughter, she didn't relish going up against someone so powerful. This overture was one of the strategies she and her best friend slash lawyer had settled on as they discussed the problem. Hopefully, he would see her effort and match it. It would make things easier for them both.

He put both hands on the table top and studied her. She wanted to pat her hair to make sure the low bun she'd wrestled her curly hair into was straight. Instead, she met his gaze, refusing to back down. He chuckled quietly, seemingly amused by her.

"Fine," he said, finally.

She nodded and blew out another breath. One hurdle down.

"Once we get the results, I'll call you," she said, standing, her purse clutched tightly.

He reached out and touched her hand. "Please stay and have lunch with me."

Her heart fluttered, its beat heavy and staccato at his touch. She licked her lips in nervousness but nodded. She settled back into her chair, and her eyes anxiously went to the security that followed him into the restaurant. They stood at opposite corners, close enough to the table to reach it should something happen but far enough away, hopefully, to not hear their conversation. Silas caught the direction of her gaze, and the corner of his lip turned up in a small smile.

"Yeah, you get used to it," he said, waving over the waitress.

She didn't know if that were possible, but it did make her wonder about her daughter's safety. "Will Sariyah have to walk around with security like that?"

He stared at her a moment before talking. "Besides my position, my father is leader of the cat shifters in this city. The both of you will need security."

She was strangely comforted by that. It would certainly make it harder for the Robinsons to access them. She took a sip of her water before reaching back into her purse.

"I read Cameron's letter to you. I'm very sorry for what you went through." She passed the paper back to him.

Silas stared down at the folded document before reaching for it. He cleared his throat. "Were you there with her? Your name is on Sariyah's birth certificate. I can only assume...."

Mila nodded. "My husband and I both were there. When Cameron came to us, she was frantic. According to her, Samantha wanted the child for reasons unknown, and I think Cameron was weary of the machinations."

"How did you know Cameron?" His gaze was sharp as he awaited her answer.

"I didn't know her personally. She was a distant cousin of Seth's. I guess she remembered his mother from when they were children. She was looking for Lauren but found us. We were living in Seth's parent's old home." She answered, smiling in memory. She had loved that old house.

"What will you do if the DNA test confirms that she's yours?"

He blinked in surprise. "You direct as shit."

She shrugged.

The waitress came up and interrupted whatever he was about to say. She ordered a salad because, honestly, she didn't think she could keep down anything at the moment. When the waitress left, she fiddled with the silverware on the table, awaiting his answer.

Silas sighed. "I want to be in my daughter's life. That's it."

"You won't take her from me?"

"Are you willing to share custody?"

That shut her up. It had taken her a week even to decide what to do. She'd talked it over with Helen. This lunch was a part of Helen's plan, and though Mila had had her reservations, it seemed the best route. It didn't make her any less nervous. Silas studied her, his dark gaze making her feel exposed, as though he was privy to her every thought.

It was intimidating, but at the same time, she felt safe from him. He had the ability to topple her whole world, and though she was wary, Mila knew he would play fair. How she knew that when she knew next to nothing about him was a mystery to her.

"Let me just say I've heard around about your family. I'm not scared of you or your money, Silas. I need you to understand that. This is for my daughter. I want to give her everything she needs to grow up healthy, including a father figure." She took a deep breath. "I think once we get to know each other and get comfortable with each other, we can work out an agreement that works for the three of us."

He smiled, and her whole body flushed and heated. God, the man was just beautiful.

"Let's get to know each other then."

seven

Silas refreshed and checked his email for a fifth time, sucking his teeth when ten came in. But none from the place he was looking for. According to the paperwork, the results of his DNA test was supposed to come in today, and to say he was anxious was an understatement. It had been a week since he'd sent in the sample. He'd talked to Mila, checking in on Sariyah every day since they'd had lunch.

Sariyah.

That was a head trip. He'd been searching for her for years, and now she was within his sights. He got daily reports from his security, but he couldn't wait until he could claim her and see her himself.

"Mr. Knight," Keisha, his assistant, called out.

He focused his attention on her and the charts she had displayed on her tablet.

"Sorry. What were we talking about?"

"Sanctuary cities," she reminded him.

He nodded for her to go on.

"There are only about twenty left in the country, so it's a small number compared to the fight we'd have on our hands."

He pulled the information she'd gathered close so he could look over them. Sanctuary cities were whole towns and cities that were shifter only. Humans weren't allowed in the towns. Most of them were inhabited by some of the smaller packs of rarer shifters who wanted no human interference. When the fights between humans and shifters first broke out, there were more sanctuary cities in the sparsely populated states.

Fighting humans was more challenging in those areas, so the shifters founded the towns, finding it easier to defend one central point.

He hadn't realized there were still as many operating. His job as Shifter Liaison required him to fight for all shifters, not just those in Eastfield.

"What's the problem?"

"The problem is, they found oil right on the edge of the city." She pointed out the spot on the map she'd marked. "The digging will require them to pay for the land usage or buy the land outright."

"The shifters there would be crazy to sell." He murmured.

"Exactly. And so, in order to get to that one town, the Senator wants to break up all the sanctuary cities."

Silas sat back, his mind finally on something other than his daughter. "He said the bill was supposed to give the cities access to federal money."

"At the cost of their independence." She told him. "He's sneaking a referendum onto their town ballots. Claiming that the will of the people should be considered."

Silas shook his head. "Ok. Get me a meeting with their alpha, and I'll work on bringing the other cities into it. We'll go with whatever they decide. If they want me to fight against it, then that's what we'll do."

Keisha nodded and made notes before preparing to move onto the next issue. Silas rubbed his eyes. Most days, he appreciated being busy. It kept his mind focused and the anger festering within him for years from breaking out. His phone rang, and he quickly snatched it from his desktop.

It was Dean.

He took a deep calming breath and answered. "Tell me."

"She's yours," Dean came right out with it. "What do you want to do?"

"I'm coming home. I'll get up with you if it goes sideways." He promised.

He didn't even have to tell his assistant anything. "Flight's in an hour. That will give you time to take the call with Senator Whitmore, and then I'll clear your schedule." She stood and left.

Silas looked up at Rock.

The slight tilt of his lips was Rock's version of a smile. "Yours?"

He nodded, overwhelmed with emotion. He'd known she was his. His panther had sensed it the moment he scented her. But now he had confirmation. His pulse was racing, and the animal within him paced and snarled, demanding Silas go home.

***

His knee bounced as he finally buckled into the seat of the private jet he used for travel. He went back and forth too much for him to fly commercially. He spun his phone in his hand, moving it from left and right, debating whether or not to call Mila. A call would be way more polite than just showing up. What would she do now that they had confirmation? She'd talked a good game about cooperating with him, but now was the time when she would have to show it.

His phone rang, the object of his thoughts on the other end.

"What's good?" He answered, covering his nervousness.

She cleared her throat. "I got the results. Congratulations. I can imagine how it feels to know you've found her after your searching."

"Thank you for that." His body tensed. "How do you feel?"

"I want a family for Sariyah." She said, but he heard the pause. He waited her out. "I guess I have to get used to sharing her."

He chuckled. "And not with just me, either. My family has been searching just as hard as I've been."

She breathed out, and Silas could almost feel her nervousness. Strangely, it calmed him, his panther softening.

"I remember when we first got word she would be ours, so I commend your patience. I expected you to show up minutes after I read the results."

He let out a relieved laugh. "It was touch and go there for a moment."

She laughed, the husky sound raising the hair on his arms. "Well, I'm a woman of my word. She has a piano recital tomorrow night," She said softly. "It's the first one she's ever had, so it's a pretty big deal to her."

He got choked up, his eyes burning with unshed tears. "Okay," was all he could get out.

"I'll text you the details." She promised. "We can go to dinner after so I can introduce the two of you."

He cleared his throat. "Will you tell her who I am?"

"I was hoping we could do that together. Sariyah knows she's adopted, so it won't be a complete shock. I try to be very open with her about the things that impact her."

Respect for Mila rose. He couldn't imagine it had been easy raising a child on her own. He took a deep breath because now that they had the results, she wouldn't be alone.

"I'm excited but nervous, know what I mean?"

She hummed. "I can't imagine how it feels from your end."

"It's surreal, that's for sure."

"Well, I don't want to hold you up. I know you're busy," she said.

"Talk to me for a second. I got time before my flight takes off." He wanted to know Mila as a woman and as the mother of his daughter. It was necessary.

"Flight? You leaving or coming back?"

"I hopped the flight the moment I got the news."

"Oh wow," she said softly.

"How has your day been? How does Sariyah like her new school?"

"My day is pretty busy, but I'm wrapping up an account, so the rest of the week will be easy. So far, so good on the school front." She paused. "You know, a part of me wondered if you would still be checking in with us if she wasn't yours."

"You don't like my calls and texts?" He had been checking in with them since he left her house a week ago.

She chuckled, and the sound flowed over him. "I'll admit that I would've missed them."

Damn, this woman was so blunt. He was getting used to it. She was so matter-of-fact, and he had to admit that it made communicating with her easier. He always knew where he stood with her.

"Who said I would've stopped if the results were different."

"Oh," she released a little gasp that went straight to his dick. "I did want to talk to you about something before we went any further."

He stilled. "Okay."

She released a breath. "I know I'm asking a lot, but please don't spoil her. Sariyah is smart and very clever. I know you'll feel the need to reassure her through gifts, but time will mean more in the long run. I'll go out of my way to ensure you and your family have time with her."

He could respect that. He should probably tell her that both his brother and father would likely spoil the little girl rotten, but he would do his best to adhere to her request.

She laughed as though she could read his mind. "Try."

He joined her in laughter. "I'll do my best."

The attendant flagged him down to let him know the flight was ready.

He nodded at her. "I gotta go. I'll call you when I land."

"Oh, okay," she said breathlessly. "See you soon."

He ended the call and stared out at the tarmac. Just the small interaction with Mila settled his animal. It was strange and not like anything he'd experienced. Now that he knew Sariyah was his, would it complicate matters?

eight

"Riyah, you have ten minutes, and we're leaving, lucky headband or not!" Mila shouted down the hallway.

She was nervous. That was a no-brainer. But, why she was nervous seemed to change every ten minutes. On the one hand, she would tell her daughter about Silas tonight after her recital. That was enough to have butterflies fluttering all through her stomach. But a small part of her...okay, a huge part of her was nervous about seeing Silas herself. They'd talked on the phone for a week, mainly about Sariyah and her likes, but Silas also took the time to get to know her. That was a little disconcerting.

From all the rumors that floated around about the Knights, she had expected him to be pushy and demanding. Silas had been neither of those things. He'd allowed her to set the pace for this thing between the three of them. It was a relief. She thought she'd have to fight him and hide from the Robinsons, all at the same time.

She sighed when the doorbell rang. She tensed. Was he here already? They had agreed to meet at Sariyah's school, where the recital was held. She let out a relieved breath when the door opened, and her best friend entered. Helen walked in, her daughter Emily trailing behind her.

"Hey, bestie!" Emily yelled down the hallway.

Her daughter's head popped out. "Come help me look for my headband, Ems."

Mila rolled her eyes and smiled at her friend. "We're ready."

"It's no rush. We have time to get to the school. Are you okay with this?" Helen's eyes roamed her face.

"I want her to have a father, and if he sticks to his side of the bargain, this can be good." She hoped anyway.

She clearly didn't do a good job of hiding her nervousness because Helen's skeptical look broadcasted what she thought of it all.

"I don't like this winging it business. I want it on paper, in front of a judge. But, we'll do it your way because the court way could get messy."

"But most especially, it will give the Robinson's a way to track us," Mila said softly to her friend. She didn't want Riyah to hear.

Helen gave her a sympathetic look. "According to Scott, they were banned from the city. I don't think they'd approach you here. And if push comes to shove, Silas is a part of the Motsi. They run this city, and we could petition with them. Well...not we. You're not a shifter."

"Exactly. I'm a human, operating in a space that's in no way built for me."

She let out a frustrated breath. This way had to work. She didn't want this to be any harder than it had to be.

The doorbell rang, and they both looked alarmed. Mila opened the door and exhaled at the beautiful bouquet the deliveryman was holding. There were happy sunflowers in a colorful pot.

"I have a delivery for Sariyah Meyers," the young man passed a card to a shocked Mila.

"Flowers for me?" Sariyah asked, peeking her head from around her mother's body, the elusive headband over the two braids in her hair. "I'm Sariyah Meyers." She announced.

The deliveryman smiled and lowered the bouquet down to her smiling daughter. Riyah grabbed the vase and squealed in delight, racing back into the house. Mila reached for her purse to tip him when he shook his head.

"It was included already. Have a great day."

He left her porch, and Mila stared after him for a moment. She looked down at the card like it was an alien.

"Flowers for me," Riyah was singing to her best friend. "It's just like your dad got you for the first day of school."

Emily properly oohed and aahed, and Mila swallowed the lump in her throat. The usual sadness she felt whenever Riyah asked about a father overtook her. She missed Seth and hated that he never had the opportunity to really be in Sariyah's life. She'd been a toddler when he died, and her daughter barely remembered him now.

Mila felt more reassured about her decision to cooperate with Silas. Her daughter would get the father she had longed for and, from the looks of the flowers, a good father. She would make sure their arrangement worked, even if she had to put aside her lustful thoughts for the man. A girl deserved her father, and Mila could finally give that to her daughter.

***

Mila smoothed down the heather gray wrap skirt she wore. The white fitted shirt she wore on top was cropped, though only a sliver of her stomach showed. August in Florida felt like summer compared to the midwest, so she had to adjust her clothing when they arrived. She shuffled her feet in nervousness, careful in her strappy heels. She could admit to being overdressed for her daughter's recital, and no, she would not be examining why she went out of her way to look good. Instead, she smoothed down her flyaway curls and patiently waited for Silas to arrive.

She'd sent Helen inside with the girls to hold seats while she waited. She didn't have to wait long. She spotted him walking through the parking lot. Her body heated as he weaved in and out of the cars still parking. He wore a dark green polo over a pair of slacks that looked tailor-made for his body. An air of power surrounded him, dominant and compelling. The confidence and swagger in his walk was the stuff dreams were made of. Certainly, her fantasies if the last week were anything to go by. She spotted the same security guard that had been with him at their lunch.

He walked up to her and kissed her cheek, lingering close to her. His cologne surrounded her, and she felt secure and a whole host of other emotions she was not supposed to feel. Her heart skipped a beat, and her breath stalled. She had to remember this was all about her...their daughter.

"How are you?" His deep voice was much more potent in person than it had been over the phone.

"Fine, fine. Thank you for the flowers. She loved them." She breathed out.

He nodded, and silence fell between them, tense and thick as they continued to stare at each other. Someone cleared their throat, and Mila realized he wasn't alone with his security. Her eyes widened, and he gave her a sheepish look.

"I'm sorry. I told them about Sariyah's recital, and then everyone was so excited," he explained.

For a moment, Mila felt overwhelmed, but then she thought of the flowers and Riyah's expression. She quickly forgave the intrusion, a little choked up that her daughter would have more family. She wondered about their family dynamic, but it showed promise that they were so quick to show up for her daughter. Sariyah would have the family Mila never had.

She sighed. "It's fine, but please—"

He cupped her chin, "I remember, and I warned them. No one will say anything yet. They're leaving right after the recital."

She looked behind him into the hopeful gazes of the five others he'd brought and nodded. They'd searched for Sariyah for years. She couldn't imagine the patience and restraint they'd been showing up until this point.

"Introduce me," she instructed him.

He breathed out in relief. "This is my mother, Adina, and my father, Dallas. There is my brother Mason, his mate Celine, and my second mother, Iris."

She smiled at the group, knowing she'd need to get their names again. "Well, let's get inside. They're starting soon. I have my friend saving seats. Hopefully, we can find a row that will fit us all."

Mila took a deep breath. The time of just her and Riyah was over. From now on, she'd have to share her baby. She got a little misty-eyed at the thought. But, at the end of the day, it would be best for her daughter. There was safety in numbers, and from what she'd heard about the Knights, they would burn the world down for their family, and now Sariyah was a part of that family.

nine

Silas was in awe as he watched Sariyah on the school stage. His daughter was beautiful and poised as she took her seat. Everything about her, from her dress to the shiny black shoes on her feet, fascinated him. The piece was simple but Mozart-worthy in Silas' eyes. Her face, so much like his, was scrunched in concentration as she studied the sheet music.

He mourned a little for the things he had missed over the years but took comfort in the fact that she was with Mila. He had had her thoroughly investigated, and everything came back clean. His eyes misted, and he felt the soft touch on his hand. He looked down as Mila grabbed his hand. He saw the compassion in her eyes and was struck again by her beauty. He tightened his grip on her hand, not thinking about it, and they held hands throughout Sariyah's performance.

They stood and clapped once it was over.

"Y'all see how good my niece is?" Mason bragged.

Silas laughed, wiping the tears from his cheek. His brother was a fool. He sat through the rest of the performances in a daze. Before he knew it, the crowd was standing and filing from the auditorium. He looked around, happy with the school Mila had chosen for their daughter. Security had been good, and the front office had been understanding and cooperative when he had his office call and arrange extra safety precautions for Sariyah.

His parents pulled him aside once they were in the hallway. As she cuddled into Dallas ' side, Adina had tears in her eyes.

"I'm going to dinner with Mila tonight to tell Sariyah, but as soon as possible, I will bring her to meet everyone." He promised them.

Dallas put his forehead against Silas'. "Congrats, son."

Silas nodded, unable to speak past the lump in his throat. Adina rubbed her cheek against his.

"She's so beautiful," she whispered. "I can't wait to spoil her."

Silas let out a watery laugh. "There you go."

"Come on, lil baby," Dallas prodded her down the hall towards Mason and Celine.

Silas turned back to Mila and smiled. "She was great."

"She's been learning since she was four. It was the only way to get her to sit still for a while." Mila told him.

She introduced him to her friend Helen, but he smiled, recognizing Helen's husband.

"Scott, what it do, play boy." He dapped him up.

"I can't call it," Scott said. "Congratulations. Helen told me everything."

"Thank you. I appreciate that."

"It's nice to meet you, Silas. Mila, we'll meet you at the restaurant?" Helen asked.

Mila nodded. "Yeah, we'll meet you guys there."

Before he could say anything, Sariyah bounded from the auditorium. A smile lit her whole face, happy damn near pouring from her.

"Did you see me, mom?" Sariyah asked, jumping into her mother's arms.

Silas could only stare as she turned her beautiful face to him. "Mr. Knight! You sent me flowers, thank you."

His hands shook with the need to touch her. She leaned from her mother's arms and into his. He grabbed her, shock freezing him. It was his first hug from his daughter. His panther moved through him, his body trembling.

Sariyah leaned back, her eyes wide. "You smell like me." She turned to her mother with questions all over her face.

"We need to talk about that, actually," Mila told her. "Not here, though. We're going out to eat."

"Luigi's?" Sariyah asked.

Mila rolled her eyes. "Yes, Luigi's."

"Is Mr. Knight coming?" She gave him a hopeful look that did him in.

He was done for.

***

Silas looked around the pizza restaurant, his panther moving through him in agitation. There were entirely too many people in this place. He could feel Rock and Leo's tension at his back. He would need to talk to Mila about places like this one. There was noise from the conversations around them, the video games that flanked the restaurant area, and the staff calling out orders. Not to mention all the scents.

They were seated in a booth right next to her best friend. Sariyah was sitting next to him, damn near bouncing in excitement. He wiped his hands down his pants, unsure how the conversation would go. How easily he'd forgotten how direct Mila was.

"So, Riyah. Remember we talked about you being adopted?"

"Mmhmm," the little girl murmured as she perused the menu.

"And how I told you that I would tell you if I learned anything new about your father?"

That caught her attention. Sariyah looked between the two adults with wide eyes. "Is that why he smells like home?"

Fuck.

Silas would break down like a bitch right in the middle of this restaurant if he didn't hold it together. Mila had no such compunction. Her eyes watered, and she gave her daughter a shaky nod.

"He's your father, and he has been looking for you and your bio mother since you were born," Mila told her.

Sariyah put a small hand on his shoulder. "I'm sorry. My bio mother passed away." She informed him solemnly.

"I found out." He whispered before clearing his throat. "I found out the same day I found you."

"Were you sad? I was, but my bio mom gave me to my new mom, so I'm very happy about that." Sariyah was as direct as her mother. "Are you going to take me from mom?"

So fucking direct.

Her uncle will love her for that alone. He could even see some of his brother in her serious gaze. There was some of Cameron in the shape of Sariyah's nose and mouth, but the eyes were all Knight. Along with the shape of her face. It was eerie.

He shook his head. "I would never take you from your mother. But, I would like the chance to get to know you and love you as she does."

"I like how you smell, and my stomach tells me that we belong together. I can give you a chance." Sariyah answered seriously.

Silas looked at Mila, who shrugged. "Her instincts." She clarified.

He was shaken. His daughter shouldn't get her panther until well into puberty, that she was already allowing her instincts to lead her made him incredibly proud and humbled.

"Following your instincts is always a good idea." He assured her. "So, what do you say? Should we give this father, daughter thing a chance?"

"We can do that." Sariyah held out her fist.

Silas laughed and lightly tapped his fist against hers. If he weren't careful, the little minx would have him wrapped around her fingers.

"I want a cheese pizza and nuggets. Can I go play with Emily now?" Sariyah was apparently done with the subject.

"Fine, you know the rules."

"Always in eyesight," Sariyah recited, sliding under the table and out of their booth.

Silas nodded for Leo to follow his daughter over to the games. "That was easier than I had built up in my head."

Mila laughed, wiping her face. "She's such an easy kid, Silas. I don't know how I got so lucky."

"I'd like to take you both to see my parents. They're anxious to meet her."

"We can do that," she said.

He could see the nervousness on her face, and he understood. The whole thing they were doing was awkward and would take some time. But none of that could dampen the feeling of having his daughter back.

ten

Observing Silas as he got to know her daughter was something that Mila couldn't put into words. Her heart clenched tightly as she realized she would have to share her baby. While Silas hadn't been invasive of their life, his presence in the past two weeks had been felt. He called her every day, sometimes twice, to check in on both of them, mostly asking questions about Sariyah's likes. It changed the way Mila looked at him. She couldn't help it.

There was nothing more endearing than observing a good Black father.

And Silas was good. Any time he was in Sariyah's presence, his attention was wholly on her. She could hear his phone buzzing away in his pocket, but he never let it disturb his time with her...their daughter.

She had to remember that.

Sariyah was theirs. She leaned her head against the wall as she watched them in Riyah's room. Earlier, when he'd arrived, their daughter had grabbed his hand immediately and taken him to her room to show him everything.

Right now, they both sat on the carpeted floor, magazines spread out in front of them, their faces identical with concentration.

"Why are we cutting these out again?" Silas' deep voice was patient and curious.

"Daddy, I explained this. We cut out the pictures and put them up on a board. That way, when I get my camera for Christmas, I can start recreating them." Sariyah pointed at her inspiration board.

"That's what you asked Santa for?"

Riyah rolled her eyes. "Not you believe in Santa, daddy."

He laughed, and Mila found herself drawn to the sound. "Ok, I'ma let you cook with that one."

He and Sariyah laughed together.

She hated to have to break up their bonding time. "It's time to get ready for bed, Riyah."

"Mom, I'm going to be eight soon. We should…" she trailed off, seeing the look on her mother's face. She sighed. "Good night, daddy. What time are you picking us up tomorrow?"

Silas gathered the mess they'd made and set it on her desk. "We're having lunch, so around ten."

Sariyah nodded and pulled him down into a hug. Mila couldn't help the tears that clogged her throat as Silas lifted her daughter and gripped her tight, his face pinched with emotion. Silas rained kisses on Sariyah's face until she giggled before setting her down.

"See you tomorrow, princess." He nuzzled her cheek before heading towards the door.

Mila moved to the side to allow him to pass. It made no sense to tempt the attraction between them by getting too close.

"I'll be back to run your bath in just a second," she told Riyah. She walked with Silas towards the front door, carefully keeping her hands to herself. "Oh, wait, I have something for you."

She rushed into the office and pulled out the little photo album she'd printed for him. Her hands shook as she held it out to him.

"What's this?"

"You missed so much. I printed out all the pictures of her that I have. I can email you some videos, too, if you'd like."

"I'd like." He whispered, looking down at the book with bemusement.

"So, about tomorrow. Ten?"

He nodded, peeling his eyes away from the book, finally. "I'll come get you. Just dress comfortably. It's not anything formal."

She tucked her hands into the pocket of her jeans to hide her sweating palms. She'd heard about his family, and she was worried, despite all his assurances.

"Thank you for this, Mila. It means a lot." He leaned over and kissed her cheek.

Mila held her breath until he'd put distance between them. The warmth of his kiss lingered on her face. She wanted to close her eyes and savor it, but that was just foolish.

"See you tomorrow."

He nodded and walked out her door, and Mila released a huff of air. God, that man was potent.

***

His study was dark, save the lamp on his desk. Silas stared at the large photobook Mila had given him. He should've opened it hours ago, but he could only stare at the evidence of all the years he'd lost with his daughter. The anger he'd lived with for the past seven years reared up, and Silas wanted to hit something. It was why he'd spent so much time in his father's boxing gym. He needed the stress outlet. Between women and boxing, he'd barely been able to contain his anger.

That anger had been missing for the past couple of weeks. It had everything to do with spending time with Sariyah and Mila.

Mila.

He wiped a hand down his face. He couldn't afford the complication of messing around with her, but even now, his animal buzzed under his skin, warming him, wanting to get closer to her. He could feel her curiosity and attraction to him when they were together, and his panther was confused about why Silas hadn't acted on it. If she were any other woman except the mother of his daughter, he would've coaxed her into his bed. Or rather hers. He didn't bring women into the place where he laid his head.

His thoughts went to Mila's home. It was warm and inviting, and he relaxed when he crossed over her threshold. He couldn't have picked a better mother for his daughter. Sariyah was smart, articulate, well-grounded, and very different from what he thought a seven-year-old would be. Not that he'd been around kids even to know. Sariyah's compassion and sweetness were a direct indication of how well Mila had been raising her. He was happy that he hadn't barged into their lives and threatened to take her. He couldn't imagine how contentious that would've made their relationship.

With shaking hands, he finally opened the book. The first thing was a baby picture of Sariyah covered in bubbles in the kitchen sink. Tears welled in his eyes as he mourned all that he had missed. She was a beautiful baby. Happy from all the pictures he saw as he turned the pages. He saw himself in her with every flip of the page. He would take this to his mother tomorrow. She would love to see it. Seth, Mila's late husband, was in many of the pictures of baby Sariyah. He could see the difference in Mila when that changed. She'd gone from smiling and light-hearted in the earlier images to a sadness that was visible through her strained smiles in the latter ones.

He looked at a photo of Sariyah's fourth birthday. Mila's face was strained, but she'd mustered a smile. He could only admire her more for it. Despite the change in her mother, Sariyah still looked happy and carefree. He imagined it took strength from Mila to make sure that their daughter hadn't suffered in their loss.

He found himself continually drawn to Mila in the pictures, wondering how a single mother made the little girl in the photos so happy. There were pictures where Mila looked slightly tired but no less happy. He needed to get his budding feelings for her under control. Just because they had a daughter together does not mean they would fall into a cozy family. He had no plans on letting another woman tie him up in knots.

He took a pull of the blunt next to him and continued flipping through the pages. He heard his front door beep and scented his brother a moment later. He didn't bother moving, knowing Mason would find him.

"The hell it's so dark in here for?"

Silas shook his head as Mason flipped on the overhead light. "You get on my damn nerves."

"What's good?"

"Chilling, or at least I was before you busted in here," Silas answered.

Mason sauntered over to his desk, unfazed by Sila's tone. "What's that?"

"Mila gave me pictures of Riyah."

"That's what's up." Mason made his way around the desk and stood next to Silas' chair. "God, she so damn cute."

Silas moved his chair to the side as his brother comfortably sat on the edge of his desk. Mason smiled as he flipped through the images.

"How has it been? Y'all adjusting?"

Silas nodded and passed his brother his blunt. "Aside from the initial shit, Mila has been mad cool about all of it. She lets me spend time with Riyah. She answers the phone when I call to talk to her and everything."

"So you got a good baby mama," Mason teased.

"Man, gone with that shit," Silas laughed. "You know my sister don't like you out this late. What you doing over here?"

Mason sucked his teeth. "Here your ass go. I ain't seen you in a couple of weeks. I just came to make sure you weren't holed up over here in the dark with Frank Ocean on repeat."

Silas couldn't stop his laugh. "Fuck you."

"I was half right, anyway," Mason told him with a smirk. "I'm excited to cash out on my niece for Christmas."

"Mila said she didn't want—"

"—aht-aht," Mason cut him off. "I'm spoiling lil baby. You might as well tell her mama that. What time we meeting tomorrow?"

Silas could only shake his head because he knew his brother was serious as hell. "Ma Dukes said lunch, so I'm picking the girls up at ten."

"The girls, huh?"

Silas avoided the question in his brother's gaze. Mason chuckled but dropped it when his phone rang.

"I'm headed home now, love bug. I stopped to make sure my big brother wasn't moping around." Mason mushed his head and got up from the desk.

Silas could only laugh as Mason's voice faded on his way down the hallway. Once the front door closed, he relaxed again, staring at the smiling face of Sariyah in a school picture. He'd missed her first years, but he wouldn't miss any more memories. And that meant not getting entangled in anything with her mother. He just had to convince his panther of that.

eleven

"What time is daddy coming over?"

It was only the tenth time her daughter had asked, but Mila's nerves were shot. Her hands were trembling, and her stomach had been doing flips all damn morning. She was at her wit's end with her baby.

"Riyah, please. He'll get here when he gets here," she said as calmly as she could manage.

She understood Sariyah's excitement, and despite her nervousness, she shared some of that excitement. Mila felt a slight twinge of regret that it wasn't Seth she was calling daddy, but at the same time, she was so glad that her daughter had a father in her life now. As a foster kid, Mila wanted Sariyah to have everything she had not. It was one of the reasons she'd been so eager to help Cameron when she'd come to her and Seth. Though they had been newly married and in no position to take care of a child, she couldn't sit aside and watch another child enter the system.

On top of the fact that Sariyah would be a shifter.

She couldn't imagine what a system that barely cared for humans would do for a shifter child.

"Sit and eat breakfast, and your father will be here soon," Mila tried to coax the anxious seven-year-old.

Throughout breakfast, her daughter's chatter helped control some of her nerves. She'd already met his family when they came to Sariyah's recital last week. But this would be different, on their home turf, as it were. Silas had assured her they would welcome her and Sariyah, but she couldn't help her worry.

Just thinking of Silas brought a flush to her cheeks. She'd spent a couple of sleepless nights reminding herself that she couldn't get involved with Sariyah's father. Not if she wanted their co-parenting situation to work out. She couldn't risk any fallout. As though she'd conjured him with her thoughts, she heard the knock on the door as she was washing their breakfast dishes.

"Daddy's here!" Sariyah shouted, racing down the hallway towards the front door.

Mila beat her there, giving her daughter a stern look. "What did your father tell you about answering the door?"

Sariyah sighed in impatience but didn't answer.

With Silas in their lives now, there were so many new security protocols they had to follow. She straightened the maxi dress she wore before she opened the door and smiled at Silas. He stood on their porch, a stunned look on his face. He blinked at Mila, and his eyes shifted colors for a moment before getting watery.

She frowned in concern. "Are you ok?"

He nodded. "I could hear her through the door. It just took me by surprise."

Sariyah bounced from behind her mother and rushed into his arms. "Hi, daddy!"

He grabbed her and closed his eyes as he inhaled their daughter's scent. "Hi, princess." He set her down after rubbing their cheeks together.

He greeted Sariyah like that all the time. She had to assume it was a shifter thing.

"Do you like my dress?" Sariyah spun in a circle.

She'd dressed her in a long-sleeved denim dress that had a pleated skirt and ruffles along the trim of her chest and arms. It was Sariyah's favorite dress and would stay relatively clean and unwrinkled with the amount of jumping around her daughter was prone to do. She'd braided her curls into two braids, with a couple of tendrils hanging around her face.

"You look beautiful," he assured her. "Are you ready to meet your grandparents?"

"I'm nervous. Mom smells more nervous than me," She informed him, grabbing his hand.

Mila's cheeks flamed, and she sighed. God, she needed the little girl to get a filter. She grabbed her purse and reached for the car seat.

"Quit telling my business, Sariyah Meyers."

Silas chuckled. "I got a booster seat put in the truck for her."

She gave him a surprised but pleased look and put the seat back down before locking the door.

He led them to a shiny new Mercedes G Class SUV. She didn't know if it was new, but she'd never seen him drive it. There was a security guard already in the passenger seat. Mila had seen him with Silas every time he came over.

"Mila, this is Rock, my best friend, and enforcer. Rock, this is Mila and my baby girl Sariyah." Silas introduced.

Rock nodded at them. Mila helped Sariyah into her seat, but Silas buckled her. She got into the back seat next to her daughter and smiled at Silas as he closed her door. He got into the driver's seat, and they were off.

"Do you think my grandparents will like me?" Sariyah whispered.

"Have you met you? They will love you, baby," Mila reassured, running a gentle hand over her hair.

Silas gave her a grateful look in the rearview mirror. Mila leaned back in her seat's soft buttery leather and tried to control her riotous emotions. Silas wore a pair of khaki pants with a black vee neck t-shirt molded to his sculpted chest. She was working hard to keep her breathing under control as his arms muscled flexed as he handled the SUV. At least it took her mind off the upcoming meeting.

When he pulled up to an ornate gate, flanked by hard-eyed security, she couldn't help her eyes widening. The guard checked over the car before they let them through. Butterflies fluttered in her stomach at the reminder of the kind of man she was dealing with. Silas was an important person in the shifter community, his parents even more so. They drove into the driveway of the palatial mansion, and Sariyah oohed.

"This house is ginormous," Sariyah whispered.

Silas pulled up to the front, and Mila saw his parents waiting outside the front door. She took deep breaths as Silas stopped the car and got out. Rock opened her door, and she stepped down onto the cobblestone circular driveway. Silas walked to their side of the vehicle and let Sariyah out.

He walked her over to Mila, and she immediately smoothed out their daughter's hair.

"Your best behavior, madam," she told Sariyah quietly.

Silas grabbed both their hands and walked them up to the front door. Mila laid her free palm across her belly to still the butterflies inside. Hopefully, the day would go well.

***

Silas's panther moved through his body in apprehension. He didn't know why he was nervous. Maybe he was picking up on Mila's anxiety. He gripped her hand tightly as he walked them to his parents. Adina's smile filled her entire face, her eyes already misty. Silas knew he wouldn't last if his mother cried. His father accused him of being a mama's boy, which was actual facts. He loved that lady more than anything else, other than now Sariyah.

He couldn't help the emotion that swamped him.

"Ma, you remember Mila. This is our daughter, Sariyah." He managed to say past the lump in his throat.

The first tear slid down Adina's cheek, and Silas had to look away. His mother lowered herself to Sariyah's level. Though that didn't take much, his daughter was tall, reaching her grandmother's chest already.

"I'm so pleased to meet you, Sariyah. Would it be okay if I hugged you?"

Sariyah nodded, and Silas released her hand as she went into his mother's arms. The hug Adina gave her was tight, and love for his mother overwhelmed Silas. Mila sniffled next to him, and he had to smile. Lord, this would be a mess if they didn't get their emotions under control. Adina stepped back, her face wet but her smile wide and happy.

Dallas stepped up next and kneeled in front of Sariyah. His father didn't ask for a hug. Instead, he placed his forehead against Sariyah's. He growled a deep rumbling that Riyah answered with a small rattle in her chest. Dallas lifted his head, his eyes wet as he put a hand against Sariyah's heart.

"That'll do, lil mama," Dallas whispered.

Silas wiped the tears from his face and sighed, the anger that had filled him for so many years dissipating.

"Come in," Adina said, holding her hand out to Mila.

Mila shot him a surprised and alarmed look before placing her hand in Adina's. "Thank you so much for inviting us."

Dallas lifted Sariyah and Silas walked behind the four of them. The house smelled amazing, and he figured Iris was cooking up a storm. It's what she did when she was anxious. Celine and Mason were standing in the living room when they came out of the foyer. Silas appreciated his brother for waiting inside instead of meeting them at the door. He didn't want to overwhelm Mila or Sariyah.

"Mila, my brother Mason and his mate Celine. Sariyah, this is your aunt and uncle," he told her.

Mason reached down and nuzzled his cheek against Sariyah's. She gripped his shoulders. "You smell almost like my daddy."

Mason laughed, his eyes wet as he straightened. "Your senses are good, princess. You're clearly a Knight."

"Hi, Sariyah," Celine shyly put her hand out.

His daughter gripped her hand and shook, her face smiling. "I've never had an aunt and uncle before."

"Well, you've got us now. That means you got two more riders on your team." Mason said.

Silas couldn't help but laugh at his brother. He loved his family, and whether Mila and Sariyah knew it, they had more than just two more riders.

twelve

Silas had made many adjustments since having Sariyah in his life. It had been two months, and his schedule had wildly changed. He had briefly considered giving up the liaison position altogether. But he loved his job and advocating for shifters across the country. He got great satisfaction seeing the laws he drafted passed throughout the government. His mother had taught him at an early age that caring for their people was a privilege, and he never took it for granted. But he needed steady hours and a way to balance it all.

For now, he was going over to Mila's house to see Sariyah. Mila had allowed him to take Riyah with him outside the house, and the two of them had been all over Eastfield together. But he wanted her able to spend the night at his home, at least weekends to start. So, he needed his schedule to be a lot more consistent than it had been. No more dropping everything and flying to Washington.

Even besides work, his life had changed in the smallest ways. He'd grown closer to Mila as they co-parented Riyah. Mila had been easy-going and accommodating to his family as they visited with Mila. Even without his prodding, she and his mother had spent time together. The only time Mila fought him was when he'd handed her a black card with her name on it. She claimed she could care for their daughter, but he wasn't having it. He was holding back on spoiling his Sariyah as she asked, but he didn't want Mila or Riyah to want for anything.

He sat back in his chair and stretched his arms. He'd been working for hours. Glancing at the clock told him that Sariyah was already home from school. He would call her in a little bit. Today was Thursday, and she had Taekwondo on Thursdays. Her poppa had signed her up for it, so Dallas should be headed to Mila's to pick her up. He smiled when his phone rang with Mila's number.

"What's good?"

"Hi, daddy." Sariyah's voice immediately relaxed him.

"Ya-Ya. How was school?"

"My security brought me home because mama didn't come in time," Sariyah told him.

Silas sat forward. "Is your mother home?"

That was so unlike Mila. She knew how he was about security. He'd given both her and Sariyah a security talk. She would've called him directly before she let security pick up their daughter.

"Mama's home, but she's sick in bed," Sariyah's voice broke a little. "She said she was okay, but she's too weak to get out of bed."

Silas cursed and jumped from his desk. Rock looked up from his spot in Sila's office. He rushed from the office with his friend on his heels.

"I'm on my way, baby. Did mama say how long she's been in bed?"

"She was fine this morning when she dropped me off at school. What should I do, daddy?"

"Just sit tight, princess. I'll be there in a few minutes." He ended the call and cursed, calling up the security guards he had on Riyah.

"Boss?" Ellis answered on the first ring.

"Get inside the house and stay until I get there. Sariyah said her mother's sick, and it doesn't sound right." He ordered.

"On it." Ellis hung up.

"Punch this shit, Rock."

Rocco didn't say anything, but the SUV shot forward as he mashed down on the gas. His panther was on edge and would be that way until he put eyes on Mila. Twenty minutes later, he jumped out of the truck as Rock stopped it in Mila's driveway. Sariyah met him at the door, her eyes wide with worry. He leaned down and nuzzled against her cheek, allowing his panther to reassure and soothe her.

He headed back to Mila's room, seeing her laid on the bed, the blankets up to her ears.

"Mila," he called softly.

She didn't answer. He looked around her room, the bohemian furniture and decorations fitting for her. He spotted an opened box of chocolate candy on her dresser. Instinct led him to it. He lifted it and took a deep inhale, pulling the scent of the candy to him. His chest rumbled as his panther warned him of the contents. He called her name again as he marched to her bed. He reached down and felt her forehead. She was hot to the touch. He called her name again, nervous when she didn't answer. He turned back to the door and spotted Ellis watching.

"We gotta get her to the hospital," he said softly, hoping not to worry Riyah. "Tell Rock."

Ellis nodded and left the room. Silas lifted Mila and carried her from the room.

"Where are we going, daddy?" Sariyah asked, her face pinched in worry.

"We're going to take mama to the doctor to make sure she feels better," he told her. "Grab mama's purse, and let's go."

Riyah didn't waste any time. She followed orders, grabbed her book bag and tablet, and followed her father from the house.

"Lock up," he ordered Ellis.

Rock got out of the car and helped Sariyah inside before jumping back into the driver's seat. Silas was gentle as he sat Mila into the back passenger seat. She moaned but was able to keep her body upright.

"Riyah," Mila whispered.

"I got her," Silas assured her. He got into the passenger seat. "Ride."

Silas was on pins and needles the whole way to the hospital. He kept turning to check on Mila, thankful she was aware enough to grip Sariyah's hand. He texted ahead for the family's healer to meet them there. He was finishing the text to the family group chat when they finally pulled in. Liam met them at the door with a stretcher and two nurses. Silas jumped out and grabbed Mila.

"I think it's poison," he told Liam, handing him the box of chocolates he'd found in her room.

Liam nodded, gently helping him lay Mila down before taking off. "I'll keep you posted," he said over his shoulder as he disappeared inside.

Rock walked around the back of the car with Sariyah in his arms. "I'll park," he said, passing Silas his daughter.

Sariyah gripped his neck tight. "Will mama be okay?"

"I promise," he told her quickly, hoping he wasn't lying to his daughter.

***

"Silas!" Mason called out.

He turned as his brother rushed towards him. He and Sariyah had been in the waiting room for the past half hour waiting to hear from Liam. He breathed out a sigh of relief.

"Pops is ten minutes behind me. He was halfway to your house to pick up Ya-Ya," Mason gripped his shoulders when he reached Silas. "How is she?"

"No word yet," Silas said grimly.

"What do you need from me?"

"I don't want Riyah here waiting." He eyed his daughter. She watched videos on her tablet, but he could feel her anxiety.

"Done. Ya-Ya," Mason called out.

Sariyah looked up and smiled. "Hi, Uncle Mase."

Mason walked over to his niece and scooped her up. "Want to go help Aunt CiCi on her farm?"

"How much will you pay me?" She asked, a mischievous grin on her face.

"That's how you do me, niece?" Mason dropped kisses across her face.

She giggled, mushing his face away. Mason grabbed her backpack and tightened his hold on her.

Silas was thankful for his brother. He brushed a hand across Riyah's head. "I'll come get you as soon as mom's done, okay?"

She nodded, her eyes sobering.

"Behave for TiTi Celine," he told her.

"What about Uncle Mason?" She nuzzled Sila's cheek.

"Give him hell."

Sariyah and Mason laughed, with his brother lifting his middle finger on his way out the door. His smile dropped the moment they left the waiting room. He wiped a hand down his face and resumed his pacing. Liam came in minutes later, his face clear.

"I'm having tests ran to see what she ingested, but we pumped her stomach and got her blood pressure stabled. I wish you had taken her to our hospital, but I understand this one was closer."

"Would you be able to treat her differently there?" Silas worried that he should've driven the distance to the Motsi hospital.

"I have more permissions there. I'm going to suggest a night here for observation, and then you should be able to take her home tomorrow. She's human, so I can't heal her like I would one of us." Liam gave him an apologetic look.

"If someone targeted her, I'm not comfortable leaving her here."

Liam hummed and furrowed his brows. "I'll release her tonight, then. But you'll need to watch her closely to make sure she's not feeling any other ill effects."

"Thank you, Liam. Which room?"

"Follow me."

Silas followed Liam through the hospital and could see what the healer meant. Most of the staff was human. He walked into Mila's room, and his panther settled with his eyes finally on her. She was awake if a little groggy. He rushed to her bedside.

"How you feeling?"

"My throat hurts," she whispered. "Where's Riyah?"

"Probably eating her aunt and uncle out of house and home by now. I'll go get her once I have you settled." He promised.

"What happened?" She looked around the hospital room.

"You ingested poison. From what I could tell, it's from the chocolates you ate."

She winced. "I got them in a delivery. I thought they were from you." Her voice was hoarse, weak.

He frowned. "That cheap ass shit."

She chuckled, but it turned into a groan as she put a hand up to her throat. "I don't know where they came from then. There was no card."

"What type of enemies you got, Mila? And why would you eat anything that didn't have a card? Do we need to have the security talk again?" Anger welled in him that she'd been targeted.

She held up a hand. "Please, not the security talk."

"The doctor is going to release you to me. You and Riyah will stay at the house." he tried to keep his excitement at that out of his voice.

It wasn't the most ideal situation, but he had to admit that having his daughter and Mila at his home gave him a fierce sense of satisfaction.

thirteen

Three days.

After three days in Silas' house, Mila was ready to climb out of her skin. She could handle Silas in small bursts when he visited her daughter. His presence would always take up her house, but she could calm herself when he left—being in his house, amid all his things and where he felt comfortable...whew. The first time she'd seen him in a simple pair of shorts and a t-shirt, she thought her body would self-combust. The man was fine, and if she didn't leave his house, she was liable to jump on him.

Every time he swaggered past her, his cologne following him in a trail of forbidden temptation, Mila prayed a little harder.

On the other hand, Sariyah was having the time of her life. Her father had already had a room prepared for her. It was larger than her bedroom at home and filled with everything a little girl could desire. Her daughter had squealed with glee when her uncle dropped her off the other day.

Mila put on a simple cotton short set that she wore around her house to be comfortable. She had already showered and put on a light bit of makeup, leaving her hair loose around her head. She'd washed it and left the curls out to air dry. She was determined to at least leave Silas's guest room today. He'd taken the doctor's advice for her to get rest to heart. He'd barely let her lift a finger in the time that they'd been at his house.

That ended today.

She marched down the stairs of his modern home and straight to his home office where he had been working. Except, she didn't find him there. Frowning, she headed towards the kitchen and the back patio doors. Silas and Riyah spent a lot of time outdoors together. Silas had a huge pool and enough property for their daughter to run out the over-abundance of energy she seemed to have. Mila's guess was correct, but she sucked in a surprised breath when she saw them. Silas was in his panther form, and Riyah was leaning against his body, reading a book.

Her heart thundered, and tears filled her eyes at the sight. She could hear her daughter's voice as Sariyah read aloud, her hands rubbing her father's fur. In a thousand years, Mila never thought she would see a sight like the one she was observing. Both Riyah and the panther looked comfortable, and even from her spot at the doors, she could feel the burgeoning bond between father and daughter. Every day Silas showed her how right her decision to cooperate had been. He was an amazing father.

It would be so easy if they could just leave it at that.

But, unfortunately for her, her feelings were getting involved. But honestly, how could they not? Watching this man move his whole life around to make a place in his life for her daughter was endearing. His family wasn't making it any easier. Regardless of how they came into these folks' lives, the Knights had taken Sariyah in without hesitation and, by extension her. She thought that they would make it hard for her and demand she give Sariyah over to them, but they'd respected her place as her mother. To be honest, she was waiting for the other shoe to drop.

Everything was going so well. It was hard not to brace for the bad.

Seemingly aware of her, Silas lifted his head and caught her gaze. Caught staring, she opened the doors and headed towards them.

"How long have you two been out here?" She asked her daughter.

Sariyah shrugged. "A while. Daddy let me wrestle with him."

She rolled her eyes, thanking God that she hadn't witnessed it. It likely would've given her a heart attack to see her daughter wrestling with the large cat, despite the fact that she knew it wasn't technically a wild animal.

"Go inside and wash up. I'm going to order pizza for lunch."

Silas watched her from within his panther. How she knew the difference, she couldn't tell, but she did. As Sariyah got up to do as she'd ordered, his eyes watched Mila. She resisted the urge to run her hands through his fur and pet him the way Riyah had. She hadn't earned that privilege and didn't know how his animal would react.

"We need to talk, Silas." Her chest thumped with the speed of her racing pulse when the animal moved closer.

He rubbed his fur against her leg, his head sliding up her thigh. He was huge, his head reaching her chest once he'd straightened. She swallowed as their eyes met again. This time, the emerald irises that studied her were one hundred percent feral animal. She froze, unsure of how it would react. She didn't know how long they stood that way, the tense silence making her ears ring, but she dropped her head, unable to hold his gaze any longer.

That seemed to satisfy him because he padded towards the back patio and the pile of clothes she hadn't noticed on the lounge chair next to the pool. Right before her eyes, he shifted. She gasped and turned her back to him as she realized he was fully naked. There was no way she could hide her reaction to his naked body. He'd been lean and cut, his brown skin covered in tattoos along his back. She wanted to lick across every one of them. She fanned her face and waited a few moments before she turned. Silas was in shorts, but he'd forgone his t-shirt. He stood next to the pool and smirked at her.

Her cheeks flamed.

"You wanted to talk?" His voice was gravelly, deep, as though he hadn't used it in a few hours.

She cleared her throat and cautiously closed the distance between them. "Yeah, I think it's time for us to go home."

His face fell, and guilt thrummed through her.

"I have work, and Riyah has school in the morning. It's easier to navigate all that from the house." she hurriedly explained.

He sighed and wiped a hand down his face. "My team hasn't been able to find out who sent those chocolates to you."

A chill went down her spine. She had been blocking that out of her mind for the two days she'd been in his house. But his words brought it back to the forefront.

"It could be a mistake. The wrong address or person." She didn't want to think she was in danger.

Her only enemies didn't even know where she was, so it couldn't be them. Besides, they had been trying to keep Silas and Riyah apart. That point was moot now.

"I'll be careful, Silas. I swear. No more eating suspiciously delicious gifts."

He shook his head, his lips lifting into a smile reluctantly. "I got Jules to assign a guard to you."

"Who is Jules?" She frowned.

"He runs the security firm my family uses."

"I don't leave home except to pick up Riyah. A guard on me would be a waste of time and your money." She argued.

"It's my money to waste," he told her, stepping closer. "You're just as important to me as Ya-Ya."

She rolled her eyes at the nickname he and his brother had taken to calling their daughter. "You've already put a security system in place. I'll be fine."

His eyes roved her face. Silence fell between them, and she held her breath. Silas leaned over and rubbed his cheek against her neck. He kept his arms at his side, and Mila was happy because her legs barely supported her as is. There was no telling what she would do if he held her. His scent seemed to surround her. It lulled her, her body damn near melting at his feet. His beard scraped against her skin, and she shuddered.

"I'll let you have it this time." He lifted his head and gripped her chin. "I don't like how you tell me no all the time, though."

Mila blinked, afraid to open her mouth. She didn't know whether a moan would fall out or a plea for him to take her clothes off, so she said nothing. As always, he seemed to read her mind. He smirked and pecked her lips lightly.

"Your eyes finna get you in trouble, Mila," he said softly as he released her.

She could only stand there as he walked back towards the house. She needed a minute to remember how to use her legs.

fourteen

Mila had a problem.

Now she had to figure out how to deal with it. At least in a way that would cause the least amount of drama. The Robinsons had found them, and according to the note left on her front porch, they weren't going anywhere. Sariyah's security guard had spotted it when they'd pulled up, forcing Mila and Riyah to stay in the car while he looked it over. Deeming it not dangerous, he'd handed over the white envelope.

Her hands shook as she sipped out of her wine glass and stared at the hastily scrawled letter on her kitchen counter. She thought hiding in plain sight was the better move, but she'd clearly miscalculated. She sighed and pulled out her phone. Helen answered on the first ring.

"We have a problem."

"The royal 'we' or me and you specifically?" Helen asked.

"The Robinsons found us."

Helen cursed. "What did they say?"

"The cowards left a note on my porch. They claim they can invalidate Sariyah's birth certificate. They want custody of her."

"Well..." Helen sighed. "You're a human, and now that the Knights have proven that Sariyah is Silas' it means she's a shifter."

Her stomach dropped, and she put her wine glass on the table. "What does that mean, Helen?"

"Silas Knight is very, very good at his job. There are a whole host of laws in place that prevent humans from taking shifters from their families and raising them. The Robinsons can lean on those laws."

Mila felt sick. "What do I do?"

"Silas will never let the Robinsons get ahold of Sariyah, so there is that. But, if they invalidate the birth certificate, they could remove her from your custody and into the system while they determine who gets to keep her full-time."

No.

She couldn't lose her daughter, not after everything she'd done to keep that from happening. She didn't believe Silas would take Sariyah from her, but did she want to risk it?

"What are they asking you for now?" Helen cut into her thoughts.

"Someone named Leland wants to meet with me. He says we can discuss it. Do you think I should?"

Helen hummed on her end. A few beats of silence passed before she sighed. "What could it hurt?"

The Robinsons were unpredictable. It was one of the reasons she and Seth had moved so much. Cameron's family wanted her daughter, and they'd gone to great lengths to make it happen. Even going so far as to have her and Seth fired every time they found them. They wanted Mila and Seth at their lowest, so giving up Sariyah seemed the more reasonable option. They would get her baby over her dead body.

"Fine, I'll meet with them."

"Turn on your location so I can track you, and call me the minute you're done," Helen demanded.

Mila readily agreed. She would meet him, but she wasn't going in stupid.

***

Ten minutes into the meeting and Mila knew she had made a mistake. Leland sat across from her, his smug handsomeness making her sick to her stomach. What made it worse was how much he favored her late husband. It was disconcerting looking into that face and listening to the threats spewing from his mouth. If this man was a representative of the family, no wonder Seth and his mother had parted ways with the Robinsons.

Leland looked and talked like a slick car salesman. His fit body and stiff Botox-laden face gave her eerie hustle vibes, and with his every assurance of the family's good intentions, she knew he was lying. It didn't help that he seemed paranoid, his gaze bouncing around the restaurant as though he was expecting someone to jump out.

"Why do you want custody of my daughter?" She cut through his bullshit.

His face didn't even shift, though she read the surprise in his eyes. "Samantha wants the part of her daughter that she lost. Sariyah is her only link to her dead daughter. Wouldn't you want to see your grandchild?"

"Samantha doesn't want visits with *my* daughter, she wants custody, and I want to know why." Mila crossed her arms over her chest.

Leland's eyes dropped to her chest before returning to her face. "You claim to worry about the girl's safety, yet you allow Silas Knight to see her."

She forced herself still, not wanting to give him the reaction he was so obviously seeking.

"You should ask the Knights about what happened to your husband." Leland dropped.

"Excuse you?" Ice slid down her spine, melted quickly by the anger that suffused her body.

It wasn't his first time insinuating that the Knights were dangerous. This one just hit a little too close to home.

He opened his mouth to answer, but his eyes widened, and his body stiffened. The hair on the back of her neck stood at attention. This time it was Mila who looked around in paranoia. Sure enough, she spotted Silas and Rock headed their way. Silas was angry, and his stride was determined as he approached them.

"Let's go, Mila." His gaze wasn't on her, though.

She looked between Leland and Silas. "Silas."

"Now, Mila," he said, cutting her off. "Rock, take her to the car."

She had never heard that tone in his voice before. She hastily stood as he ordered, following Rock out of the restaurant. She looked back and saw Silas talking to Leland. She reached the valet station and paused.

"I drove."

"Silas'll handle it," Rock said with his rough voice.

She shuddered. She didn't know why this man didn't scare her daughter, but Riyah loved Rock, so she would trust that.

"What do...?"

He gave her a look that closed her mouth. She sighed and got into the back seat of the Jag. Silas slid into the car next to her moments later.

"Ride, Rock."

She could tell he was angry. "What was that about?"

"For one, I told you about moving around without security."

She swallowed. "I didn't think—"

"I'm glad you acknowledge that," he said, cutting her off.

Now, wait a damn minute.

"I don't know why you got an attitude with me."

Between his anger and the things Leland had implied, she was flustered and couldn't get her thoughts together. She put aside his anger, turned to him, and asked him the most pressing question Leland had raised.

"Did you have my husband killed?"

He stiffened next to her. "How do you know Leland?"

She blinked in confusion and swallowed a frustrated growl. "What?"

"How do you know him?"

"I don't know him. He contacted me on behalf of the Robinsons. He's one of Seth's cousins." she ran a shaking hand over her hair. "Did you have Seth killed?"

"A cousin," he said softly to himself. "I didn't know your husband," he said louder to her. "I'm not in the habit of killing people I don't know."

Rock snorted in the front seat, and it caught her attention.

"Is that what that pussy told you?"

She stiffened. "He strongly implied it."

"How did your husband die?" Silas asked.

She turned her head towards the window at first, not answering. Leland brought it up carelessly as though her husband's death had been some simple chess move and not something that had devastated her for years. She hated talking about it, and she certainly didn't want to cry about it. She shook her head at her glassy-eyed reflection.

Her throat was tight when she turned her gaze back to Silas. "It was a convenience store robbery. The thing is, the robber didn't take anything. He shot Seth and left the store." She hastily wiped the falling tear from her face.

He touched her chin and turned her head to him. "I'm a lot of shit, Mila. But a pussy I ain't never been. I would never do no coward shit like that. Every motherfucker I been after has known who came after them."

None of those words should make her feel as horny as they did. Her stomach clenched, and moisture gathered at the apex of her thighs. Desperate, fervent yearning set her body ablaze. She closed her legs tightly, sucking in a sharp breath. She believed every word of what he said.

She couldn't help the small smile that tilted her lips. "Silas, is that supposed to reassure me?"

He leaned down and gave her a soft kiss on her lips. "Ain't no sense in me lying to you. You need to know what kind of man you're stuck with."

Stuck with?

She somehow knew he wasn't talking about just their co-parenting. She refused to let her foolish heart skip a beat over his words.

"Silas," she warned softly.

He kissed her again, a hard peck on her lips.

"You need to send someone to get my car," she muttered and changed the subject. She turned her head back towards the window.

Lord have mercy. She was fucked.

fifteen

Silas shook his head and settled his panther as Rock drove them toward Mila's house. He thought his words would've scared some sense into her, but he didn't sense any fear from her, just residual anger and grief. He couldn't imagine talking about her husband's death was pleasant.

He could also sense her annoyance underneath all that. That was alright; he anticipated them butting heads often. Her lil fine ass was stubborn as hell. He sighed and shed his own anger. He could admit that part of his anger stemmed from his jealousy from seeing Mila out with another man. He knew he didn't have rights to her, but that didn't stop the rage that had consumed his body when he saw her.

Luckily for him, Ellis had given him a heads up on the envelope she had received and the meeting she'd rushed out of the house for. He'd been leaving the restaurant to go looking for her when he spotted them. It had taken him a moment to remember that Ellis said it wasn't a date. Not that it dimmed his anger any.

He should've put security on her despite her protests, especially if she continued to move recklessly.

"What else did he say to you?"

"I don't want to talk about it," she muttered, laying her forehead on the window's glass.

He dropped it for now because he knew he would get it out of her one way or the other.

"Where's my baby while you out gallivanting with goofy?"

She rolled her eyes. He saw it in the dark glass of her window.

"Helen has her," she told him. "What did you say to him?"

"Him who," he played dumb.

"Yeah, okay," she muttered.

"What's your relationship like with the Robinsons?"

"I don't have a relationship with them. They have been trying to get us to give Sariyah back to them since they found out Cameron gave her to us. When Seth died, their attempts became less about persuasion to outright bullying."

"Have they threatened you?" His panther bucked at the thought.

She shrugged. "Depends on your definition."

She didn't elaborate, so Silas dropped it. He got out of the car once Rock pulled up to the house. He opened Mila's door and nodded towards the vehicle pulling into her driveway.

"Your car," he told her.

"You better be glad." She raked a look over him that had him on brick.

He had to smile because her attitude was something he very much enjoyed. Instead of going to her front door, she walked next door. He followed her, and she turned to him and sighed.

He smirked at her, "I know you didn't think I was just going to drop you off and not see my baby."

"I don't know what I was thinking," she muttered sarcastically.

He nodded at the security that watched Mila's house. They'd switched to Helen's house, and he appreciated their efficiency. She knocked on the door, and Helen's husband answered.

Scott dapped Silas and let them in. "She literally just fell asleep."

Mila sighed. "Lord, she gon' be so heavy."

He sucked his teeth. "I got her."

He followed Scott upstairs and smiled as he saw Riyah in the top bunk of her best friend's room. Riyah talked about Emily enough for him to feel as though he knew the kid. He sighed at how beautiful his daughter was. No matter that she'd been back in their lives for nearly two months. It took his breath away every time he saw her. He wanted her in his home, under his protection. He lifted her, and her head came up.

"Daddy," she said softly, squeezing his neck.

"Bedtime, princess."

"You went to dinner with mama?" She was never too tired to be nosy.

He smiled. "No, we just happened to be eating at the same restaurant."

She hummed and went back to sleep. Silas carried her down the stairs, thanking Scott and Helen. He walked her over to Mila's house and down the hall to her bedroom. He tucked her in bed, and she kissed him before rolling over and going back to sleep. His heart stuttered. He walked back to the living room. Mila had taken off her shoes and was taking her hair out of the bun.

His dick hardened when she shook out the straightened hair. It reached her shoulders. He wanted to tug on it as he was fucking her. He licked his lips and stepped towards her. They had more pressing matters to deal with at the moment.

"I don't want you anywhere near Leland or the Robinsons."

She frowned. "Trust me. I would never purposely seek out the Robinsons."

"All the same."

She nodded.

He tilted his head. "No argument."

"I'm tired as hell, Silas. Good night. We can discuss this in the morning when you come to get your daughter."

He walked her back to the wall. She stared up at him, and he down at her. His eyes traced her face taking in her beautiful features.

"You gon' get enough of talking to me like that," he murmured, gripping her chin.

She sucked her teeth. "Your family may run this city, Silas, but you don't run shit here."

The pulse point at her neck thundered beneath his thumb, and he chuckled at her fake bravado. He leaned down, hovering over her lips, their breath mingling.

"Tell your body that, lil mama, because she calling you a liar." He kissed her. "You better behave."

"I'm always good," she whispered.

Lord have mercy. He was going to fuck the shit out of her the first chance she gave him.

***

Silas rechecked the time and sighed loudly. His daughter was probably up and packed, ready to come with him for the weekend. It was their first weekend together, and he was excited. He could well imagine her impatient ass bugging her mother about when he would arrive. Silas released a growl. Riyah had come by that impatience naturally.

He could admit that he wasn't in the best mood. He'd gone to bed horny as hell, thinking about Mila. He wanted her, and his panther was fully on board, pushing him toward her. He'd been in Julian's home office since dawn, waking his friend up for information on Leland Robinson.

Mila had no business meeting that jackass, and Silas wanted to know all he could about the man before he approached her again. He didn't believe Leland would heed the warning he'd given him last night.

Julian looked up from his computer and smirked. "Don't come in here rushing me. I told you I'd send the shit over when I found it."

"How long it take to get information?"

"You don't just want information, Si. You want all the dirt I can find and anything that will give you leverage. That takes time." Julian said calmly.

Silas stood and stretched. "Fine, I gotta go get my baby."

Julian smiled at him. "How is that going?"

"We're getting along. All of us."

"Mason said her mama fine as hell. How is that working out for you?" Julian didn't hide his smile.

Silas cursed. "You and Mason's messy asses talk too much. Send me that information as soon as you get it."

He turned his back on Julian's laughter and headed out the door. Rock was laid out on Julian's sofa, his eyes closed, though he wasn't sleeping. He got up immediately without a word and headed for the door. But then, Rock didn't use a lot of words.

Thankfully Saturday morning traffic was light, so they were at Mila's house in under half an hour. He smiled at the Halloween decorations she'd already put up. They hadn't been up last night. His foot hit the front porch when he heard his daughter announce his arrival. His heart thumped hard as love filled him. He would never get used to her calling him daddy. The front door opened to her smiling face.

"Hi, daddy!" Riyah jumped into his arms.

He hugged her tight, breathing in her scent. "Hey, princess."

Sariyah slid down his body. "I'm already packed and ready. Hi, Uncle Rock!" She moved around him to speak to his best friend.

Rock lifted her and walked her back to the car. Riyah would chat the quiet enforcer's ear off, giving him time to deal with her mother. He stepped into the house and closed the door behind him. He found Mila in the living room on the floor, picking up trash from the Halloween decorations that they'd clearly just taken out of the box. She looked up as he loomed over her.

"It was the only way to keep her from asking me every five minutes where her daddy was," she said, shaking her head.

"We need to talk about last night," he told her.

She tilted her head and studied his face before pushing off the floor to stand. "Okay."

All the feelings from last night bubbled up as her scent reached him. The panther wanted her with him. Yes, he wanted his daughter, but he also wanted her mother. Something about Mila called to him. But they had Sariyah between them, making it all hard. He didn't want anything to interrupt his relationship with his daughter. His panther was talking forever, so he didn't think it could go wrong, but it was hard to call.

"I don't want you meeting with any of the Robinsons anymore."

"Like I said last night, I have no intentions of getting buddy-buddy with the Robinsons. And you finna get on my nerves with all these orders." She crossed her arms over her chest.

He took a deep breath and worked to corral his temper because this woman stayed trying him. "My family got a lot of history with them. It's not safe."

She snorted. "I've been taking care of my daughter for seven years. I don't need to be told how to keep her safe."

The growl that rumbled his chest was entirely his panther. "Our, Mila. You gon' get that shit straight right now—we talking about our kid. And ain't shit about Sariyah that I'ma take lightly. That means meeting with the Robinsons is dead. I don't give a fuck what they promise you to lure you out. We clear on that?"

"Silas," she sighed.

"We clear or not, Mila?"

"We're clear."

He took a deep breath. "They took her from me once before. A second time ain't gon' happen. Nobody coming out of that alive, including me," he finished softly.

He hated that he'd admitted that, but he needed her to understand that when it came to their daughter, he had no patience and would take no chances. His panther was riding him, even the thought of a threat to Riyah setting the animal on edge. He took a deep breath, fighting to control it.

She nodded. "I'm sorry, Silas. It won't happen again."

Her gaze roamed his face, and he knew she could see the animal in his eyes, but there was no help for it. Between the need for Mila stealing his sleep and worry over his daughter, he was finding control elusive.

sixteen

His chest was moving up and down hard as he suppressed his cat. Mila wanted to go to him, to soothe his anger, but she wasn't...they weren't...She didn't have any rights where Silas was concerned. No matter that, she went to bed thinking of him every night. Or that she spent her mornings wishing she was with him. None of that wishful thinking gave her rights to him.

"Let's talk about what you were hiding from me last night."

She couldn't control the spike of fear that sped her heartbeat. She'd hidden most of what Leland had told her from Silas last night, but it didn't look like he had forgotten it.

"I wasn't hiding it, per se. I didn't want to talk about it. And frankly, Riyah is probably in the car driving Rock crazy. We can talk about it later."

She tried, but nothing in her dealings with Silas told her he would drop it. She sat down in the chair in her living room, her knee bouncing.

"Now you know by now that I don't like repeating myself, Mila. What did he say?"

That deep growly voice set off pings of arousal all through her bloodstream. It was highly inconvenient. Especially for the conversation they needed to have.

She sighed. "It's not just what he said, but what he threatened. He said they would invalidate Riyah's birth certificate and claim fraud. According to Helen, there are laws in place about humans taking shifter babies, even by legal adoption. He threatened to have Riyah taken from here until the courts could figure it out." She admitted.

God, please don't let him take her baby. Her eyes burned, but she refused to shed a tear. She wouldn't want him to think she was manipulating him. He sat across from her and stared.

"Marry me...no," he shook his head. "We'd have to mate," he muttered more to himself.

"Silas, do you hear yourself?"

"You're the only mother Sariyah knows, and I'm her father. If we're mated, ain't shit they can do to take her from us."

She stopped her leg. She was intrigued by him, but then she always had been. From the very first moment she'd seen him on TV. But mating? Did she even know how to do that? Was it possible for them to mate? She was human. Would his panther accept her? His people? Silas was a prominent figure in the shifter community.

"Say something," he said softly.

That hint of vulnerability that softened his eyes; she'd never seen that look on him before.

Her heart thundered. "I'll do anything to keep, Riyah, but are you sure? You have every advantage here."

He licked his lips and looked away. "Mating wasn't really a priority for me," he said after a long moment. "This shit with Riyah had me up at night. I couldn't think about anything but finding her. But, from the moment we met...I don't know, Mila, you don't feel this between us?"

"It could make it all so messy, Silas," she told him, worry and hope warring within her chest.

"I don't do anything by half measure, so if we do this, we all the way in it. I already see what type of time they finna be on, and I don't want to fight them and you."

She nodded because she could perfectly understand that sentiment. "What would I need to do?"

He smiled, and her stomach dipped. He was dangerous to her in a lot of ways, and yet, she was all in for it.

"Just fuck with ya' boy," he said.

He stood, and she did the same. The tension that was already in the room ratcheted up until Mila had a hard time catching her breath. Silas stepped closer to her until barely a hair's breadth separated them. He lifted her chin with one finger, his eyes molten.

He licked his lips. "That means you'll be mine, Mila."

What could she say to that? Instead of trying to find words, Mila went up on her toes and kissed him. Silas let her control the kiss at first, his full lips passive as she sealed their mouths together. It wasn't until she licked across his bottom lip that he'd taken over. He opened his mouth and sucked her tongue inside. Any chance Mila had to resist him was gone as he devoured her mouth. Their tongues dueled, and she was swept into a maelstrom of sensations as Silas took over her every thought. She wrapped her arms around his neck and leaned into him, moaning once her nipples brushed his chest.

Silas pulled back, and Mila was thankful he had his arms around her waist because it was the only thing holding her up.

"Go pack a bag," he demanded.

He nipped her bottom lip, licking across it to soothe the sharp pain. It took her a moment to come to her senses.

"A bag for what?"

"What part of 'all the way' did you misunderstand, shawty?" he buried his head into the crook of her shoulder.

He scraped his teeth along her skin, and her clit jumped.

"Better hurry up because you know how impatient my baby is." The arrogant smile that tilted his lips should've aggravated her.

Instead, she rushed from the living room to do as he said. She whipped out her phone the second she got into her bedroom. Helen answered quickly, her face bunched in concern.

"Silas's car is still in your driveway. What's going on?" Helen asked.

"Your nosy ass." Mila laughed.

"I'm just looking out for my friend. You're welcome."

Mila sighed. "Girl."

"Oh shit, do I need to come over?"

"No, I'm headed to spend the weekend at Silas's house," Mila told her.

Helen rolled her eyes. "I thought you were giving them time alone."

"So, Silas asked me to marry him." She dropped the bomb and held her breath.

Helen's eyes widened. "Biiiiiitch. When?"

"Just now. I told him about the threats from the Robinsons, and he says that mating will keep Sariyah out of their hands."

"Wait," Helen held up a hand. "Did he say marry or mate?"

"Semantics."

"Semantics hell, bitch. There is a clear difference between the two. Which did he say?" Helen's face was serious.

Mila's stomach fluttered. Should she be worried? "Mating."

"Oh.my.God."

The background on Helen's screen blurred as she took off. She passed the pictures lining her stairs, stopping with a huff at the foot of her bed. Her husband, Scott, was there, watching TV.

"Scott! Silas is going to mate with Mila," Helen said, breathing hard.

"What?" Scott sat forward.

"Should I be worried over here?" She cut into their conversation.

"Hell nah," Scott reassured her. "Silas good people. It's just that..." he looked to his wife for help.

"Just that?" She leaned closer to the phone.

"Nothing. This is a good thing. I'm very excited for you, friend," Helen hastily added.

That felt suspicious as hell, but she didn't have time to question her friend. "You're my lawyer, Helen. What's the move here?"

"He's rich as hell, good-looking —"

"—not too much!" Scott cut in.

Helen rolled her eyes. "He's clearly determined to be in your daughter's life. It's not a bad way to start a marriage. Plus, honestly, it would solve the issue with the Robinsons and him quickly, cleanly."

Mila chewed her bottom lip and nodded. She was thankful for that breakdown because it reinforced her decision. She was doing what was best for her and her daughter; bonus, she really wanted to be with Silas. It was a win for them all.

seventeen

Silas wiped a hand down his face as he came down the stairs. He'd finally convinced his daughter to take a bath. She was still on ten and asking her father to play with her. He was beat. But in the best way. Even though he'd brought Mila with them, she'd let him have his alone time with Riyah. They'd spent their day traipsing across art galleries in Eastfield. He loved discovering more about Riyah and what she liked. His baby loved art, and so she'd had a great time.

Now that he had his daughter taken care of, he could focus on this mating situation. He didn't know who was more surprised when the words had come out of his mouth, him or Mila. But, once he'd said them, his panther had settled in relief, and Silas realized the animal had been trying to get him to see the signs since he'd first laid eyes on Mila. He and Riyah had stopped off at his parents' house so he could ask them how that worked with a human. He needed to tell Mila what would happen. It wasn't something the shifters advertised, so he was sure she would be shocked.

He found her in the kitchen, prepping dinner. He smiled because his big ass kitchen had seen next to no action. His mother and Iris had taught him and Mason to cook, but with his schedule, he didn't even bother. Luckily for him, the person he'd gotten to decorate the place had thought ahead to stock the kitchen with essential appliances. He watched her work, fascinated with how beautiful she was. Her hair was braided down into two braids, leaving her face open to his perusal. Her brows were furrowed in concentration, her full lips pursed as she sliced vegetables. He desperately wanted to feel those thick lips against his.

She was in another dress, one of those soft cotton ones he noticed she liked to wear around her house. He flexed his fingers, the urge to touch her filling him. He adjusted his dick in his pants and entered the kitchen.

He cleared his throat. "Finally got Ya-ya in the shower."

She smiled but continued chopping. "Did you enjoy your day?"

"I did." He sat across from her on the island and watched her work.

"I can feel you staring," she murmured, a whimsical smile on her face.

"Can you tell me why you and Seth never mated?"

She looked surprised and then uncomfortable. "I loved him, and we were married quickly. I wanted security and had never really had a home. Seth gave me that."

"But he never offered to mate with you?"

"Why is that such a sticking point? Does it make that much of a difference?" She asked, exasperated.

Silas frowned. "Yes. As my mate, you'll be transformed into a shifter."

She gasped in surprise and looked up, giving him her full attention.

"He didn't tell you that."

"I... no, he never said a word." She admitted. "He didn't really talk about his animal at all."

Curious, but not his business. Silas counted it as Seth's loss and his gain. That did answer one of his more pressing questions about Mila. He wondered why she'd stayed human, but her late husband hadn't even given her the option of becoming a shifter. It could possibly change her answer to Silas, but he sensed the strength in her. He didn't think she'd back out of their mating from fear, especially with Sariyah's well-being on the line.

Was that selfish of him? To use her desperation? His instincts told him she felt something for him, or she wouldn't have agreed to mate.

Mila never had a problem telling Silas no.

She continued chopping her vegetables, so he thought she would drop the subject, but she stopped cutting. "So you would change me into a shifter?"

He nodded. "Will that be an issue?"

She shook her head quickly. "It will certainly knock out one of my worries. Does it hurt?"

"I don't know. It's not something that's widely talked about. We rarely mate with humans."

She nodded and went back to prepping food. "Christmas is coming up. Are your parents excited about their first holiday with Riyah?"

He let her change the subject. He imagined going from a human to a shifter was a lot to process, so he would give her that time.

"You don't even know the half. To give you a heads up, you might want to put that black card I gave you to some use."

"I'm not broke. I can do for my...our daughter." She huffed as she dumped the chicken she'd chopped into a waiting wok.

He shook his head because this woman stayed trying him. "I didn't say you were, ma. I want to do for my daughter in a way that doesn't step on your toes."

"What does that mean?" She washed her hands before turning back to him.

"She's the first grandkid. Dallas and Adina finna show their ass. I just want you to be able to match energy so you won't feel no type of way."

Plus, he already knew how his brother was coming. It would be shocking if the tree could fit all the presents underneath it. He was still debating what he wanted to get Riyah. He wanted it to be unique for their first Christmas together. He wanted something a little more thoughtful than just toys.

"Duly noted," she said dryly.

She turned to him and braced her hands on the counter between them. "Can you...I don't want to pry, but all of this is so confusing to me. How did you lose her, Sariyah, I mean?"

He sighed and felt heated anger mixed with embarrassment. "Cameron and I were supposed to marry. It was a way to kind of solidify my father's position. He was still getting a lot of shit about how he'd gained it. He'd defeated Cameron's father in the duel, and he thought a marriage merger between the families would settle the Motsi members. Cameron and I messed around. I mean, we...the lust was there. We were going to get married anyway, so..." He shrugged. "Last minute, her brother makes a play for my dad's position. Pops put him down, her mother took Cameron, and they left town."

"And you didn't know anything until you got the letter?"

He nodded, his panther filling him. He needed to run, or he would soon be a ball of horny anger. Mila opened her mouth to ask another question, but Sariyah's loud footsteps could be heard on the stairs. They could talk later when their daughter went to bed.

***

Silas took another deep breath as he stepped out of the shower. He'd been wrestling with his panther since his conversation with Mila. For a person who had no interest in mating, he and his panther sure were impatient. He'd run around the property for a while to burn off energy and anticipation, trying to steal his control. Still, his panther filled his body with power. He wrapped a towel around his waist and left the bathroom, pausing when he noticed Mila standing at the open door of his bedroom.

Her nervousness was apparent. The tension and attraction between them couldn't be denied. He wanted her and had from the first look at her. He'd never been one to beat around the bush, so he sat on the bench in front of his bed and beckoned her forward. She came with tentative steps. He pulled her down so that she was straddling him.

"I know the bold woman who been talking shit to me not finna act shy?"

Her lips twitched as she tried to fight a smile. "This is a big deal, Silas."

"I'm not saying it's not, Mila, but I'm gon' be honest. I can't even get to the logistics past this overwhelming need I feel for you." He skimmed his hands up and down her back.

Her breath caught, and her hands drifted up into his hair. His panther damn near purred at the touch. He rubbed their cheeks together to mark her with his scent.

"I don't know what to do," she whispered.

He chuckled but continued to nuzzle against her. "I can show you all that, ma."

She snorted and hit his shoulder. "That's not what I meant. Are you sure you want to do this?"

He pulled back and looked into her eyes, seeing the worry. "I may have been distracted with getting to know our daughter, but my panther has been on this path from the first moment. I'm sure."

She let out a relieved breath. "This attraction I have for you is so different than anything I've ever felt. I wasn't sure..." she sighed. "It feels so big."

He nodded. He could well understand that. He gripped her chin between his fingers, "the security you need, the love you crave; I can give you all that shit, Mila. Just give me your heart and let me worry about everything else."

Her body shuddered on top of his, her eyes heating. The scent of her arousal rose between them, and she bit her lip. A mischievous glint lit her eyes.

She wiggled her body. "I want all that, but I also need you to back up all the shit you've been promising me in these whore pants you're wearing."

He laughed, the tension easing. "Oh, don't worry, I'm finna fuck you six ways to Sunday. If you can walk in the morning, then we'll start over."

He stood and lifted her, turning towards the bed. He laid her on it gently, his eyes raking over her form. She wore a simple silky gown and nothing else. Her nipples beaded beneath the fabric making his mouth water. He reached down and pulled up the hem, hissing as more of her gorgeous brown skin was revealed.

"Fuck, Mila," he whispered, going to his knees.

He parted her legs and licked his lips. He was starved for a taste of her. He kissed his way up her thigh, sucking on the skin to leave his marks as he headed straight for her wet center. Her hands tangled in his hair, tugging him faster towards his destination. He allowed it, just as needy as she was.

From his first taste of her, Silas knew he would be addicted. He buried his face in her pussy, not even bothering to hide his enthusiasm. Especially when she canted her hips and whispered his name in longing. He ate her like he had something to prove. Which, perhaps, he did. He wanted to leave his imprint on her.

He sucked her clit into his mouth, and she went wild, her legs closing around his head. It didn't take much to send her into an orgasm. He barely let her come down before sliding up her body and sharing her taste with her.

Mila pulled back. "I want you inside."

Who was he to deny her? Silas fit his dick at the entrance of her pussy and pushed forward. He closed his eyes as her heated walls surrounded him. He was home. The feeling of it overtook his body, and for a moment, he couldn't move. He braced his body over her, savoring their closeness.

Impatient, Mila lifted her hips and took him deeper. Silas could only chuckle at her whimper.

"More, mama?" he teased, pulling out before plunging back in deeper, harder.

She moaned and wrapped her legs tight around his waist, her hands squeezing his shoulders. Silas took his time with Mila, his hips moving leisurely with every thrust. There would be time for fucking her later. Right now was for basking and luxuriating in their connection.

At least, that's what he told himself.

Mila pulled him down on top of her, kissing him, bucking beneath him, begging for more without words. Their tongues dueled as she got nastier with her kiss. She feasted on his mouth, kicking up the intensity between them. She was done with slow. Silas chuckled and picked up speed, his dick driving deeper, harder.

"God, yes," she whispered, rocking into him.

His panther filled his body until energy was crackling between them. Silas lifted her leg so he could get deeper. She took his every stroke, her pussy starting to flutter around his dick as she got closer to orgasm. He hissed with every pull of her sex. Her nails scored down his back, and the bite of pain pushed him to go harder. His canines lowered as his panther demanded they seal the mating between them.

He leaned down and skimmed his teeth across her neck and down to her shoulder. "Ready, love?"

"Yes!" she moaned, grinding her hips against him.

Silas reached down between them and pressed his thumb into her clit right as he sank his teeth into her shoulder. Mila went up in flames, screaming his name. Her pussy tightened on his dick, and Silas's body went taut as his orgasm stripped him of the rest of his control. He drove into her until her legs tensed and her back bowed in pleasure.

She yelled his name, and the bond between them snapped into place. There was no soft melding of souls. No, this was a tsunami that swept through them both, reshaping their cells until Silas could feel her down to his soul. He pulled his teeth from her shoulder and licked over the wound. He rubbed his forehead against her chest, sliding his cheek over her skin. He pulled her tightly into his body, their hearts beating together. Love for her engulfed him, and even more miraculously, he could feel it from her. It beat down their newly forged connection, leaving him full of emotion and speechless.

He could only hold her as he tried to catch his breath.

Mason had tried to warn him about the potency of the bond between mates, but Silas didn't think anything would have prepared him for the uninhibited love and desperation that overwhelmed him.

"Silas." Mila clutched him tightly, nuzzling her face against his. "This is...my God."

He nodded because he understood every word she couldn't mutter. He rolled over and pulled her with him until she lay on top of him. She rained kisses across his chest.

"Will I turn into a shifter now?"

He grunted. "It takes a while for it to develop. I was ordered to bring you to my mother when you got your bearings so she could walk you through the process."

She hummed, in no hurry to move from on top of him.

"How do you feel?" He murmured.

"Like my body is made of putty. But don't worry, I'll be ready for that fucking you promised."

He laughed and held her tighter. "Let's start in the shower, then."

eighteen

Silas rubbed his eyes and sat back from his desk. He'd been in his office for hours, poring over the legalese for the bill he was writing. He was anxious to get home as well. He'd been gone for a few days, meeting with the mayors of the last remaining sanctuary cities in the United States. He missed his girls, but work had to go on. He couldn't wait to see them this afternoon. Once court was finished, he was headed home. Usually, he'd be in the office well after his father, making sure the decisions they'd made in court were started, but today, he'd forgo that to get home. He'd already video called them when he'd landed this morning.

It was a month into his new mating, and Silas was content and happy. It was a new feeling, and now he understood his brother's rush to get home. Thanksgiving had been fun, and he'd been proud to attend dinner at his brother's home with his mate and child in tow. He couldn't wait until Christmas.

He looked up at the knock on his door. Dallas entered and stood in front of his desk.

"They're already starting?" he asked, checking his watch.

Dallas closed the door and sighed. "I just got word that the Robinsons are on the docket again."

Silas frowned. "What for?"

"Micah gave me a heads up so we wouldn't be blindsided. They're trying to say that a human is preventing them from access to Cameron's child."

Silas cursed. "The fuck are they pushing this for?"

Dallas held up his hand. "I don't want you to attend court today. They're going to try and get a rise out of us both, which is why Micah gave me the heads up."

"So you want me to stand around while they try again to take my child?"

Dallas shot him a warning look.

"I'm sorry, Pop, I know you better than that. What do you want me to do?"

"I want you to stand by while I make some shit shake. I'll let you know what happens."

Silas growled but nodded his head. He knew he could only push his father but so far. Dallas held his gaze a little longer before nodding himself.

"I got you, son."

And he knew that. Dallas wouldn't let anything happen to his daughter, but still, he was beyond aggravated.

"One more thing," Dallas started. "Has Mila shifted yet?"

He shook his head. "I can feel her panther, but it hasn't emerged."

Dallas hummed but nodded his head. "Okay. That will help. I'll keep you posted." He said, leaving.

Silas wanted to throw something, but instead, he pushed back from his desk and spun his chair around to the large painting behind him. The whole thing was supposed to mimic a window high up in a high rise. Some days he could pretend the print compensated for the loss of the view, but today that wouldn't work. He pulled out his phone and sighed, hating the call he needed to make. He knew Mila was working. He'd added a second desk to his office for her until she figured out which of the other bedrooms in their house she wanted to convert into an office for herself.

She answered, a smile in her voice. "Hi, babe."

He felt stronger just hearing her voice.

"That's amazing," she breathed.

"What?"

"I can feel you," she said in wonder. "What's wrong?"

Knowing there was someone in the world just for him struck something inside him that he didn't even realize was there. He'd always loved to see his parent's relationship and Mason's when he and Celine had gotten together, and now he had that. It was amazing.

"Work shit. We may have a problem with the Robinsons."

She sighed. "What's happened?"

"I don't know yet. Pops says they're on the docket."

"Your mind automatically went to the worse."

"It did." He admitted, leaning his head back onto his chair.

He let the sound of her voice wash over him and soothe him. Just like she could feel him, their bond went two ways. Her calm filled him and settled his panther.

"You think they're still going after Riyah? What can the Motsi do? I'm still a little fuzzy about what they do as a whole. I mean, I know they govern the shifters in a way, but no more than that. Shifters are so secretive."

"For good reason," he muttered.

His mind went through all the legal hoops the Robinsons could jump through to disrupt their lives. They didn't have a chance in hell in the human courts. He was her father, and her bio mother was dead. No court would grant them anything. But shifters were different. Especially the Motsi. Money turned heads, and the Robinsons had it. At least enough of it to turn some wheels.

"Silas," Mila prodded.

He sighed and brushed his hand across his hair. "The only thing I can see the council granting them is some kind of visitation."

Her anger spiked down their bond. "That's bull. They don't know my daughter, and for all their threats, they've never expressed the desire to get to know her. They want to own her. They didn't care for our daughter then. I don't know why they're pretending to care now."

He smiled because she finally said 'our.' "I'll let you know what I find out. Court can take hours."

"Are you staying until they're done? We missed you while you were gone."

He shook his head. He wanted to see his mate. "What time Riyah get home today?" He checked his watch.

"Why?" He could hear the smile in her voice.

"I'm trying to slide and spend some time with my mate. What you wearing?"

She laughed. "If you on the way, I can be persuaded to take what I got on off."

That's what the fuck he was talking about. "I'm on the way then."

He hung up the phone and stood, headed for the door. "Let's ride, Rock."

Rock nodded and followed him out. He wished he could tell his friend he'd go alone, but his job was much more dangerous than Mason's. Going without security was asking for some shit to pop off, and now he had too much to lose for that. He got into the passenger seat of his Jag, and Rock took off.

***

Mila hung up the phone smiling ear to ear. Being mated to Silas was amazing, and she was happy they'd taken the chance. She closed out the documents she was working on, noting where she had left off. She'd catch up with work tomorrow.

She rushed upstairs and into the shower. She'd been outside all morning trying to coax her stubborn panther forward. She could feel the thing getting stronger every day, but according to Adina, it wouldn't emerge until it, and her body was ready for the change.

She didn't know what she had to do to show the animal that she was ready, but every morning after she dropped Riyah off or when Silas took her to school, Mila headed outdoors to sit in the grass and meditate. Adina had been a godsend with the whole process. The woman was so attuned to the animal that resided within herself, and so all the tips she'd been giving Mila had been working. Her panther was developing, and the two of them were bonding, just as the older woman had predicted.

All that was left was the shift, and Adina cautioned her to quit rushing the process. She said that, eventually, the meditations would work.

Either way, Mila needed a quick shower to get the grass and smell of the outdoors off her. She'd barely stepped out of the stall when she felt her mate's presence. Silas' energy was unmistakable. And her body shuddered in anticipation.

Silas stalked into the bathroom while she was wrapping the towel around her chest. He growled, and the sound made her throb. He smiled, and that smile was one that she would never tire of. He took off his shirt as she watched, licking her lips, wanting a taste of every inch of the chest he exposed. Her breathing was loud, panting, really.

"You got here faster than I anticipated."

He didn't say anything, just grunted. His eyes glowed, and Mila saw the green shining, his panther making its presence known. She had to admit that she loved when he lost control. That feral part of him brought out a matching one inside of her. When he got to his pants, she loosened her grip on her towel. It dropped to the ground, and he growled, low and long. He leapt the distance between them, pinning her against the shower stall wall. He scraped his teeth down her neck.

"I came in here to make love to you, Mila," he grumbled in her ear. "But I don't think I have it in me to be gentle."

He nipped her shoulder, his tongue licking across the mating mark he'd left on her skin. His lick was like a live wire connected to her clit. For every swipe of his tongue, that bud thumped and swelled. Her hands went to his pants, and she unbuckled them, shoving the fabric down his hips. His dick fell out, hard and thick. She swore her mouth watered. She dropped to her knees, needing the feel of him on her tongue. There was no preamble; she sucked him deep into her mouth, her tongue swiping the underside. Silas hissed and grabbed her wet hair, tugging it tightly.

That bite of pain went straight to her pussy, and she could feel the moisture sliding down her thighs. She hummed her pleasure, and that seemed to set him off. He cursed and lifted her. She wrapped her legs around his waist and sucked in a sharp breath when his dick prodded at her center.

"I'm finna beat this pussy down, Mila," he warned, the dark carnal thoughts all in his eyes for her to see.

In response, her pussy clenched tightly. Silas chuckled, gripping her throat and kissing her. His tongue speared her mouth, and he pushed into her at the same time. She moaned as he filled her, their tongues twining together. His face was a mask of concentration as he made good on his promise. He stroked her deep and slow, holding onto her thighs so that she had no choice but to be wide open to him.

"My shit," he whispered, pulling out of their kiss.

He turned them, putting her down on the counter between the double sinks. He looked down at their joined hips, groaning as he watched his dick's in and out of her.

"So fucking pretty," he muttered, punching his hips into her. "So fucking, mine," he said, giving her a smile that had her walls contracting around his dick.

Mila threw her head back as their new position shifted the places his dick reached within her. Soon, he was sliding over that button deep within her that was going to set her off.

"Silas," she warned.

"I can feel this good pussy squeezing me, mama. Let that shit go," he ordered.

His words.

Those fucking words set her blood on fire, and she obeyed, her body going up in flames. She screamed his name as she came, and Silas, sweet, amazing Silas, didn't let it phase him. He kept up the steady rhythm, the cocky smile on his lips well-earned.

"Again, lil baby," he whispered, leaning to kiss her.

She met him halfway, sucking his tongue into her mouth. Love for him filled her as her body tightened again. She wanted him with her this time, so she canted her hips, purposefully squeezing down on him. He cursed, his strokes getting harder, faster.

"Come for me," she whispered in his ear before biting his neck.

His hands gripped her tighter.

"Shit, shit, shit, woman," he shouted, finally coming. He laid his forehead against hers. "I missed you." He whispered.

She chuckled. "I can tell." She kissed him softly. "Feel better?"

"Always feel better inside of you."

Her cheeks heated.

"We got time for another round," he murmured against her lips, lifting her from the sink and heading back to the shower.

Giddy happiness filled her, and she readily agreed.

twenty

Mila was humming to herself as she started the oven. She'd already had the wings she was making for dinner seasoned and waiting in the fridge. Her body was deliciously languid, and she couldn't help the smile covering her face. Agreeing to raise Sariyah had been the single best day of her life, but deciding to mate with Silas was easily among the next. He'd done everything he'd promised her he would. She was secure, content, and well-loved. None of it had taken away her feelings for Seth. He'd had his place in her life, and she appreciated every moment she'd had with him. But Silas...it was as if he had been made especially for her. She could feel her panther under her skin, relaxed and tranquil. Silas had a way of calming the animal growing within her.

She was chopping veggies for a salad when the doorbell rang. She checked the feed on the small monitor next to the fridge. She frowned when she recognized her new father-in-law.

She wiped her hands and walked to the door.

"Mr. Knight."

"Dallas is fine, Mila." He rubbed his cheek against hers, and she felt her panther raise up and brush against his. "Won't be long now. Silas was right. She's right there under the surface."

She was curious about what else Silas had told his father about her panther, but she was scared to ask, so instead, she stepped back to allow Dallas entry.

"Come in. Silas and Rock went to get Riyah, and I'm making dinner. Would you like to stay?"

She'd learned weeks ago to always prepare for someone extra to stop by their house. Silas' family was so close, and she loved it. If it wasn't his parents or Mason and Celine, it could be any of Silas's friends who dropped by.

Dallas looked down at his watch. "Yeah, I don't want to miss my baby."

She smiled. She loved the way they treated her daughter. "Would you like something to drink?"

"I got it. Carry on with what you're doing."

She nodded. Slightly nervous. He was a powerful man with an intense stare. He fixed a whiskey and sat at the island and watched her work. He stared at her, his gaze keen and introspective. It was so reminiscent of her daughter that she smiled.

"You're where she gets it from, then."

His eyes flashed with surprise. "What do you mean?"

"Your granddaughter watches people the same way you do."

Pleasure filled his gaze, emotion warming his face and relaxing his body a moment before he hid it under his normal stoicism.

"How was court?" She asked.

He grunted. "I need to talk to you and Silas about it."

She stopped what she was doing. "Should I worry?"

"Not about this. If you don't know nothing about me, know that I always take care of my family."

She nodded, not necessarily relieved by that. If he thought there was something to take care of, the Robinsons had succeeded in starting some trouble. She should've known they were too quiet after she met with Leland.

"What are you cooking?"

"I'm baking wings and making wild rice," she said absently.

He nodded. "Tell me about yourself."

She paused, unsure what to say. She hadn't spent any amount of time with Silas's father alone, so she wasn't sure what to say or where to start. "Umm..."

"Where are you from?"

"Texas. Well, as far as I know. That's where I was found."

He frowned. "You were abandoned?"

"According to the records I could find. I was two years old. I was in foster care until I aged out."

"You've done well for yourself, despite how your life started. I admire that."

Her cheeks heated. "Thank you."

"Riyah showed me her paintings last time I was here. How long has she been into it?"

She smiled. "From the first moment she got a hold of crayons. She wants to explore photography now, but she never strays too far from painting."

His smile transformed his face. Silas looked so much like his father that Mila looked forward to him aging. As fine as his daddy was, she knew Silas would age like fine wine.

"You didn't birth Sariyah, but I can see you in her. Especially over the phone. She talks just like you."

Mila laughed. "Might be a little too late to watch my mouth around her."

He laughed. They both looked up as the door beeped. Riyah's hurried footsteps could be heard as she came down the hallway.

"Poppa, I can smell you." She said excitedly, coming around the corner.

She jumped at him, and he caught her as he spun on the stool.

"Hey, my baby." He hugged her tight.

Riyah rubbed her cheek against her grandfather's, and Mila got a little misty. Their love for each other was plain for anyone to see. Their bond tight despite them just coming into each other's lives.

"Are you staying for dinner?" Riyah asked excitedly.

"I am."

"What about G-mom?"

"I'll call her over now."

"Yay," she cheered.

"Good afternoon to you too, little girl," Mila said.

Her daughter gave her a sheepish smile. "Sorry, mom. Good afternoon."

"Before you start demanding play time from your Poppa, wash your hands and face and change clothes."

"I know, I know." Riyah slid out of her grandfather's arms.

"And?"

"And I'll finish my homework." She said, hugging her mother and rubbing her face all over her stomach.

Silas had explained that it was Riyah's way of leaving her scent on her mother. She had been doing it more since Mila had been transformed. It was like she gained reassurance from the action. There were so many little mannerisms that Mila had been puzzled by regarding her daughter that was the direct result of Sariyah being a young shifter. She'd been so fascinated as Adina explained it all to her. Silas and Dallas had been ecstatic to find that Sariyah was already showing signs of having a strong animal. The three men played rough with her as though she already had the animal, and it had taken Mila a little time to get used to that, but she was settling into their new life.

Silas chuckled, coming over, prying their daughter away from her waist. "Get off my mate," he ordered his daughter.

Riyah laughed and gripped Mila tighter as her father tickled her.

"Ah, the sweet sound of karma," Dallas said, laughing along with them.

"Both of you get off me so I can finish making dinner." She fussed.

Silas gripped her chin and kissed her deeply. Her body melted, and she sighed into his mouth.

"Ew," Riyah said, giving up her spot.

Silas laughed as he backed away. "You and your Poppa some haters."

Dallas laughed.

"Up to your room, princess," Silas ordered.

And, of course, her daughter didn't give her father any lip, just picking up her backpack and going off to do her homework. They waited until Sariyah left, and then Dallas sighed.

"What happened?" Silas asked, leaning onto the counter.

"Cyrus granted them mediation."

Silas sucked his teeth.

"Who is Cyrus?"

"The wolf representative on the tri-council," Silas answered. "What was their petition?"

"They want visitation with Riyah. Says that Mila has been purposefully keeping them from seeing their last tie to their daughter."

Mila cursed. "That's bullshit. They've been threatening me from the moment Seth died. They went out of their way to make our lives hell. They were actively making it hard for us to raise our daughter. Did they tell your council that?"

Dallas held up his hand. "Either way. We have to go through mediation."

She opened her mouth, but Silas pulled her into his arms. "When?"

"The end of the week."

Silas kissed her temple. "That's soon."

"They tried to do it next month. Which means they're stalling."

"For what?" Silas asked.

Dallas shook his head. "Exactly my thoughts, so I pushed for it to happen quickly to disrupt whatever game they're playing, hopefully."

"We'll be ready," Silas assured them both.

"I have no doubt. Your mind is its own treasure, my boy. I'm not worried about it on our end."

Silas hummed. "But I am curious as to their end goal."

Dallas tapped his temple. "Exactly. Mila, did they give any hints in their threats to you?"

Mila shook her head and sighed as Silas rubbed her back. "I know Cameron told us her mother was trying to use them both, but she never said what for."

Dallas and Silas shared a look that she couldn't decipher. They stopped talking as they heard Riyah stomping down the stairs.

"I gotta teach my baby to move quieter than that," Dallas said off-handedly.

"Please don't," Mila said. "I can't have two of them sneaking up on me."

They all laughed.

twenty-one

Silas had wanted to leave Mila home. He didn't know in which direction the mediation would go, and his first instinct had been to protect her from the process. Adina had nixed that idea, reminding him that Mila would have to stand next to him through worse, so she needed to understand her role as his mate. Plus, it was Sariyah they were talking about. It wasn't fair to leave her out of anything to do with their daughter.

She fidgeted next to him. "How long do you think this will take?"

"It depends on how nice we can all remain," he said softly as they walked up to the conference room.

The rules of mediation regarding arrivals and departures were strict. Each party had a twenty-minute window from each other in an effort to prevent them from crossing outside of the conference room. So the Robinson family were all seated at the table when Silas and his family entered. It should've been just Silas and Mila, along with Dallas, as he was their councilman. But the rest of his family had been waiting in his office when he'd arrived.

He couldn't do anything but smile because his family would always ride for each other.

Silas helped Mila into a seat and sat beside her in the middle chair. The rest of the family settled in seats on the opposite side of the table from the Robinsons. Their enforcers lined the back wall. Silas narrowed his eyes at Leland, wondering what, if anything, he had to do with his daughter.

Cyrus cleared his throat at the head of the table. Micah growled on the other end, his aggravation with the proceedings evident.

"Councilman Crespo and Booth will serve as mediators for this proceeding," Micah said to the group.

"Let's get started," Cyrus ordered. "This council is aware of all the circumstances regarding the failed marriage merger between the two families. When was the presence of a child found out?"

Silas spoke first. "Cameron sent me a letter with a picture of my daughter, but according to our investigation, it was well after the baby's adoption." He slid all the documents, including the letters, over to both councilmen. "I couldn't tell you when these assholes found out about the baby."

"Let's not start with name-calling," Leland tutted.

Samantha adjusted in her chair. "I knew from the beginning."

His mother scoffed.

Micah flipped through the documents. "So why, then, weren't the Knights informed?"

"They killed my mate and sons. I didn't think it was in the child's best interest," Samantha said. "They're dangerous, and I refuse to have any blood of mine under their influence."

Adina growled. "All shifters are dangerous. At least the ones who are not puppets for humans."

"Puppets? Why, because my husband wanted to negotiate with humans?"

"At the cost of our lives," Dallas said calmly. "Rob didn't deserve the position, and if he were strong enough, he would still have it. There is a reason we are separate from humans. Their laws should have nothing to do with how we govern our people."

Samantha said nothing. She simply looked at Cyrus and held her hand out as if to tell him, 'see?'.

"Separating a shifter child from their parent is illegal. Custodial kidnapping is illegal. Since I am Sariyah's only living parent, this mediation is useless. I will not give up my daughter."

"Out of his own mouth. He is keeping her from us," Leland said.

Cyrus held up his hand. "You have admitted to keeping the child from them."

"You're welcome to do something about it." Silas shrugged.

Mila gripped his hand underneath the table, her nervousness and anger bombarding him through their bond. Cyrus growled, his eyes changing color.

"The Robinsons have requested visita—"

"No," Mila said, her voice firm, with no hint of her anxiety.

"You have no say in this at all, human. You shouldn't have even been allowed in the building," Samantha growled.

"The child was given to this female. She has some say," Micah said mildly.

"A human can't keep the girl. You made the rules yourself, Silas," Cyrus said.

Silas growled. "The human is my mate, so the moniker no longer applies."

The smug smile dropped from Leland's face. "You haven't mated her."

"If your animal ain't strong enough to smell my son's mate on him, just say that," Adina mocked.

Leland turned his attention to Adina and bared his teeth.

Dallas leaned his elbows onto the table. "I wish the fuck you would. I promise you don't want this smoke."

Silas smiled. "Now, ain't no more mediating. Stay the fuck away from my daughter and my mate, and you might live to see another birthday."

Leland stood and braced his hands on the table. Samantha gripped his forearm to call him off, but he shook away her hand.

"All this talk with your security around."

Mason laughed. "Security not here for us, playboy. They here to make sure my brother don't blow your shit back for messing with lil baby."

Leland sneered, pulling his lip up to show his growing fangs.

Silas chuckled, not at all intimidated. "You must not know who the fuck I am."

"I don't care about you or your bitch," Leland growled.

Silas moved swiftly, partially shifting his hands. He jumped across the table, pushing Leland back against the wall.

"Call her one more muhfucking thing other than her name, and I'll rip your tongue out."

"Silas," Dallas called calmly.

His father's voice reigned him in.

"No violence during mediation." Cyrus snapped.

Those pesky rules. Wasn't shit saying ol' boy couldn't see him after, though, so Silas smiled, his canines slipping down.

"Keep fucking with me, and like my brother said, I'ma push your wig back," Silas said as he pushed his pointer finger into Leland's forehead, his bloody claw leaving a point.

He backed away and wiped his bloody claws on the man's shirt to clean them off. Silas stared at Leland the whole time, daring him to say shit. Yeah, his father had reigned him in, but his panther was waiting for one slip-up, and he would lose his shit.

Silas walked back around the table and took his seat next to his mate. Mila's heart was racing, her fear wafting from her pores. He wanted to tend to her and at least get her to get her emotions under control. But she'd only been a shifter for a month. She was still learning.

Samantha ran a nervous hand over her hair. "We will drop the claim over Sariyah if Dallas agrees to a challenge. Leland will be our family's representative. And we're not going through the hierarchy."

Ah, and now they were getting to the root of it all.

Mason sucked his teeth. "Whole family full of bitch asses."

"Mason," Adina cautioned, sharing a look with Dallas. "You've done all this just to circumvent the duel laws? I knew y'all weren't shit, but to use an innocent child...." Adina shook her head.

"Wait, so chasing me across the country, threatening me...that was all so that you could come back here for some kind of petty revenge?" Mila's anger took over all her fear.

"There is nothing petty about it. Dallas does not belong in my mate's chair," Samantha hissed.

Adina sat forward. "And yet, there my mate sits, and there he will remain."

Silas held his hand up to pause the room because he already knew his mother could get rowdy if the need arose. "Do I need to say it slower for you? Y'all ain't got no claim over my daughter. Cameron is gone, and I'm her only surviving parent."

"Cameron signed the child over to me before she died." Samantha slid a document toward Silas before giving a copy to the mediators.

Silas snatched it up.

"There is no way Cameron would've done that," Mila spat. "She didn't want our daughter anywhere near you."

Samantha growled in fury but said nothing.

Silas skimmed the paperwork, frowning at Cameron's signature. "Mila's name is on the birth certificate. This means nothing unless you can prove Cameron is the mother."

"And we both know that the Motsi can demand a blood test. The hum...Mila does not share your daughter's DNA. Once they declare that birth certificate a forgery and a fraud, then what?" Samantha asked, smug satisfaction on her face.

He could easily fight and beat this, but it would take time. And he didn't put it past Cyrus to demand they remove his daughter from their home in the meantime. The wolf had it out for their family and would do it if only to piss off Dallas. Mila made a small sound of distress but recovered quickly. He looked at Dallas, who gave him a reassuring look.

Dallas smiled. "I can hold this territory. I'm not worried."

Micah held his hand up. "No."

Cyrus whipped his attention to him. "What? There are no rules against it."

"And do you imagine I'm going to be fighting challenges every month from young assholes trying to blackmail me into it?" Micah scoffed. "You mean to tell me that you want to give a city full of hungry wolves a direct path to you and your seat? What the fuck is the hierarchy for, then?"

Cyrus growled but remained silent, Micah's point well-taken.

"I earned my position. You think the cats will allow you more than a moment on my throne if you get lucky enough to win?" Dallas chuckled. "Your coward ass would be gone within a day."

"Hour." Mason and Silas growled together.

Dallas's smile made Silas almost feel sorry for the Robinsons. That smile promised retribution, and regardless of the outcome of the mediation, they would be hearing from his father and all the goons Dallas thought he hid from his sons.

"What y'all wanna do, then?" Dallas asked.

Samantha and Leland shared a look. They came to some kind of unspoken consensus.

"Fine. We'll go through your second, but no other," Samantha finally said.

"This is bullshit. They've admitted to only wanting my daughter as some kind of bargaining chip. This whole proceeding should be tossed out," Mila protested.

Dallas chuckled. "I'm definitely not worried. Silas?"

"I agree to the terms."

Mila gasped next to him before schooling her reaction. Her leg bounced beneath the table, and she gripped his hand. Unlike his mate, he wasn't worried. He was his father's son, and nobody in the room put fear in his heart.

"The deal is made," Cyrus agreed hastily before Micah could intervene.

It was done.

twenty-two

Mila shook her head, her heart stalling, then thumping really hard as she sat next to Silas in the car. They'd had to wait thirty minutes after the Robinsons left before they were allowed to leave the conference room. It had been the longest thirty minutes of her life. She had already embarrassed herself and probably Silas because she couldn't keep her emotions to herself during the meeting. She couldn't break down further in front of his family.

The panther she was still getting used to bucked against her so hard that Mila flinched. Everything that happened in mediation flashed back to her. She barely managed to keep it together on the car ride home. As soon as Rock pulled into Silas's garage, she jumped from the car and rushed into the house. She needed to be back in her safe space. As soon as her feet touched the kitchen tile, she broke.

Silas stepped to her quickly. "breathe, mama," he whispered and pushed his nose into her neck. His cat reached out to hers, and the animal settled. "I'll be fine, I swear."

Of course, he knew why she was freaking out. He was in her head, their bond probably broadcasting her every fear. She didn't bother trying to mask it.

"You don't know that. I've heard about shifter challenges. You could be killed," she whispered. Her breath hitched, her chest tightening.

"Breathe, Mila," Silas said stronger, his teeth nipping against her skin The sharp pain brought her back to herself.

"Losing Seth hurt, but I don't think I could survive losing you, Silas." Tears crested her eyes, and she hated that.

Silas lifted her, and she wrapped her legs around his waist, settling her head into his neck. Mila inhaled his scent, allowing it to wash over her.

"I love you, Silas," she whimpered, fear continuing to steal her air.

"Settle," he told her, his voice a growl that reached deep within her.

She lifted from his neck and cupped his cheeks with both hands. Her eyes stared into his and that of his animal. Her panther responded, and Mila leaned down and kissed him, devouring his mouth.

Silas pulled apart from her, alarm on his face. He set her feet on the floor. "Baby, she's close. You need to calm yourself."

"I can't," she whispered as a fiery wave shot through her bloodstream.

"Outside, now," he said, rushing her towards the backdoor.

She screamed as the pain hit her. She racked her mind for the tips Adina had given her.

Breathing.

She needed to breathe.

Before she could take her first deep breath, her back bowed as her bones started aching.

"Silas," she whimpered.

"You've bonded with her already. Calm yourself and her, Mila." His voice was stern, but what was more, the animal was within it.

His growl filled her body. It triggered her panther, and pain seized her muscles. She breathed deeply and closed her eyes. Adina told her it was like coaxing a child to her. She remembered many days of talking Sariyah from under the bed when she got overwhelmed. Tears streaked down Mila's cheeks, but she pushed her fear aside, focusing on that. She reached for the connection she had with her animal, gasping when she saw her bond with Silas. It was a light within her that encompassed her panther. His love flowed down that bond, and the light got brighter.

She breathed deeper in and out and called the panther to her. A dark spot separated from the light and rushed toward her. Heat filled her until it felt like her skin was melting. Her mouth opened to scream, but no sound came out. She opened her eyes, and she was closer to the grass. She looked around and then up...up at Silas. Was she on the ground?

He smiled at her and stooped. His mouth was moving, but her panther was in control, so his words didn't penetrate. He butted his forehead against hers and growled. Her panther understood that easily, giving him submission. She lifted her head slowly, exposing her neck to him. Silas rubbed her fur, and his words filtered through to the panther. At the same time, she realized that she and the panther were back on an even keel, their bond tight, their souls intertwined. Inside the animal's body, she felt joy...freedom.

He was amazed by his mate. He guessed the stress of the day finally brought the animal forward. Her emotions had been all over the place at the meeting, so he could well understand. She was not used to dealing with the Motsi the same way their family was. He would teach her, though. He rubbed his hand over her head, delighting in the soft fur.

Their bond, though already tight, seemed to fuse tighter. Her panther butted against him, his cat whining for him to change. He rubbed his cheek against Mila's. He gripped the animal's chin and stared into its eyes.

"Stay on the property. And we not finna be out here all night, understand?"

She chuffed and licked his face. He laughed and backed away, stripping. Mila's cat watched him, its eyes glowing. He quickly shifted and walked to her, allowing his animal time to acquaint itself with its mate. Their bodies rubbed together, and Mila licked his skin, marking her scent all over him. She took off, and Silas was right behind her, ensuring she followed his instructions to stay on his property.

He could scent Rock and Leo on the property and knew they would cover them if something happened. His mate was worried, and her cat wouldn't settle. He could feel it all through their bond. He walked to her and nipped her flank, but she hissed at him and took off. They spent hours playing in their animal form until her exhaustion filled their connection. He herded her back towards the house and the back door.

Sariyah was now home. He could scent his baby in the air, along with her uncle, who must have dropped her off. When they got to the back porch, he helped Mila shift back, coaching her through the change. Mila was either a fast learner, or her body was too tired to fight the change. She shifted quickly. He lifted her limp body, smiling as she nuzzled into his neck.

"Behave," he told her, kissing her neck.

He took her into the master bathroom and washed her off. Her body was pliant and tired, yet she reached for his dick.

He moved her hands, laughing. "No. Sleep for you, lil baby. You're too tired for all that."

She growled though it was a weak protest. Her eyes lit momentarily, her cat showing off before backing away. He settled her in bed, tucking her under the blankets. He headed to their closet to put on some clothes. When he came out of the closet dressed, his daughter was at his door. She watched her mother, her face a mask of worry.

"What's wrong, princess?"

"Why was mama upset?"

He sighed because they couldn't get anything past the little girl. He lifted her and carried her towards her room. She already smelled of lavender and cocoa butter, so he knew she'd taken a bath at her grandparent's house. It was still another hour before her bedtime, but he was sure he could convince her to watch movies with him in her bed.

"You smell good, daddy," she murmured, nuzzling into his chest.

"Want to watch movies with me?"

Her eyes lit up as he laid her on her bed. "I get to pick?"

He nodded, resigning himself to whatever musical his daughter was obsessed with presently.

She gave a happy squeal and dove under the covers. He squeezed onto her full-size bed, closing his eyes as she cuddled close. He held her tight as she flipped through streaming services to find the one she wanted.

"I overheard Poppa talking about someone trying to take me." She said off-hand. Her body tensed.

"That's never going to happen," he reassured her.

She picked a movie and lay on his chest, wrapping her body around him. "I love it here with you, daddy. Mom is so much happier, and it feels like home."

Silas closed his eyes and clutched his daughter tight. They would take his daughter over his dead body.

twenty-three

Mila downed the champagne in her glass and looked around the room. Silas had told her they would need to do it big for their mating celebration, but she hadn't envisioned anything like the decked-out ballroom she currently circled. She didn't know anyone except Helen, her husband, and of course, the Knight family. But, because of Silas's position, the room was filled with red gowns and tuxedos, dripping diamonds and rubies, and the elites among the shifters. She was happy they'd been able to have their marriage ceremony small and short. She didn't mind parties, but this was a little out of her league.

The first hour of the party had been a whirlwind of Silas and Adina taking her around the room and introducing her to various family members. The second hour had been slower as Silas had to make his way through the Motsi. He pointed out the ones important to his job, and she was even introduced to a couple of state senators. Her new husband was a big deal, and she was nearly overwhelmed by the thought.

She took comfort in the fact that his position was also keeping her and Sariyah safe.

"There you are," Silas kissed the spot beneath her ear. "Let me holla at you for a minute."

Mila groaned. "Not more people to meet."

He chuckled, leading her away from the crowds. She frowned when they went down the hallway towards the bathroom. Silas led her into a bathroom, closing and locking the door behind them.

"What are you doing?" She raised an eyebrow, fighting a smile.

Silas stalked over to her. She took a step back. The smile he gave her caused heat to pool low in her belly.

"Silas," she warned.

A growl rumbled through him as he backed her up to the counter between the sinks. Her butt bumped into the sink, and she held up her hand.

"There is a whole ballroom full of people out there, Silas Knight. What if someone wants to use the restroom?"

He smiled and said nothing, only reaching around her to wash his hands. She frowned in confusion. She started to move, but he moved quicker, trapping her between him and the counter. Silas slid his hand into the slit of her dress, parting the velvet fabric. His eyebrow lifted in pleased surprise to find her in a simple thong. She'd complained when he'd picked out the dress that she would need shapewear, but the corset top held everything together, so she'd forgone it. His fingers teased the edges of her panties; his eyes focused wholly on her. It was intoxicating. She gasped when his finger slipped inside her panties.

"Silas," she tried again.

"She's wet, Mila. She don't care about all that other shit you talking." His finger dipped into her sex.

She swallowed her moan. His words, audacious and daring, made her stomach clench. He pushed her panties aside and pushed two fingers into her.

He chuckled and sucked on her neck. "See, she's thumping against my fingers because she wants the dick. Her person is being so selfish."

She had to laugh, which turned into a gasp as he hooked his fingers forward, rubbing against her g spot.

"Silas," she hissed, widening her legs.

He bit down on her neck, leaving yet another mark on her skin.

"I'll be quick." He said, pulling his dick from his pants.

"Liar," she hissed, throwing her head back as his teeth scraped the front of her neck.

"I don't know, sometimes the way you be gripping this shit have me gone," he murmured.

Lord, this man, and his words.

She grabbed his dick and guided it to her sex. He slid in to the hilt, and Mila almost swallowed her tongue. Jesus, the man knew what to do with what he was packing.

He closed his eyes, biting down on his bottom lip. "Fuck, Mila, she so greedy for me."

She needed him to shut up before his words sent her spiraling. She pulled his face up and kissed him, which was an even bigger mistake. A quiet Silas was a concentrating, determined Silas. And that meant...

Fuuuck.

His thumb circled her clit, pressing down with the precision of a man who knew everything about her body. Her moan slipped out as she crashed into an orgasm. Silas kept his strokes slow and deep, prolonging the orgasm. She pulled back from their kiss, sucking in desperate air.

"This my shit." He whispered into her ear, his strokes finally speeding. "Say it, Mila."

She gripped his shoulders, rocking her hips. "Your shit," she gasped as he hit that spot deep in her that had her vision darkening.

Silas gripped her hips tightly and pounded into her, kissing her again.

"Yes," she whispered.

He bucked a final time, growling softly as he came.

"My God, woman." He finally breathed out. He nuzzled against her neck, leaving his scent on her.

"Are you marking your territory, Silas?"

He hummed, and she hit his shoulder.

"You are ridiculous," she chided him.

"I just realized I'm a little greedy with you."

She snorted because that was an understatement. It seemed he only wanted to share her with their daughter.

Mila pushed against his chest. "Get out of here so I can clean up. Otherwise, a room full of people will know what we've been in here doing."

His eyes lit with pleasure, and she narrowed hers. He'd done it on purpose.

"A whole Neanderthal," she fussed.

He slid from her body, a charming smile on his face. He cleaned himself, kissed her deeply, and walked out, his cocky swagger making her reconsider calling him back for another round. Mila straightened herself as much as she could before leaving the bathroom. Her heart sped its rhythm when she spotted Leland waiting for her directly across from the door. There was no way Silas' family had invited him.

She looked around. "You shouldn't be here."

She tried to go around him, but he stepped in her way.

***

Silas pulled a blunt from his pocket to light up. His body was relaxed, and his panther settled now that he'd marked his mate up some more. Now that she was a shifter, the innate grace Mila had prior was magnified tenfold. Every eye followed her as she moved around the room. She was beautiful before, but with the cat residing in her, she was more alluring. It was making his panther jealous. It wasn't an emotion familiar to him. After the shit had gone down with Cameron, before he found out about Sariyah, Silas had never lacked for female company. After Sariyah, he'd changed all that, focused wholly on finding his daughter.

He hadn't time for relationships, never mind being jealous. Mila had called him a Neanderthal, and he'd be that. He wanted people to know she was his. He spotted his sister in her usual corner, seated with a drink in her hand. He walked over and plopped down into the chair next to her.

"Your mother-in-law must not know you're over here hiding."

Celine smiled the sweet smile that Silas knew his brother loved. He loved her for Mason.

"See what you know. Papa D had them add these chairs over here."

He laughed. His father spoiled the shit out of Celine now that she was a part of the family. He talked all that shit about Mason making sure she was strong enough, but Dallas folded so easily with her. He smoked his blunt, enjoying that easy, relaxing quiet that only Celine seemed to bring out of their family. He watched the entrance to the ballroom waiting for Mila to re-enter. His panther perked up in alarm when after ten minutes, she still hadn't emerged.

Her irritation filtered down through their bond, and he stood.

"What's wrong?" Celine asked, standing with him.

"Mila should be out of the bathroom by now," he murmured, heading in that direction.

They marched over to the bathroom, him none too gently pushing through the crowd. Silas growled when he reached the back hallway and saw Leland gripping Mila's arm trying to drag her down the hallway toward the back entrance. He was about to intervene when Mila reached into her corset and pulled out a knife. In a quick movement, she sliced across the man's arm.

Leland hissed and pulled his hand from her.

"Don't ever put your hands on me," Mila hissed.

She snapped her switchblade back into place and slid it back into her corset. She hadn't raised her voice, and he didn't feel an ounce of fear from their bond. His panther reared forward despite that, fury suffusing him.

Silas growled and rushed forward, grabbing Leland around the throat. Anger had a red haze over his mind.

"Don't kill him yet, Silas," Dallas told him, entering the hallway.

Mason was directly behind their father. "Nah, Pop, he violated. Fuck him up, Si."

"If you kill him outside of the challenge, then we forfeit. He's goading you," Adina said, running to him as fast as her skirt would allow. She laid a hand on his shoulder.

Silas squeezed down on Leland's neck, enjoying the blood running between his fingers. He hadn't even realized that his claws had come out. He didn't smell any fear from Leland, only apprehension. That set his panther off. It wanted the male scared. Silas let his canines descend, lifting Leland from the ground. Once his feet were dangling, Leland's expression changed, and he reached his hands out to hold on to Silas's forearm.

"Silas," Mila spoke up. "It's done, love."

He inhaled sharply through his nose and pulled back his panther. Leland slid to the ground, choking on air, holding his bleeding throat. Silas clocked the smug look on his face. His mother had been right; the pussy had been goading him.

"Rock," he called, knowing his best friend wouldn't be far. He backed away from temptation, putting a few steps between them.

"Make sure your mate doesn't touch any other packages left on her porch," Leland taunted.

Silas dove for him, held back by his father. Dallas had him in a tight grip, dragging him away. Rocco lifted Leland roughly and carried him towards the back exit. It wasn't until the male was out of his eyesight that Silas's panther calmed. He held up his hands so that his father would release him. Dallas stepped back, handing Silas his handkerchief. Silas wiped his hands and turned to inspect his mate.

Mila cupped his cheek. "I handled it. I'm fine."

"Next time, let your panther loose," he said, his voice growly with his own animal.

She took a shaky breath. "Still getting used to that. My first instinct is to pull out my knife."

"Speaking of," he smiled, his good mood breaking through the anger. "You been carrying that in your titties this whole time, Mila Knight?"

His mother laughed, running a shaky hand across her hair to ensure it was still in place. "A woman after my own heart."

"I don't know, Silas. You might have to sleep with one eye open dealing with this one." Mason said, shaking his head.

Mila laughed, a relieved sound. "Don't do me, Mason."

"Well, I'm thoroughly impressed," Celine told her, looping her arm through hers.

Adina grabbed her other arm, and the three of them walked away. Silas' heart was still beating hard from adrenaline.

His father squeezed his shoulder. "Don't worry, Si. He'll pay for touching your mate and more when you beat his ass next week."

"Ain't no ass beating, Pop. I'm taking him the fuck out."

"In front of everyone, so the next person knows not to fuck with us," Mason told him, dapping him up. "Now, come on, so we can be done with this party shit. My baby 'bout ready to go."

Silas laughed. Celine didn't have a long social battery, so he wasn't surprised. He wiped his hand down his face and fixed his tuxedo, coaxing his animal into retreating for the rest of the evening.

twenty-four

Mila opened her eyes and sighed. Tonight was the night of the challenge. Time had moved like it had some shit to do, and the week had flown by before she could even get her bearings straight. Everything in her wanted to beg Silas to change his mind, to back out, but after the long talk Celine and Adina had given her last night, she was resigned to their fate.

Being a Knight came with a level of power and influence that had to be held in place by blood and sacrifice. In agreeing to mate with Silas and stay in Sariyah's life, she had taken the unwritten covenant on her back. She was tough, had been her whole sad life, but never before had she had so much to lose.

This was her first forever family.

The Knights had damn near adopted her. She'd gone shopping with her new mother-in-law, baking and candle-making with her new sister, and the men had taken her in with no reserve in their hearts. She couldn't do any less than ride for them, and she would...she just needed a moment—a small moment to sit in this morning silence and gather herself together.

She turned on her side, propping her chin on her hand. Mila's eyes traced over her mate and daughter. They were cuddled together, with identical beautiful faces. The three of them had spent what could be their last night together. Mila shook her head. She wouldn't think that way. She refused to doubt Silas. He told her he could handle it and he hadn't lied to her once. Not even when lying would've made getting his daughter easier. He was a man with integrity. That didn't mean he wouldn't get his hands dirty. It just meant he wouldn't lie about it.

She smiled and skimmed her fingers down his arm slung across Sariyah. The contact woke him. He lifted his lids, his sleepy gaze meeting hers.

"You're worrying, my love," he whispered.

"A little," she admitted.

Silas slid out of bed on his side and came around to her. She turned her body to meet him on the other side. He kneeled next to the bed and cupped her chin.

"Leave your doubt here, ma, understand? When we leave this house, we're a united front, and ain't shit we fear, hear?" He gripped her hand.

She nodded, cursing the tear that slid down her face. Being bonded to Silas had come with so many rewards she would willingly pay any price required to keep her family together.

"Ain't shit we fear," she whispered.

"Ain't shit we fear," Sariyah said groggily, climbing Mila's back and adding her hand to theirs.

Mila released a watery laugh. "No cussing, little girl."

Silas leaned over and pecked her lips, standing and lifting their daughter. "Grandma Iris is coming over to make breakfast. Let's go brush our teeth and get ready for the day."

Mila rolled her eyes. Silas was so spoiled, but she couldn't fault Iris or Adina. Silas's charisma had her all outside of herself, doing things she'd never done before for Seth. She sighed and got out of bed. As he said, they needed to get ready for the day.

***

It was surreal.

That was all she could think as she entered the same ballroom where she'd celebrated her mating just a week ago. At the head of the ballroom, a dais had been erected, and three oversized chairs spaced out evenly sat on it. Dallas was in the middle of the stage, his face placid, with no hint of worry for his son. The other two councilmen flanked him.

Where there had been lavish decorations, loads of food and drink, now there was a crowd of bloodthirsty spectators. Oh, there was still plenty of booze. The bar was up and functioning. From the sound of the conversations, bets were being placed along with speculation about what Dallas would do if his son fell. Mila shivered as Silas clutched her hand and moved through the crowd. Rock was in front of them, making a path, his big body moving any who didn't step aside fast enough.

They met up with the rest of the Knights on the side of the stage. They'd spent the day together as a family, decorating their house for Christmas. Sariyah had loved it, and Mila had to admit that it had helped soothe her nerves. She held that memory tight to her chest, using it as a talisman. There would be many more Christmases with her family.

Silas turned her body to face him. "I don't know how long it will take, and I don't know what you'll feel through our bond, but I need you strong."

She nodded and schooled her face. "You got this. Ain't shit we fear," she whispered.

The smile he gave her was the twin of his daughter; for a moment, she nearly faltered. She took a deep breath and focused on their bond. She felt his determination and the strength he was gathering to get through the challenge. There was no worry or apprehension, which bolstered her waning confidence.

Straightening her shoulders, she leaned forward and kissed him. Silas cupped the back of her head, tilting it to kiss her deeper. Her body warmed, and Mila poured every ounce of love she felt for him into it. Silas pulled back and guided her over to the rest of his family. Adina, Celine, and Mason were all standing on the side of the dais. Adina shot her a warning look, and Mila nodded, fixing her face. They would present a strong front together. Mason pulled Silas to him, whispering something before tapping their foreheads together.

Celine gripped Silas's shoulder, her eyes pools of calm. "You know how much I hate crowds, so let's not take all night."

Silas laughed and rubbed their cheeks together. "I got you, sis-in-law."

He moved to his mother. "I love you."

She cupped his cheek and nodded. "I love you. Do whatever you have to do, hear?"

He nodded and gave them one final look before heading to the dais.

"Come, let's take our seats," Adina instructed.

Mila followed them to a door she hadn't noticed last week. That door led them up a flight of stairs to the second floor. There was balcony seating four rows deep that went around the whole ballroom. She remembered wondering what the seats had been for. Now she knew. They took their seats at the front row, and the enforcers the family employed posted up on either side of them, six deep. Their usual stoic faces had been replaced with something she couldn't quite name. It wasn't nervousness or worry, but their normal unreadable faces held a wealth of emotion. The Knights treated each of their guards like family. Sariyah did the same, treating Ellis like a bonus cousin, so she imagined they were invested in the outcome of the duel.

Mila focused on the floor below, ignoring the crowd filling the balcony seats. Those that didn't fit stood along the wall and in the aisles.

"They thick in this bitch." Mason sucked his teeth. "I wonder how many they didn't let in?"

"Vultures," Adina snapped. "They came for the spectacle."

"Si gon' give 'em a show," Mason said confidently.

The guards growled in agreement, the sound bringing attention to them. A heightened frenzy of whispers was the result.

The councilman for the bears stood, and the crowd automatically shushed, turning their attention to the councilman. Mila took another shaky breath. Celine grabbed her hand and squeezed.

"The Robinson family has issued a challenge for Councilman Knight's position." Micah turned his attention to the Robinsons. "Send your champion forward."

Leland separated from the family and ascended to the first step of the dais. Micah turned and nodded at Silas, who did the same. They were equally matched in height, but Leland had Silas by a few pounds. The other man's bulky muscles were apparent in his tight black t-shirt. But Mila had seen Silas at the boxing gym. She knew that his speed was unmatched.

"This council sanctions the challenge. The only rule for combat is no weapons. The fight will be to submission."

Giddy excitement moved through the crowd, and Mila pressed her free hand against her stomach. She was glad that they'd left Riyah home with enforcers on her. It was the only worry that Dallas had expressed about the whole process. He speculated that the Robinsons could still try and take Sariyah when they failed the challenge. He hadn't said 'if.'

"Any interference from anyone other than the fighters, the challenger forfeits." Micah's voice took her out of her thoughts.

She straightened her shoulders and took a deep breath. Silas had reminded her that their bond went both ways, so she prepared herself to send only confidence on her end. She would do nothing to distract him.

Silas and Leland descended the dais and circled each other in the middle of the ballroom floor. They seemed to size each other up. Silas smirked, sending a quick jab toward Leland. It connected, and then the fighting started in earnest. Both men bobbed and weaved, their combos connecting, the loud slaps of each blow carrying all the way up to the balcony. Mila winced at the sound.

She relaxed slightly. She wasn't worried if they were going to keep it at boxing. She should've shelved that thought because Silas reached out and slapped Leland open-handed. The sound thundered, getting an audible reaction from the crowd. Some gasped, some straight up laughed.

That set Leland off. He growled and what had been a simple boxing match turned rougher, bloodier. Shit was getting real.

twenty-five

Silas blocked out all thoughts as he fought. He couldn't afford even a moment's distraction. Leland had been cocky in their every interaction, so he knew the male had some fighting experience. Silas knew one mistake could cost him, so he kept his eye on the prize. For every hit he took, he gave Leland back four. The male had pounds on him, and he hit harder than a motherfucker, but Silas moved quickly, and in the end, that would give him an edge. Plus, thanks to his sister-in-law, he had the stamina to go for hours. Celine had been determined to get stronger, and their sessions sometimes went as long as two hours.

Leland growled in frustration as Silas caught him with two jabs. He flashed claws raking across Silas' thigh quicker than he'd anticipated. Silas hissed as blood slipped down his leg. He backed off to assess the damage, and Leland used that advantage to press forward, punching with one hand, using the claws on his other to slash across Silas wherever he could reach.

Silas dodged his downward swipe aimed for his face and delivered two punches to Leland's kidneys. Leland fell, pulling Silas down with him. Leland used the momentum to shift into his panther, weighing Silas to the floor and aiming his claws for his throat.

Still in his human form, Silas used his legs to toss the off-balance creature over his head. Leland sailed over him, his animal righting itself immediately. He jumped for Silas, trying to get at him before Silas gained his feet. Instead of fighting against the floor slick with their blood, Silas shifted to gain purchase with his claws. The two animals collided, and the fighting got bloodier—teeth and claws upping the ante. Silas lost track of time as they fought. His panther understood the stakes and would not give up. He saw the moment Leland's strength waned.

Leland's panther backed away and swayed on its feet. The male shifted to human and held up his hands.

"I submit," he whispered in pain.

Silas stalked closer to the fallen male, his steps cautious but no less determined.

"The fight is called." Cyrus stood from his chair.

Micah and Dallas both stood. Silas kept his eyes on Leland, almost willing the male to try and stand. Not that he needed any other reason to kill the male.

Dallas stepped forward, and Silas placed his paw on Leland's chest.

"I've already yielded." Leland wheezed, his eyes wide.

Silas leaned down into his face and growled but didn't move his paw. Submission was no longer enough for him or his panther. The male had fucked with what was his; an example needed to be made.

Dallas smiled at his son before looking up at the crowd. "Your challenger has been defeated." He directed his words to the Robinsons, sitting across from the fighting. He then turned his attention to the rest of the crowd. "I know you're wondering why the Robinsons didn't go through the hierarchy to get this far. I've heard the speculation. You've all seen them for the cowards they are."

The crowd murmured. Silas leaned his weight on his paw, his panther relishing the fear they could feel from the male under them.

"If they really cared for the cat shifters of this city, then they would've done the challenge correctly. Wouldn't you agree?" Dallas continued.

The cats in the crowd went wild. Though the panther was impatient, both it and Silas knew their father was nothing, if not a showman. They waited for Dallas' orders.

"The Knights are here to stay. We built our shit by blood and have no problem using blood to stay in place." Dallas nodded at him. "You know what to do."

Silas took pleasure in swiping his claws across Leland's throat. The crowd gasped, their sounds covering the male gasping for his life. Silence descended as Leland took his last breath. His father crooked his finger, and Silas ambered to the dais next to his father.

"Let this be a warning to the next challenger who thinks to cheat the duel laws. There is no submission, only death." Dallas didn't need to shout, but his words went through the crowd in a shockwave.

Now that the fighting was done, Silas focused his attention on his bond with his mate. Though the fear was there, he could feel her resolution. He looked up into the crowd and spotted her. None of the fear showed on her face. Dallas reached down and patted the top of his head, indicating that he could leave. His father would take care of the rest.

Instead of shifting back to human, Silas bounded from the room in his animal form. Mila met him in the hallway with Rock behind, her body trembling. He guided her from the ballroom and down the hallway, pushing her into an empty waiting room. Mila dropped to the ground the moment she closed the door behind him. He went to her, and she gripped his neck, crying into his fur.

"I was so worried," she whispered.

His panther licked across her face and down over their mark, though her clothes hid it. Aggravated, Silas used his teeth and ripped away at her shirt. He growled when his mark showed. He licked over it, and she shuddered, holding onto him.

"I love you," she told him.

He nuzzled his head into her neck, his panther leaving its scent all over their mate. It took a few minutes before the animal relented its control. Silas was finally able to change back.

"I thought you would stay in your animal form all night," she told him, her hands roaming his body, checking for wounds.

He winced because there were still cuts and deep scratches across his body, but they would heal soon.

She cupped his cheek. "Are you okay?"

"Of course, love," he told her. He wanted to kiss her badly, but he could still taste the blood from Leland. "I need a shower first."

She nodded and stood with him. "You're going out there naked?"

He chuckled tiredly at the streak of jealousy that flashed through their bond from her end. A knock sounded at the door, and Mason entered, handing him a robe. Rock was standing outside the door on his job like always.

"It's clear here," Mason told him

Silas nodded. That meant his brother and Rock had made a path for him to his office. He could wash off in the shower in his bathroom there and then take a longer bath at home, in the arms of his mate. He couldn't wait. He stepped out into the hallway, Mila trailing him.

"Jules said they still tried to hit the house," his brother told him, falling into step with him.

Mila gasped.

Fury filled him. They'd tried to get his daughter again, just as Dallas had predicted. Bunch of pussies. Their desperation would cost the rest of that family their lives. He didn't plan to leave anyone around to try this plan again once they'd regrouped. An example needed to be made. His daughter would serve as a pawn for no one.

"How many?"

"Doesn't matter, they dead." Rock informed him. His face was a mask of indignation.

Riyah had already wrapped Rock around her fingers, so Silas knew the bear was pissed.

"It's taken care of," Mason said. "They already took Ya-ya to Pop's. Mom wants you to stay with them while she gets someone to fix the house."

Silas stopped walking. "They fucked my shit up like that?"

"Jules handled it," Mason assured him, wincing. He was no stranger to his home being invaded.

Silas sighed because he had been looking forward to alone time with his mate.

His brother must have read his mind. "You can stay at my condo tomorrow, but you know mama. Give her tonight."

He nodded. Adina had stayed stoic throughout the whole process, but he knew she would want to make sure he was fine in private. Silas reached back for Mila's hand. She gripped him tightly.

"Anything you want Celine to get for you?" Mason asked Mila.

She blinked, still in shock. "Umm, just clothes, please." She said quietly.

Mason nodded and butted his forehead against Silas and Mila before taking off.

"Got the door," Rock growled, standing guard.

Silas nodded and pulled his mate into his office. Mila was docile next to him, her steps slow. He knew she barely slept last night. Between that and the anxiety and shock, she was due to crash soon.

"Let me shower, and then we can go, love." He said.

She followed him into the small bathroom and started stripping. He raised his eyebrow, and she raised her brow right back. His lips tilted in a small smile, allowing her into the small shower with him. Her touch wasn't sexual. It was reverent and careful as she washed the blood from his body. He relaxed as she gently stroked over him with the washcloth. She sent soothing waves down their mating bond, and Silas closed his eyes to bask in her loving.

"Rinse off," she ordered, stepping from the stall. She passed him the toothbrush and toothpaste she found in the drawer under the sink. "I'll be right outside," she said quietly.

Silas followed her order. When he was finished, he got dressed in the spare clothes he kept in the small closet. By the time he exited the bathroom, he was exhausted. Mila was pacing his office in one of his dress shirts and her jeans. He could hear his baby on the phone.

"Here's your daddy now." She passed the phone to him.

Riyah's worried face filled the screen.

"I'm fine, Ya-ya." He told her.

"I just wanted to see for myself. Mr. Ellis brought me to Poppa's house in a rush. I think something happened."

"That's not for you to worry about, princess. We'll be there soon. I love you."

"I love you too, daddy."

He hung up the phone and reached his hand out for Mila's. She walked into his arms and cupped his cheeks, bringing his face to hers for a kiss. It was a deep, healing kiss. There was no heat, just comfort.

"I was so scared." She whispered.

"Thank you for waiting until we were in private to show it."

She nodded. "I'm a Knight now. I gotta act with some decorum."

He laughed because some would say otherwise about his family. "I love you."

She sighed and snuggled closer, kissing him softly. "I love you so much."

"Let's go to our baby." He murmured against her lips.

His body ached, but just saying those words healed him. After so many years of searching, his daughter was home. And she'd brought him a gift he'd never thought to ask for. Despite how much his family would have to clean up behind all of this, he couldn't find room in his heart for anything but love.

epilogue

Christmas, one year later.

Silas cradled the baby gently, humming as he walked around the kitchen.

"You're going to spoil him," Iris said as she started breakfast.

It was early Christmas morning, and he and his lil homie were the only ones in the house, other than Iris who was awake. Surprisingly. He thought for sure Riyah would've beat him down the stairs this morning. She'd talked incessantly last night about what she thought was in the boxes under the tree. He'd tired of the speculation and had sent her to bed with her Poppa and grandmother so he didn't have to hear it. She had her own room at her grandparent's house, but according to Ya-ya, she was owed a sleepover.

They only lived two streets over from his parents, but it was Christmas, and Adina wanted all her family under one roof. She'd started the new tradition two years ago when Mason had mated, so now they were all camped out until tomorrow.

"I know you ain't talking about spoiling," Silas joked, kissing the top of Iris's head.

She and Adina were ridiculous when it came to this little boy.

"Man, if you don't quit hogging my baby," Mason grumbled, shuffling into the kitchen.

"He wanted to spend time with Uncle Silas, ain't that right, man-man," Silas cooed at his nephew.

His heart turned over as his nephew stared up into his face. Soon, Antonio would have a playmate to join him, and Silas couldn't wait.

"You fed him?" Mason asked, sitting at the kitchen island, laying his head on the granite.

Silas chuckled and nodded. Little Antonio was kicking his parents' asses. "He started whimpering as I passed the nursery, so I grabbed him before he could wake up sis-in-law."

"Thank you. CiCi can hopefully get another couple hours of sleep before your monster wakes up yelling about opening presents."

He thought a couple of hours was generous. If Ya-Ya gave them at least one, he would be shocked.

"I hope you're this helpful when I finally evict this greedy demon," Mila said as she entered the kitchen.

She walked over to Silas, her normal graceful walk a little awkward with her seven-month pregnant belly. She kissed his shoulder and rubbed a gentle hand across Antonio's head.

"Not too much on my baby," Iris told her. "Sit. I already made my grandbaby some grits."

Silas shook his head and hid his smile. He called Iris his second mother because she'd been that from the moment he'd been born. She was technically his mother's cousin, but he couldn't imagine their life without her. He didn't know who was happier about having grandkids in the house, her or his parents. She spoiled Celine and Mila through their whole pregnancies.

The grits were his mate's major craving as she carried their son. And Iris made sure she had it every time they came over.

"With extra cheese?" Mila rubbed her hands together.

"Baby ain't even here yet. How he eat before us?" Mason teased.

Mila shoved his shoulder. "You carry around a passenger in your uterus for nine months, and I'll feed you first."

Iris laughed as she set a bowl of steaming grits in front of his mate.

"Gimme my boy," Dallas said, coming into the kitchen. "You got about two minutes before Ya-ya finishes brushing her teeth and storms down them stairs."

Silas smiled and passed his nephew over. He rounded the corner in time to see his daughter leap from the last three steps.

"Good morning, princess. Breakfast before presents," he instructed, lifting his baby.

She was eight and not a baby anymore, but he would never tire of having her in his arms.

"I can't possibly eat, daddy. You already know what time it is. Present time," she argued.

"Remind me to limit your time with Uncle Mase. You're starting to sound like him." He grumbled, rubbing their cheeks together. He walked back to the kitchen.

"Morning, everyone!" Riyah called out. "Do you want help, Grandma Iris?"

"You can make the waffles," Iris told her.

Sariyah cheered and wiggled out of his arms, racing to the pantry to get the footstool Iris kept there for her.

Silas walked over to his mate and wrapped his arms around her, settling his chin on her shoulder. He rubbed her belly, smiling as his son kicked against his palm. God, he couldn't wait to meet him.

Love overwhelmed him.

His family was together, and there were no missing pieces. He couldn't have asked for anything more for Christmas.

Destiny Series

Destiny Awakened

A Destiny Revealed

Escaping Destiny

Haven Series

Haven

SoulBonded

HellBound

Georgia Arcane Series

Surrender to the Moonlight

Magic in the Moonlight

Standalones

Hers to Call

Chasing Savannah

Novellas

Hamilton Brothers

The Friend Contract

The Alpha's Affair

Porsha's Wolf- A short

Knight Brothers
To Her Rescue
For Her Safety

ABOUT THE AUTHOR

I am a full-time photographer and a mom of two. I've been writing my whole life, and after the birth of my first kid, I decided I couldn't very well bring up a fearless human without first trying the things that scared me. So, I wrote my first book and then subsequently more.

I try to write stories I love to read: love stories that feature brown girls like me. Some of my stories feature gods and goddesses and creatures I derived from old African folk tales remixed and thrust into a modern world. Visit my website, www.driaandersen.com, for more information on my other novels.

Join my newsletter for free short stories and more...